WHERE MY HEART BELONGS

Encounters of the Heart Series - Book 4

BESTSELLING AUTHOR

Ann Marie Bryan

Victorious By Design
Tallahassee, FL

To order copies of this book, please contact:
Victorious By Design, LLC
P.O. Box 6141
Tallahassee, FL 32314
Lighting the path to your next level

Visit our website at www.victoriousbydesign.com
Email us at: orders@victoriousbydesign.com

Cover photo courtesy of bigstockphoto.com
Cover creation by Global Multi Media Enterprises

ISBN-13: 978-0985146894
ISBN-10: 0985146893

ENCOUNTERS OF THE HEART SERIES
#1 AMAZON BESTSELLING SERIES
(AFRICAN AMERICAN CHRISTIAN FICTION)

PRAISE FOR BOOK 1

SHADES OF THE HEART

"This book in one word: POWERFUL! As a married woman, this book ministered to my soul. I loved how the author took us through every emotion of dealing with the extreme lows in crisis to the extreme highs. The personal battle to move towards forgiveness, restoring, rebuilding and ultimately the true meaning of love were all brought in full circle showcasing that love truly endures all things. This is an excellent display of how our faith and relationship with God can develop and the importance of having strong and true supporters in your corner. I loved Blake and Gabby together but what I loved most was their individual story of growth. Excellent job and excellent read!" *Author Untamed*

"I loved this fabulously written Christian romance novel centered on a married couple dealing with infidelity by the wife. Although it contained prayers, Scriptures, and a few short sermons, it wasn't preachy but right on time for me. I loved reading about the trials and tribulations of Christian marriages and this one covered all of the emotional basis to draw me in and keep me turning the pages. I couldn't wait to read the beautiful ending. Just a fabulous story that pulled on all the heartstrings!" *Author Barbara Joe Williams*

PRAISE FOR BOOK 2

MIRRORED HEARTS: SEALED BY FIRE

"...I found this novel to be particularly meaningful, because it urged me to look at myself—a Christian, a wife, a mother, a writer, a teacher—in a different light. I can honestly say it caused me to enter into some deep self-examination as it relates to being judgmental of the sins of others while carrying around sin that is no more or less 'sinful' than theirs. I love a book that makes me think. This novel did more than that—it made me pray.... A true wordsmith, she has the ability to transport you 'smack-dab' into the middle of a scene. There were times I felt as if I was in the room watching the characters interact with each other. I could hear the emotion in their voices and feel the tension in the air.... I was amazed that by simply shifting perspectives, the writer was able to get me to feel sympathetic towards a character... whom I absolutely did not like.... You absolutely ROCK, Ms. Bryan!" *Amazon Customer*

"Ann Marie Bryan's second installment in the Encounters of the Hearts series is [a] powerful story of one married couple's struggle to overcome the double betrayal of their wedding vows.... Bryan makes it very clear throughout this moving story that love and faith are keeping this marriage afloat as Larry and Rozene navigate these turbulent waters. The characters constantly turn to their faith to guide them in their darkest moments and to give them the strength to persevere, to find the sun waiting for them just over the horizon. This is a beautifully written and powerful story! I highly recommend it!" *Amazon Customer*

PRAISE FOR BOOK 3

A PLACE FOR MY HEART

"I purchased this book because the first two books were so good. I was disappointed in Chandler character at first but as in life, you really need to get to know a person before judging them. The author showed how childhood issues has a lot to do with your adult outlook on life. It was a great book on forgiveness, communication and a lot of spiritual insights on accountability. My grandson's name is Chandler so I was interested in reading his outcome. This is a great series for book club readers." *Amazon Customer*

"Author Ann Marie Has done 'IT' again... she has written an exceptionally strong book. A Place For My Heart takes one from the guilt and shame of sin to the infallible grace of God. Howbeit just like God to allow the sins of your past, to collide you with the promise of your future and this book is the purest example of just that.

Not only is this an awesome book for singles ministries all over the world, it's a glimpse of hope for the over thirty woman who feels God has left them out of the marriage class. Ever fresh on my mind is this, 'If you wait on the Lord and be of good courage, He will strengthen thine heart; wait I say on the Lord.' (Psalm 27:14)

Thanks woman of God for a delightful weekend read that captivates hearts, could very well save souls, and produces hope... be blessed!" *Author Danyelle Scroggins*

DEDICATION

I dedicate this book to my nieces and nephews. I am glad to
have you all in my life.

CONTENTS

ACKNOWLEDGEMENTS

Many individuals contributed to the completion of this book.

My Heavenly Father – I am constantly amazed by You. I love You. Thank You for making my life a ministry for You.

Orville, my husband, my beloved – Thank you for your love, support, prayers, and inspiration. I love you.

My mom Estrina Johnson and siblings – I love you. I am deeply grateful to my eldest sister (second mom), Mrs. Icylin Morgan. I enjoyed discussing the characters in this story with you. Thanks for your encouragement and invaluable feedback.

Thank you to my pastor, Bishop John E. Baker, and his beautiful wife, First Lady Elder Ann-Marie Baker, for continuing to deliver timely messages that influence my life. Thanks to my church family, New Hope International Outreach Ministries.

Special thanks to author Tonya Franklin, for selecting the title of this book, and to author Melinda Michelle of Global Multi Media Enterprises (GMME), for designing the cover.

A big thank you and shout out to the members of my Facebook readers' group (<u>Ann Marie Bryan's Readers' Café</u>) for your love, support, laughter, encouragement, and prayers. You have motivated me to continue writing stories that will inspire and empower. Thanks, too, for making the café one of my happy places to visit. You all rock.

Heartfelt thanks to my literary sisters – Authors J.L. Campbell, W. Mason Dunn, Cassie Edwards Whitlow, Tesa Erven, Tonya Franklin, Angela Y. Hodge, M.A. Malcolm, Melissa Mallory, Melinda Michelle, Ramona Poole, Danyelle Scroggins, Lorine Thomas, Denise Walker, and Genevieve Woods, for your encouragement and friendship.

I love my sisters who are my beta readers and first round editors – Millicent Battick and Paula Owen. Thanks for your prayers, insightful skills, and enthusiasm. Ooh, thanks for the hearty laughter, too.

I am grateful for the outstanding guidance and creative input of my official editors – Authors J.L. Campbell, M. A. Malcolm, and Melissa Mallory. Thank you for helping me bring life-changing books to the world.

ABOUT LOVE

"Love suffers long and is kind; love does not envy; love does not parade itself, is not puffed up; does not behave rudely, does not seek its own, is not provoked, thinks no evil; does not rejoice in iniquity, but rejoices in the truth;"
(1 Corinthians 13:4-6)

PROLOGUE

"Em."

Tyler Bradshaw was unaware he had said her name aloud. He stared blindly as the avalanche of memories he had tried to bury blasted their way to the present.

Hiding was no longer an option.

When he awoke this morning, the last thing he'd expected was his past catching up with him. It was a cold January day like so many others in the last few months. He had gotten up to his normal rituals—pray, workout, eat, shower, and dress—and was about to head through his bedroom door when his cell phone rang.

He'd barely said hello, before everything stopped.

Everything.

To say he had feared this day would come would be an understatement. He had prayed about it but not hoped for it. Yet, perhaps deep down, his heart longed for it. All because back in the day, he had made certain decisions. Decisions he regretted. Decisions he wished he could take back.

His heart rate kicked up and he raked a hand over his head as dread shot through his veins. Still, wisdom demanded he move speedily to help, even if the situation would force him to come face-to-face with someone he was unprepared to see.

"God, help her," he prayed aloud, before jumping into action.

He moved swiftly to grab his Jeep keys from the coffee table then rushed through the door. He did not relish the journey that now lay before him. Nor did he wish to confront the one thing that would never let him rest—the one painful remorse that continually aggravated his gut. The one thing in his life he needed to fix—his relationship with the woman he had nicknamed Em.

Madison Emma Kanate. She was his first love....

Once his soul found her, he loved her.

One look and he was helpless to her pull. She had caught his attention and lingered in his heart ever since. He had endured two years of being near Madison—drowning in her love. She always stirred him. Around her, he constantly felt the flutter of butterfly wings in his stomach. She made him feel things he longed for...things he couldn't have.

Despite all the love she offered him, he could not bring himself to reach for her. Fear held him bound, propelling him to escape the source of his misery.

At the first opportunity, he had left it all behind.

He ran.

He had run away like a frightened animal.

And he had kept moving. He hadn't looked back.

But, he couldn't outrun the memories or the guilt that haunted him.

She had an untouchable hold on his heart.

Daily, the memories of their friendship burned through his heart, but he had drowned them with a busy career. Life had brought him varying degrees of hopelessness that had caused him to give up instead of reaching out. That was easier. Even better, he had learned to keep his heart hidden. He knew firsthand the torture of abandonment that left him yearning for anyone who was willing to look into his soul and see him...and love him.

As he sped out of his driveway in his black Jeep Wrangler Sahara, Tyler thought of the many moments that shaped his life. Meeting Em had been the most life-changing.

Recently, he had come to realize he should have at least tried to take their friendship to the next level—anything but give up. His bravery to face her now did not surprise him. The current situation made the barriers he had erected seem small.

Still, God had given him another chance—a golden opportunity—and he was taking it.

He left no stone unturned, weaving in and out of the traffic, before he careened into the parking lot at Zeinatra Memorial Hospital. In a blink, he got through at the information desk and was at the nurses' station. Thanks to Mason Kanate, Em's brother, they were expecting him.

Uneasiness spread through his stomach as he followed the nurse down the passageway. The stillness in the air made the pounding of his heart sound louder in his ears.

They moved through a small waiting area and the nurse stopped at a white door. "Mr. Bradshaw, this is Ms. Kanate's room."

"Thank you!" Tyler said, and then knocked on the door.

When no response came, he looked at the nurse.

"She was sleeping when I checked on her around fifteen minutes ago," the nurse told him.

"Okay, I'll go in and wait quietly," he responded, turning the doorknob.

He entered the room, closed the door behind him, and laid eyes on Em. His heart smiled, whipping back and forth in his chest as he gazed tenderly at her.

Seven years ago, he had been at this juncture, but he had not crossed the finish line. Today, he had another chance and one more chance was all he needed. After all, Em made him believe in miracles.

CHAPTER 1

The stillness of the breathtaking sky-blue room engulfed Tyler, crowding out the edginess that made his stomach churn. He stepped closer and closer to Madison's bed. It was as exhilarating as it was nerve-racking, tearing at his heart.

She was resting peacefully on her side, a white sheet pulled up to her waist. Seven years later and he could tell she was still in tip-top shape.

A wave of happy thoughts swept through him as he drank in the sight of her.

Soft, full lips slightly opened.

Her straight nose, perfectly positioned, on her beautiful oval-shaped face.

Her caramel complexion was flawless, and he almost reached out a hand to smooth her long, wavy, honey-brown hair, which was splashed all over the white pillowcase. He smiled, thinking her hair was usually much curlier.

He pulled himself away from the foot of the bed and quietly moved the blue chair that was near the door closer, so he would be on hand when she woke up.

As he gazed at her face once again, he realized there were no scratches or marks. His eyes quickly scanned her body and there were no casts indicating broken limbs. He knitted his brow, and then chuckled inwardly. Mason had outsmarted him.

By Mason's description of the car accident that Madison was involved in, he had feared the worst. Nevertheless, he was glad, for his heart might not have taken the strain if anything serious had happened to her. He could only hope the damage was not internal. One thing was sure—he was glad to be on hand to help. Mason had been like a brother to him, ever since they had met at MIT.

Tyler sat and prayed silently for Madison.

He had disappeared from her life after college but that didn't mean she was not always on his mind. He constantly felt a vast wilderness in his soul as he longed to be in her presence.

This situation might have pushed him towards seeing her again, but he felt ready to wave the white flag and surrender.

His eyes scanned the room that was designed for rest, before landing on a book on the table next to her bed. He peered at it. *Our Secret Place: A Contemporary Christian Romance* by A. M. Pollick.

He smiled inwardly. Madison loved to read. That was expected, with her mother, Rozene Kanate, being an international bestselling author.

Madison pushed out a soft sigh then smiled as she settled back to sleep.

Unable to help himself, Tyler leaned forward for a close-up. *Simply beautiful,* he thought.

In a heartbeat, Madison's eyes fluttered to life, and she let out a heart-stopping smile.

His heart lurched. *That smile.* Hypnotizing and mesmerizing, just as he remembered. Instinctively, he smiled back.

Madison's forehead furrowed, and immediately her smile disappeared. She closed her eyes, and then slowly opened them again, clearly rationalizing the situation.

Tyler watched her, his heart in his throat, beating at what seemed like a hundred times the regular rate.

He started counting under his breath.

Seconds ticked by.

Then her eyes popped. Wide. Vacant.

She stared at him for what seemed like an eternity.

When her head jolted, he tried for peace. "Hello. Welcome back," he said softly, smiling yet bracing himself for the onslaught.

Her brows scrunching, she gaped at him as if she had seen fifty shades of crazy. Then in a sudden move, she rolled on her back and dragged the bedcover up to her neck.

Tyler stood. "You had us worried. Thank God you're awake," he said, looking at her. Her body shook as she held back a lethal dose of displeasure.

"What are you doing here, Tyler?"

It was hard to miss the coldness in her tone, but he decided to ignore it. Ignoring, too, the fact she was looking everywhere but at him.

"Mason was worried about you," he offered quietly. "He asked me to check on you since he is out of town." *Correction. He had me running in here, thinking you were at death's door.*

Her brows creased. "I wonder why my brother would think that. I told him I was fine. I'm here to appease Mom and Dad, because I didn't want them driving all this way for nothing." She gave Tyler a bored glance. "It was just a fender-bender, so you need not concern yourself."

Go away, he interpreted.

Shoving the daunting thought aside, he added, "I'm glad to fill in for Mason. Plus, it would be a great opportunity for us to…"

He paused as she cut her eyes at him.

"I'm okay, so you can leave."

Swallowing hard, he refocused. "I got strict orders to take you home."

"Mason is not my father. I can take care of myself." Her voice was tight. "The doctor will be here shortly to discharge me. I'll grab a cab."

"I'm here. Why would you think of calling…?"

"I'll grab a cab, Tyler." Her voice had risen an octave. "I don't know you."

"How long are you going to stay mad at me, Em?" he asked quietly.

"Don't call me that. I am Madison to you," she shot back. "I don't need you or Mason running my life. Okay?"

"We're doing no such thing. I am here to help, and Mason is concerned about your well-being. If you were my sister, I would be, too."

Her eyebrows scrunched as she visibly held back the contempt she felt for him. "I'm almost twenty-eight years old, Tyler. I've got this."

"Okay, Em…Madison." *Of course, she can manage herself.* After all, she was the president and founder of a thriving multi-national business — La'Roz Interior Design Corporation. According to her business website — truly a one-of-a-kind custom experience. Exclusive. Elegant. Exquisite…unequalled expertise and unparalleled excellent service.

He had no doubt those words were true.

Madison pursed her lips in annoyance. "I'm tired of Mason and his foolishness. You can leave now."

"He's being protective, Madison. He has always been like that with you. You being twins, and all." He recalled Mason's shenanigans with Madison during their college days. "Weren't you the one who told me he's always insisting he's *your* big brother?"

"Yes, by all of ten minutes. You would think it was ten years," she said with forced patience. "Anyway, you were leaving."

Tyler watched, remembering the ease with which they had once related. He came out of his recollection, realizing she was watching him, puzzled.

Before she could speak he said, "Let me take you to your home." His voice sounded strong and slightly commanding in his own ears.

Defiance flashed in her eyes. "I already said no, Tyler. I'll grab a cab."

"There's no need for that. I am here. I promise, I will be a perfect gentleman. I'll drop you at your doorstep and leave."

"I haven't seen you in seven years, so please stop pretending I know you."

He shook off the insult. "Okay, Em, I mean Madison. I'll drive behind whomever is taking you home so I can report to Mason that you are home safely."

"You don't have to do that. I'll call Mason and—"

A rap on the door caused her to pause.

In strutted a middle-aged, slender, Caucasian man in a white coat, a stethoscope draped around his neck. "Hello, my favorite patient."

"Dr. Wray!" Madison beamed, pulling herself in a sitting position.

He gave Madison a toothy grin. "Hello to you, too, sunshine. Are you ready to be out of here?"

"You know I am," she told him, smiling.

Dr. Wray glanced at Tyler, inquisitively, then smiled and extended his hand. "Hello! I'm Devon Wray."

"Tyler Bradshaw." Tyler shook his hand and released it.

"Please give me a few minutes with Ms. Kanate and she will be all yours."

"'Er…" Madison began with raised eyebrows.

"Thanks, Dr. Wray. I'll be waiting outside."

Madison was too surprised to respond, but Tyler knew this was not the end of their conversation.

With that, Tyler took his leave and sat in the small waiting area outside her door.

Fifteen minutes later, a nurse entered the room and Dr. Wray left, waving goodbye to Tyler.

Tyler waited patiently for the door to reopen.

After another fifteen minutes, he heard voices nearing the door and he stood as it opened.

With feline grace, out walked Madison, tall and stately, in a pair of navy-blue tailored pants and a white silk blouse. Her navy-blue jacket rested on her arm. She balanced her black purse and workbag in the other hand.

She looked gorgeous.

Her hair was pulled back in a ponytail but the mass of honey-brown curls behind her made her look like she was sporting a foxtail. Her hazel-colored eyes held a simmering storm yet to be unleashed.

Tyler smiled at her and...it could have been his imagination, but he was almost sure she blushed before looking away.

"You look great," he told her softly, while attempting to take her workbag from her hand.

"Thank you. I can carry it," she said.

"I want to help," he insisted quietly.

She released the workbag and stared at him.

The nurse came from behind Madison, and cleared her throat to get their attention. She clutched a clipboard to her chest, which Tyler assumed was Madison's medical records. The nurse looked from Tyler to Madison, before settling on Tyler. "We need Ms. Kanate's signature on a few documents, and then she's all yours."

All yours! Wasn't that what the doctor had said? Tyler thought. *How I wished that was true.*

A scowl lit Madison's face and he knew she recalled it, too.

"Lead the way, Nurse." Tyler said, smiling at her.

Taken by Tyler's charms, a grin popped on the nurse's face before she put on a professional front. "Nurse

Sandra Bailey," she filled in. "Please follow me, lady and gent."

Madison looked straight ahead as if she had not witnessed the exchange.

Fifteen minutes later, after following the nurse's directions, Tyler pulled around to a private exit to pick up Madison. He slid from behind the steering wheel, and walked past the front of his Jeep towards her. Before he could speak, she marched away from him, huffing and puffing her way to the passenger side of the vehicle. He moved swiftly to open the door for her, but she was hardly on the seat before she snatched the door from his hand and slammed it shut.

Flabbergasted, he stared at the door before moving away. *Help me, Lord!*

Tyler was still praying silently as he settled on the driver's seat and switched on the ignition. He glanced at Madison before pulling away. She was hugging the passenger door and staring outside. The air between them was as thick as ever.

He had driven for five minutes before he attempted a conversation with her. "How have you been?" he asked sincerely.

A long pause, then finally a tight. "Good."

"I've been doing well," he ventured.

Silence greeted him.

Nearly ten minutes later, her head swung towards him as if someone had slapped her. "How do you know where I live?" she asked.

"Mason texted me your address."

She let out a long-suffering sigh before her lips pressed together in a tight line.

"I'm only taking you home, Madison." He tried to keep the hurt from his voice. "I will not turn up uninvited."

She grimaced but remained silent, still staring through the window.

Shortly thereafter, her phone vibrated and a text message popped up.

He could not see whom the text was from, but Madison's expression indicated she was not in the least impressed.

She responded to the text with much vigor before shaking her head and continuing to stare through the window.

Soon Tyler veered right and came upon the wide entrance gate to The Crichton, a small, exclusive housing development in a picturesque neighborhood. The gate was manned by armed security officers, and there was no doubt in his mind the property was wired with cameras.

After they cleared security, Tyler had driven almost a mile when Madison spoke.

"Take the next right, please."

He did and came upon another gate, secluded among trees.

"Oh, right!" Madison muttered, grabbing her purse when she realized he could not proceed. She searched her purse and came up with a remote that was attached to a set of keys, and squeezed one of the buttons to open the gate.

Almost ten minutes later, Tyler pulled up to a two-story, Mediterranean-style luxury residence. *Unapologetically exquisite,* was all Tyler could think as he stopped his Jeep on the terracotta-tiled courtyard.

Breathtakingly beautiful, Madison's home was designed with great imagination—striking exterior walls painted in a light shade of cream, high arched windows, and an elaborate low-pitched tile roof. Her home looked like it had been constructed elsewhere and placed on the well-manicured lawn.

"Very nice," Tyler remarked.

"Thank you."

He alighted from the Jeep and opened the door for her. She misjudged the distance to the ground and stumbled.

Only too glad to assist, Tyler caught her slender, five-foot-seven body in his arms, absorbing her muffled cries in his chest.

"I've got you," he murmured gently, feeling her trembling. She was a perfect fit for his arms. Perfect. *God, she smells good, too.* He wanted to hold her forever.

Neither of them moved for several seconds.

Then, Madison's struggles made him realize they were not at all on the same page. "I'm good," she all but yelled, pushing at his chest.

"Okay, okay," he said, letting her go.

She bit her bottom lip before swallowing hard, the soft skin at her throat moving up and down.

"I'll get your workbag," he said, knowing they both needed distance.

By the time he returned to her side, she was back to wearing her icy gaze. He gestured towards the huge verandah and walked silently beside her towards it.

From the verandah, she opened the double doors to her home, and stepped in to disarm the alarm system near the door.

Tyler waited.

She then turned her attention to the bag in his hand. "Thank you," she said reaching for it, and not looking at him.

He made no move to hand it to her.

She eyed him cautiously. "Thanks for taking me home."

"Look at you paying me lip service," he teased.

"Not at all. I'm grateful, but if you don't mind, I have a lot…"

He noticed she had skillfully ignored the teasing drop in his voice. He tried for a softer approach. "I understand. I just wanted to make sure you're home safely."

He handed the workbag to her and she gripped it by the handle.

"Thank you." She dropped the bag on the ground, near a mahogany console table, and then made movements to close the door.

"I don't want us to relate this way," Tyler said.

"I don't know what you're talking about, Tyler." Madison cocked a brow, her gaze humoring him. "In any case, I doubt we'll see each other again."

He held her gaze for an extra moment. "You know what I mean. You need to let it go."

"Which part?" she fired back. "Oh, I know—the part where you ripped my heart out," she told him sarcastically. "Not to worry, I survived. Goodbye."

Her words landed with a hard thud in his heart.

And just in case he didn't get it the first time, she closed the door with an even firmer thud.

Tyler heard the locks click into place. His service was no longer needed.

Instead of being disturbed, a strange sense of calm washed over him. He turned away from the door and walked to his Jeep. A smile curved his lips. *It is unexpected, this peace,* he thought. *Awesome.*

CHAPTER 2

I need to tiptoe past this day, Madison thought, leaning against the front door. It felt like she was dreaming—floating and drifting. Floating and falling.

Tyler had skewed her equilibrium.

Sliding down the door is definitely in order. She crushed the thought since she didn't have the energy. Instead, she moved what felt like wooden legs through the oval entryway of her home to the open-concept living room and dropped on the first seat she saw—a cream-colored love seat.

Just like that, seven years fell away. It had happened so fast her head was still spinning. Long-buried memories whispered around her like a cool mist, refusing to let her go. She'd submerged Tyler in the sea of forgetfulness, but she'd always known that one day, they would cross paths. She had played the scene in her mind, but it looked nothing like what had occurred today. She would have been fabulously dressed, instead of looking like someone who had gotten dressed in the dark.

Yet, she couldn't deny that when he held her in the courtyard, her senses were awakened by his nearness. *What's up with the burst of pleasure?* That thought caused her to cringe and she sank against the back of the love seat, clutching her purse. *Lord, have mercy! No, this is not happening.*

She couldn't recall most of the nurse's instructions—at times, she had no idea what she had said. She had gone temporarily deaf because she was busy thinking about cutting. Yes, the urge to run had mushroomed in her chest, but she knew Tyler was somewhere watching the door. So, she focused on protecting her emotions. She would no longer be affected by his swoon-worthy voice.

Yes, he still had it...and the heat of his touch still lingered.

And there it was—the clear memory of that moment she had first thought he was the love of her life...the first time their eyes collided across the hall at church.

There was no denying their elemental reaction to each other. She knew she should be running out of the room, but good heaven, not with her body pushing out a resounding *yeesss*—a serious call to action. He was fine—a tall glass of water that would quench her thirst.

The instinct to flee totally left her when her eyes landed on the expanse of his bowlegs. She couldn't help taking him in...she along with all the other females in the room. With long strides, he crossed the room, nodding and smiling his greetings to the other guests. His teeth were immaculate. White and glistening.

A smile lit her face as they stood face-to-face. He was mesmerizing and incredibly beautiful in a masculine sort of way. His dark-brown eyes were engaging, and his lips...ooh, sweet Lord! She shivered.

Glancing down, the picture only got better. His cheeks and jaws were defined, his moustache thin, and the jut of his chin almost hidden by a not-too-thick beard.

And she should have stopped looking right there.

No such thing.

Her delightful tour continued.

Obviously, his workout routine was paying off, because his biceps filled out his Polo shirt. His shoulders were broad and his waist trim. Everything on his glorious, all-chocolate body was in the right place.

She raised her eyes just in time to witness his slight smile turning into an expression of disbelief, highlighting the point of his straight nose.

Feeling strange and now uncomfortable, her cheeks flushed.

"Hi," she ventured, extending her hand. "I am Madison Kanate."

He quickly gathered himself. "Great to meet you, Madison. I'm Tyler Bradshaw."

His smoky voice almost halted her thoughts, but she recovered quickly. "Nice to meet you," she responded, shifting uneasily under his gaze. "Is something wrong?" she asked, curiously.

He smiled at her. "No. Everything is...perfect."

He had her heart racing full throttle.

Since that day, they were inexplicably connected.

She fell in love with him fast.

She fell hard.

The vibrating of her cell phone brought Madison out of her reflections. She pulled out the phone from her purse. It was her mom. *Oops, I forgot to call Mom and Dad.*

She tried for a happy voice. "Hi, Mom."

"Madison, are you okay? Are you home now?"

"Yes, Mom, I'm home and I'm feeling great."

"Praise the Lord. I was glad to get the text that you were about to be discharged, but I would still have preferred to talk with you. Dad got your text, too, but I told him I would call you."

"I'm fine, Mom. Remember, I told you it was a fender-bender."

"I know, but I'm still happy Mason convinced you to go to the hospital. You never know. Thank God, you're okay."

"Everything is good. The doctor gave me a clean slate."

"Wonderful. Brittany and Briana are all squashed up on my side, trying to get a chance to speak with you."

Mumbling protests of "Ooh, Mooommy!" reached Madison's ears.

She smiled, thinking of her seven-year-old identical twin sisters, whose personalities were as different as night and day.

"I'm putting you on speaker," her mother said.

"Okay, Mom," Madison responded, pausing briefly before exclaiming, "Hi, girls. How are you?"

"Hello, Madison," they said in unison.

"We were worried about you," Briana told her.

"Mommy said that you were in an accident," Brittany said.

"Thanks, loves, but I am fine. All my parts are intact. Thank God."

"Yes, thank God," Briana said with conviction.

"Madison, did the doctor confirm that?" Brittany questioned.

Madison almost laughed aloud. *You are your father's child.* "Yes, Brit. The doctor said that I am good to go."

"That is wonderful," Brittany responded with much self-importance.

Madison could imagine Briana rolling her eyes.

"Are you girls on early release from school?" Madison asked. Both girls were in second grade at the prestigious Pine Hill Academy.

"Yes, it was on the school's..." Briana paused.

"Teacher planning or something, they say," Brittany butted in.

"Brittany, please let your sister finish speaking before you chime in," their mother cautioned.

"Okay, Mommy," Brittany said, humbly. "What were you saying, Bri?"

"I was saying that the early release was on our school's calendar," Briana said softly.

"Yes, it was," Brittany agreed. "Madison, now that we know you're fine, we're off to finish up our homework. Remember our date with you next Saturday?"

Madison laughed softly. *The world better be ready for Brittany.* "Yes, I remember. Okay, go ahead and finish your homework."

"We will," Briana said cheerfully. "Call us later."

She enjoyed her nightly chats with the girls, albeit, she had missed quite a few because of evening engagements or traveling for business.

"I will," Madison reassured her.

"Bye, Madison. Talk with you later," Brittany squealed.

"Bye, Madison!" Briana echoed.

"Bye, girls. Later."

Madison heard her mother shrieking,

"Girrrrls!" their mother roared, causing a snicker to burst from Madison. She knew exactly what the twins were doing—hugging their mother tightly and placing wet kisses on her cheeks.

"Mom, are you okay?" Madison tried to sound helpful.

"I know you're enjoying this," her mother complained. "What I want you to do is take them off my hands"

"We can hear you, Mommy," Brittany said, laughter in her voice.

"Unfortunately," Rozene grumbled.

"We love you, Mommy," Briana said, chuckling loudly.

"Love you, too. Now leave me in peace. Let me talk with your sister."

"Yes, Mommy. We'll see you in a bit," Brittany said.

A few seconds later, Madison heard her mother sigh before asking, "Are you there, Madison?"

"Yes, Mom." She giggled softly. "I see the girls have you all whipped."

"They think they do. I don't know what I was thinking having kids after forty."

Madison chuckled loudly, because this was an all-too-familiar conversation. However, she knew her parents would not have had it any other way. Brittany and Briana were their pride and joy, their little princesses.

"They are pretty hyped about the movie date next Saturday," her mother informed her. Chuckling, she divulged, "They have begun selecting their outfits."

Madison laughed. "They need to, with their schedule. They are involved everywhere – school, church, our dance company, and the list goes on."

"Yes, they do keep us busy. Thankfully, we are running our own ship, so time is what we have."

"Sounds great, Mom."

"Mason told me that Tyler took you home from the hospital. I didn't even know he had moved here. Mason said that he moved into town around three months ago. The great thing is, he likes it here. But who wouldn't like Orlando?"

Madison froze, and then opted to talk about Mason. "You heard from Mason? I thought he was busy with Kelani. In fact, so much so, he couldn't talk…well, at least to me."

She had called Mason while getting ready at the hospital, but he did not respond. Of course he hadn't; he was clearly trying to avoid her. However, when she was heading home with Tyler, a text message had popped up from Mason.

Mason: *Baby sister, I hear you're doing great.* ☺ *Phew, that's a relief. I'll swing by later, after I drop Kel home. Be kind to Tyler. He's trying to help.*

The last sentence had thinned her lips. *Sure, Mason,* was her only thought.

She'd texted him back: *Yes, please stop by. We need to talk.*

A few seconds later, Mason responded: *I know.*

She could hardly wait to see him to wring his neck.

The sound of her mother's chatter took Madison out of her reverie.

"Mason, too busy to talk?" Her mother sounded puzzled.

"Yes," Madison responded. "He said that he would swing by me later."

A bit distraught when the accident had happened, the only person Madison thought of calling was Mason. The other motorist had broken the red light, but she had seen him on time and swerved to avoid a collision. He had only clipped a little piece of her back bumper.

Mason had arrived at the scene, just after the police took her report. Her belligerent big brother insisted that she go to the hospital, even though she was fine.

Then trouble started.

"How is Tyler doing?" Her mother sounded nonchalant, but Madison knew better.

She tried for a casual tone. "He's okay, I guess."

Rozene persisted. "You guys haven't seen each other in forever. It would be so nice for you both to catch up."

Catch up? That would be a negative. "Ahhh, Mom, we don't know each other like that. It has been years."

"Okay. You must have grown, way up, because I remember you saying you were smitten by Tyler. In fact, I remember you grabbing your chest and telling me. 'I want to tattoo his name on my forehead.'"

Madison let out a loud sigh. "That was then, Mom. We are both grown now."

Her parents did not know what had transpired between her and Tyler. She had avoided telling them the truth with imaginative sketches, which boiled down to a series of white lies. Like—school work is piling high, no time for a relationship. Tyler? Who? Oh, that Tyler. Nuh-uh, not in touch. Why would I be in touch with him anyway?

The only truth in those statements was that she and Tyler were definitely not in touch.

"You may have been only nineteen, baby, but you were in love with that young man. I recall your words, 'Mom, I love him endlessly. My code name for him is HC—hot chocolate.' Baby, I watched you glowing across the table and I knew it was very serious. Do you know, that was the first time and last time you have confessed to being in love...ever? You didn't even have the courage to confess that you loved Carlton. I sense you have unfinished business with Tyler."

Madison bit back a sigh. "Mom—"

"You do, Madison, or you're going to keep having debacle after debacle—the sort you had with Carlton."

Madison's lips swiped to one side. True, she had shied away from a committed relationship. Shied away from the maddening chaos because of what she had experienced when Tyler had left her for dead.

"Sorry, Mom. Carlton didn't deserve that. Neither did his family. He was a kind and loving soul, but—"

"He was not Tyler."

"Mom, why would you even say something like that?"

"Okay. I am going to leave that alone."

"Thanks, Mom. I promise, I am fine. The situation with Carlton had nothing to do with Tyler."

"Okay, Love. Rest well."

"Have a good evening, Mom."

With that, Madison disconnected the call.

She sank deeper on the love seat, clutching her purse. *Argh! Why did he have to turn up?* Immediately, a painful memory about him stabbed her.

You closed that chapter a long time ago, she reminded herself, springing from the love seat and making her way across the living room. She ascended the stairs, running a hand along the polished wood railing that curved all the way to the second floor.

She entered her opulent master suite with arch treatment between bedroom and sitting area. Vaulted ceilings, classically-inspired moldings, thick cream-colored carpet, and dark luxury furniture turned her bedroom into an oasis.

The walls were painted off-white except one with a hint of pastel green that served as the perfect backdrop for her impressive upholstered bed. The bold use of green, gold, and off-white accent pieces was seamlessly incorporated. Elegant green and off-white drapes, complemented by intricate inner sheer white curtains, framed the windows to create a sleep-inducing atmosphere.

She had taken it up a notch by adding a large cluster of framed family pictures on one wall, but the showstoppers were the two stunning burnished gold marble lamps on the nightstands. Topped off by rectangular green linen shades, they had a pair of vertical shelves at their bases, which would clearly be desirable to a bibliophile.

Closing the door with a soft thud, Madison strolled across her bedroom, dropped her purse on the king-size bed, and toed off her heels. She moved to close the drapes, shutting out the daylight and the amazing view of her property, and then spread out on her back atop the pretty, embroidered green comforter.

Drinking in the cool air, she closed her eyes, firmly thrusting aside all thoughts of Tyler.

Then, she left it all behind in prayer.

CHAPTER 3

"You almost killed me," Tyler grunted as Mason hauled his tall frame through the front door of his two-story condominium. "But, I said not today. Even though I'm still doing deep-breathing exercises to calm my nerves."

"That's a relief." Mason chuckled, attempting to lighten the moment. He walked into the living room and sat on the plush gray-toned sofa.

"Man, I still can't believe you set me up like that," Tyler complained, sitting across from him. "You had better be glad you're my brother for life. I was seriously thinking of giving you a beatdown."

Mason pulled forward on the sofa. "Bro, come on! I did you a favor."

Tyler's eyebrows shot upwards. "If you pull a stunt like that again, I will leave this brotherhood. Man, I felt blindsided. That was not a good feeling."

Mason watched him for a few moments. "I've been dropping hints all over the place about you catching up with Madison. I'm tired of you not picking up any of my hints."

"I heard your hints. They were very subtle."

Mason laughed. "Come on, bro, I'm trying to help."

Tyler looked at him. "I don't know what you think you know about me and Em—Madison, but I want you to stop this foolishness."

"You have it bad for my sister. That's why you are not settling down. And that's why God relocated you here."

"Why don't you just tell me how you really feel?" Tyler said sarcastically, as he felt his pulse leap in his throat. He hoped Mason hadn't noticed.

"I am, as they say, helping love along," Mason said.

Tyler shook his head, but he did not deny Mason's statement. "She really put the knife in me today. And I was unprepared."

"Shoot! And you pulled it right back out," Mason exclaimed, his hazel-colored eyes twinkling. "That's what I'm talking about." He gave Tyler two thumbs-up.

"No. Noooo." Tyler shook his head. "This is not a thumbs-up moment. She was slowly killing me with every insertion of that knife."

"So she overreacted. It was great seeing her though, right?"

Tyler looked at Mason as if he was hearing things. "I didn't mind seeing her again, but not when we were both unprepared. She got me so edgy, I may have started speaking in a different accent in the middle of our conversation."

Mason laughed out. "Very moving. Deeply moving. I'm feeling hopeful. But I've never known you to back away from a challenge." Mason looked pleased with himself. "I have all confidence in you."

Tyler's eyes narrowed. "Haven't you heard anything I said? She hates me. I'm not sure why you're feeling hopeful. The wall she built around her heart is impossible to scale."

"She turned into a fighting machine. That's her defense mechanism."

"Defense mechanism?"

"Yes. I couldn't figure out why my sister had shut her heart away from the possibility of love, bro…suitor after suitor. Poor fellas." He eyed Tyler. "But I put two and two together when the blow-up happened between her and Carlton."

"Poor Carlton."

"*Poor Carlton?* Now, don't act like you weren't relieved that things didn't work out between them. You can't deny it. I heard it in your voice. You may have been miles away, but you sounded lovesick."

"I don't know what you're talking about. She just didn't love the guy."

"Whatever you say. You are the key to unlocking her heart. I suggest you get to praying, if you haven't started doing so."

"I don't know about all of that. What I do know is—Madison does not want you meddling in her affairs. She made that plain today." Tyler chuckled. "But, you've been doing that forever."

"It has been working, even if no one wants to admit it."

"You've finally found the lady of your dreams, so now you're bent on being a matchmaker. You—who used to run away from getting into a relationship."

"I was on the run until the day Kelani walked her fine self out of Madison's kitchen."

He laughed and Tyler joined in the laughter.

"Madison pulled a fast one on you, huh?" Tyler asked, remembering a previous conversation they had.

"I think she did, even though she won't admit it."

"So, you're doing the same thing to her?"

"No!" Mason lifted a hand. "You both did that for yourselves. Anyway, Kelani and I have something special. I asked the Lord to show me my special lady when the time was right. That had always been my prayer."

"Good for you and Kelani."

Suddenly the living room grew silent.

"Sorry, bro," Mason said. "I am trying to bring you two together not only for your good, but also for the good of me and Kelani."

"This is getting interesting."

A big grin covered Mason's face and he stood. "I proposed to her today."

"Bro!" Tyler gave a long whistle. "Congrats!" He walked over to Mason and slapped his back. "From what you have told me about her, she sounds great."

Mason looked proud of himself as they sat on the sofa again. "I want you to be my best man and I know for a fact that Kel wants Madison to be her maid of honor. So you see, we need you both to work together."

"Does Madison know this?"

"No. I am about to visit her now."

"Well, I'm sure she will be happy for you and Kelani. *After* she gives you a beatdown."

"You know she will. I fully expect it."

"Happy for you, bro. Your parents will be happy, too."

Mason's face filled with joy. "Yes, they are. They both love Kel. I mentioned my plans to them two weeks ago. I have their full support."

"That's great." Tyler smiled at him. "When is the wedding?"

"We are hoping for August. Lots of planning to do. Kel is bursting to tell Madison, but I have asked her to wait until I see Madison tonight."

"That I can understand. I would be honored to be your best man. That's if I survive Madison."

Mason laughed aloud. "I know my sister. You'll be okay."

"For your sake, I hope so," Tyler said solemnly.

"Of course, you will be okay," Mason confirmed. "Thanks, man. I can't wait to introduce you to Kel. I can't see myself living without her...and I know you feel the same way about Madison. There's nothing like seeing two people who I love, in love with each other."

Mason laughed loudly, then shook his head.

"What?" Tyler asked puzzled.

"You need to contain your enthusiasm. I feel like I'm at a Macy's Christmas tree lighting ceremony every time I mention Madison to you."

"Man, please." Tyler knew his nonchalant behavior was lost on Mason. "You know what I think—you are seeing everything through your glasses of love. I'm happy for you and Kelani."

"Thanks. But I must go."

"Sure, bro."

They rose and headed to the front door.

"Love you, too, man," Tyler said. "Even though you are threatening this brotherhood with your insane ideas."

"No such thing." Mason said, throwing a glance behind him at Tyler. "You should be thanking me. At least your obsessive inner monologues about Madison will cease."

A chuckle escaped Tyler. "Keep that up."

Grinning, Mason stepped onto the patio. "Pray for me. That my next stop will end well."

Tyler grinned because of Mason's serious expression. "I am tempted to say it's your fault, but that would be too trivial. Go with God."

Mason laughed loudly. "I did set myself up for that one. I'll go with God."

With that, he gave Tyler a fist bump and was gone.

CHAPTER 4

"Shhh! Shhhhhh!" Mason attempted to quiet Madison as he stepped through the front door of her home.

A surge of anger bubbled within her. "Shhh?! Don't shush me!" she spat.

"Your neighbors are about to call 9-1-1," he warned her, strolling into her living room.

"Neighbors?" she scolded at his back as she followed him. "I have no neighbors for at least a mile on each side, so stop trying to change the subject."

"I never felt so misunderstood in my life," Mason feigned hurt as he took a seat on the plush, cream-colored, U-shaped sofa.

"Really, Mason? We have had this conversation." She groaned in frustration, plopping down on the other end of the sofa. "Stop meddling in my business. And stop, please stop all your plans for driving me crazy."

She glared at his stoic six-foot-three frame. The stubble covering his square jaw, and the thin moustache did not conceal his handsome features.

"I had to stop you from marinating on the couch. That's all you do when you're not on one of your save-the-world missions."

Madison's mouth fell open and she snapped it shut.

Mason watched her for a moment. "You will thank me one day. I'm helping to position you for success."

"Listen to me, Mason," she said through gritted teeth. "Stop meddling in my business. And for the record— nothing will be happening between me and Tyler."

"Now, isn't that an assault on the truth—this premeditated cluelessness. Let that be the last lie you tell yourself, Madison. You both need to go before the Lord in prayer. I've been trying haaaard to get you two together. At the rate you're going, I'll be two hundred years old before that happens."

Madison glared at him. "No—you'll be five hundred years old." Her voice rose an octave. "Stop this foolishness."

"You can't fool me. You want to walk in the moonlight with Tyler. You want to hold his hand and stroll along the beach. You've been thinking about him."

Madison scrunched up her face. "No, I haven't been."

"I know something happened between you two, even though none of you are saying it. In college, you guys had it bad for each other, so don't bother denying it. You were everywhere together."

Madison propped her hands on her hips. "Look, Mason, I'm—"

"Do you remember how he used to help you with staging the dance and drama productions at church during our college days? You guys were a ministry team, back then. The young people loved him, as their youth leader, and you helped him with his youth programs." Mason gave her a hard stare. "Didn't he moderate the last production you staged, right before he graduated?"

Madison eyes hardened. "That was then—"

"Don't give me the 'That was then; this is now' speech. You guys were inseparable for a year and a half. It's as if you were dating, even though you weren't... or you never admitted it to me, at least." Mason covered his face with both hands, then swiftly pulled them apart. "Then poof! Everything stopped between both of you. In fact, I will venture to say, you both disappeared."

Madison moved to retrieve a bottled water from the oval glass coffee table. "Thanks for the trip down memory lane," she said with a hint of sarcasm.

"Trip?" Mason echoed. "Madison, God has blessed you with wisdom, but for certain life events like this one—your relationship with Tyler—you will need not only wisdom, but faith and trust in the Lord."

She remained quiet, staring past him.

"I admit I can be overbearing where you are concerned. Sometimes I can't help it. But I'm going to take my foot off the gas and apply the brakes concerning your relationship with Tyler. I'm going to let you both handle it."

"Please do," Madison told him. "There's nothing to handle. Capiche?"

"Got it. But one question—did you guys have a fight?"

Madison put on a stone face and looked Mason in the eye. "Why would you ask that? He graduated." She uncorked the bottled water and sipped.

Mason's silence caused her to pause mid-swallow. She could see the disbelief in his eyes.

"He graduated," Mason echoed. "Is that all you have?"

Madison took her time to cap the bottle and place it on the coffee table. Mason's frustrated sigh was not lost on her.

"I love you," Mason said, quietly, "so I need to tell you—you need to cut out that haughty spirit and what you are doing in terms of your love life."

"Man, please get a life. Anyway, what love life?" she countered sarcastically.

He smiled. "Exactly my point."

A hollow chuckle came from Madison. "You're a love guru now?"

"No. I wouldn't say that, but I know whatever happened between you and Tyler, spoiled you for any other man."

Madison stared at him, blinking rapidly to hold back tears.

In her heart, she and Tyler had been in a relationship, even though he never officially asked her into one. Before his graduation, she had put her pride aside and attempted to find out the status of their 'friendship'. Suffice it to say, that had not ended well, and her twenty-year-old heart had been crushed.

She was baffled, because on numerous occasions, she had seen the light of love in his eyes. He had looked at her as if she was everything he had ever wanted. But that day, he had made it clear that his dream didn't include her.

Anger clawed slowly through Madison, causing her lips to tremble. *I suppose that's the thing that lay between us,* she thought, *he ripped out my heart and left me for dead.*

"Baby sis." Mason quietly called her out of her reverie. "Things happened back then, but God is presenting another opportunity for both of you. You should take it, before the moment passes."

Madison could not come up with a suitable response.

"I'll be praying," Mason continued.

"Thanks," Madison heard herself say, the shock of it all causing her to look past him.

Mason drummed his hands on the back of the sofa, flashing a boyish grin, before clapping loudly. "I have great news."

The air was filled with his excitement, and Madison was immediately drawn in. "What?" She waited, her eyes begging for the news.

"I proposed to Kel today." Mason stood and patted himself on the back. "Of course, she said…yes."

"Woot! Woot!" Madison moved in, gave him a tight squeeze, and released him. "Congratulations, big brother!"

"Thank you." Mason smiled widely.

"Yesssss!" Madison threw her hands in the air, smiling. "Happy times!"

"Yes. Happy times."

"Oh, I see what's happening here." Madison's smile dwindled. "That's why you're trying to get me and Tyler together. You think we'll have a double wedding, huh?"

"Absolutely not." Mason grinned at her. "I was not thinking about you two when I got down on one knee today."

"Awww. How sweet. I can't wait to chat with my bestie."

"Kel can't wait to talk with you. I told her I needed to talk with you first."

"Sorry to spoil your day."

"Don't say that. It has been a great day." He smiled at her, leaning deeper into the sofa. "God spared your life and I got engaged."

"Great day, indeed." Madison returned his smile. "But if you pull another stunt like the one you pulled today, you will bring my inner gangster out."

Mason chuckled loudly. "That I would love to see."

CHAPTER 5

Tyler weaved in and out of traffic on a cool Monday evening. *Frosty,* he thought. Back in the day, Madison had been heartwarmingly feminine. An utterly beautiful spirit. He could hardly believe how she had changed. She was definitely testier and there was a slight hardness in her gaze.

After pulling into a parking space at Zilano Italian Restaurant, he reached towards the back seat for his navy, dot-print Neiman Marcus jacket that matched his pants. He stepped out of his Jeep and hauled the jacket onto his six-foot-three body. He had taken it off when he had made a visit to the construction site his team was overseeing in downtown Orlando.

Thanks to his reputation as 'the fixer', this project, which was running behind, had landed him in Orlando three months ago.

According to the project plan, the hotel should have taken an estimated three years to build. However, with a year and a half left to completion, the project was running behind due to the staff turnover issue that had been plaguing the Orlando office of Holt Architects & Engineers.

Tyler had originally run back and forth from Boston to Orlando, but got tired of traveling, so the company decided to temporarily relocate him in Orlando. His team was assigned to complete the building of Grand Orvann Hotel and Suites, a consummate luxury hotel that would offer incomparable relaxation and recreational activities for guests.

Mason had been super excited about Tyler's relocation. Over the years, they had been in touch, and two years ago, had even caught up with each other in Boston, where Mason had attended a business conference.

Tyler walked through the double glass doors of the restaurant and was greeted by Jennifer, one of the smiling hostesses.

"Thanks, Jennifer," Tyler said responding to her welcome. "I'm meeting with a group, under the name Mason Kanate."

"Yes, Mr. Bradshaw, we have been expecting you. Please follow me."

Tyler nodded, then followed her through the elegantly furnished restaurant to a private room.

Jennifer knocked on the door, and then opened it after Mason gave a firm, "Come in."

"Thanks, Jennifer," Tyler said, stepping into the large room.

"You're welcome," she responded, closing the door behind him.

"Hey, bro," Mason hollered, getting to his feet.

"Hey, man," Tyler's baritone voice rang out as he moved deeper into the room and glanced around the table. "Good evening, everyone."

"I'm glad you made it," Mason said. "You had me worried for a while."

"Why? I've never missed an important dinner," Tyler responded. "My stop at the site took a bit longer than I anticipated." His smile swept the group. "Enough about, me. Hello, Madison."

"Hi," Madison greeted him with a cold expression.

Yeah, this is going to be fun, Tyler thought.

From her countenance, it seemed his appearance was a surprise to her.

He could see Mason and Kelani's gazes swing between both of them.

"And you must be Kelani Norwood?" Tyler said, still smiling.

Kelani's face brightened instantly, highlighting the warm glow of her cheeks.

"Yes," she gushed, extending her hand to Tyler. "Nice to meet you." Her light-brown, almond-shaped eyes seemed to pop from her oblong-shaped face.

Tyler shook her hand. "Glad to finally meet you."

Pleasure lit Kelani's face, so Tyler knew he had scored.

Tyler released her hand, noting she was all girl—slender with skin a light shade of bronze. She was rocking dark-brown braids that swept way past her petite shoulders, some curling at her neck.

"I can see why my brother is smitten," Tyler told Kelani. "I'm here to make sure he treats you well."

Girlish giggles erupted from Kelani.

"It's not even eight p.m. and my inner gangster is being tested," Mason grumbled playfully as Tyler sat next to him and across from Madison.

"No worries, bro," Tyler told him. "Just making sure Kelani knows I have her back."

"Can you both drop the he-man act?" Madison snapped.

That wiped the silly grins off everyone's face.

Three pairs of eyes watched Madison in an epic staring contest.

Good Lord! "This is what you call a really awkward moment." Tyler's eyes arrested Madison as he chose his words carefully. "Let's pretend that didn't just happen."

Madison's head swung towards him. "And who made you leader?" Her voice was sharp, seven years of pent-up anger on full display.

"It's harmless fun," Kelani jumped in, looking at Madison.

"Whatever makes you all happy," Madison declared, not sparing anyone a glance.

47

"Em," Tyler said softly. "Let's call a truce. Okay?"

"Tyler, I already asked you to refer to me as Madison," she said in a curt, professional tone.

A tiny muscle jerked at the corner of Tyler's mouth. "Okay, Madison, I'll try to remember. You know this is a race to the bottom. No one wins."

"Well, if you're going to focus on all the negatives..." Madison said sweetly.

Tyler knew Madison was attempting to fix the little scene she'd created, but he had to make sure it did not reoccur. "For the sake of the bride and groom, let's call a truce," he appealed to her.

Air burst from her lips and Madison gave a little laugh. "Okay. I can't be here long. Something else has come up that I need to take care of."

"Another one of your save-the-world missions," Mason teased.

Madison cranked a smile. "If you must put it like that."

Sighs of relief all around.

After Mason prayed, they left the table to fill their plates at the buffet, which displayed several Italian dishes.

When they were halfway through their meals, Mason cleared his throat. "Pardon me for a moment while I step up on my soapbox," he said, smiling.

They were all ears.

"Kelani and I are grateful to you both for taking on the roles of best man and maid of honor."

Madison gasped; clearly, she was the only one who didn't know Tyler was the best man.

"O-kay then," she said dramatically, then pushed out, "Please continue. I'm good."

"We have some details that we think you guys need to know." Mason glanced at Kelani, who had her tablet beside her plate.

"We sure do, Boo." Kelani smiled at him, then touched the screen on her tablet. "First of all, note that I will be emailing all we will be talking about. Not to worry Tyler, Mason already gave me your email address."

"Great!" Tyler said.

Kelani smiled at him before continuing. "Our wedding date will be on a Saturday in mid to late August. We are still trying to finalize the date."

"Awww!" came from Madison before she could stop herself. She grinned self-consciously as everyone stared at her. "I love fall and summer weddings," she confessed.

"Me too," Kelani told her, smiling. "Our colors are apple-red and gold. We thought they would be timeless."

"Timeless, indeed," Madison agreed.

"You guys have been busy," Tyler said, before pushing a piece of grilled salmon into his mouth.

"Since I proposed, I have been held hostage every night on the phone," Mason divulged, then chuckled softly. "I'm under new management."

Kelani stroked his hand, which rested on the table. "But remember, you love the new management," she said, smiling wickedly.

Mason all but climbed across the table. "I do. I really do."

"Is that what we'll be facing for the rest of our lives?" Tyler said to Madison, who was about to sip sweet tea.

"Yup. Thank God you're coming in at this time," she responded drily. "I've had to deal with this for the last year and a half."

"That is very interesting, you two." Kelani grinned at them. "Even though I have no idea what you are talking about."

"Sure, Lani," Madison teased.

"No idea," Mason jumped in.

"Yes, Boo, that's our story and we're sticking to it," Kelani giggled girlishly, then cleared her throat dramatically. "I digressed. Let's continue. I have compiled a list of duties for both of you, concerning our wonderful occasion; however, we want you to be on hand as often as you can, to meet with Susan Bowen, our wedding planner from All Things Divine."

"Susan is pretty awesome," Madison said smiling. "Her company did Mom and Dad's renewal of vows ceremony, and just the other day, I went to the Women in Business awards gala and I understand they helped pulled off that function. It was awesome, too."

Kelani returned her smile. "Your mom recommended her. I went to their website and I was sold."

"Speaking of Mom," Mason said, "she and Dad want to throw us an engagement party, the first weekend in March. Mom is still working on the location."

"Sweet," Madison said, smiling at Mason before her gaze shifted to Kelani. "We have a little over a month to go for that."

"Correct." Kelani beamed. "Mason and I think we should spend the weekend with your parents. Say, Thursday to Sunday. No doubt the function will be on the Saturday. Your mom assured us it would be okay for Tyler to stay, too."

Madison pursed her lips.

"I'm in," Tyler announced with exuberance, which brought much laughter from Mason and Kelani.

"And I'm excited to announce," Kelani expression registered happiness, "our wedding will take place at Chateau de Kanate." She glanced at a smiling Madison. "I was thrilled when your mom suggested it, but I bet it was Grandma Darlene's idea."

"Good for you both," Madison said joyfully. "I know how much you love the Chateau. We do, too. Plus, Grandma rocks."

"She's wonderful," Kelani agreed. "I could sit all day and talk with her about the Lord. Especially in one of her favorite spots—near a pear tree—in the garden."

"That's Grandma for you," Mason stated before eating a piece of peach cobbler.

Kelani continued. "Mason and I think you should both be responsible for planning our bachelor and bachelorette parties. You will also be responsible for helping to select the bridal party gifts and activities for the week of the wedding." She looked at Madison. "Your mom and dad and grandparents are in charge of the wedding rehearsal dinner. And, since the wedding is on a Saturday, we would like our bridal party to be together from the Monday before our wedding. And…that's all we have." Her eyes swept from Madison to Tyler. "Questions?"

"Clear on this side," Tyler said, looking across the table at Madison.

"Great," Madison responded, stuffing a piece of peach cobbler into her mouth.

Mason watched her. "Would that *great* be referring to our wedding plans or the peach cobbler? Please differentiate."

Tyler chuckled. "I see nothing has changed. You're still eating a lot and not gaining an ounce."

Madison harrumphed and gave him a look that warned, *Stop pretending you know me like that.*

She eyeballed Mason and smiled sweetly. "*Great* with respect to the planning. I'm proud of you guys. I'll make sure I am ready to handle your business. But now, I need to leave. Please email me everything. I'm all in."

"Madison, please remind me to send you my smile-and-smell-the-roses app," Mason said with a straight face.

Madison's brow furrowed as she launched off. "I beg—"

"Don't say it, Madison," Kelani intervened. "I think we're finished."

"Yes, we are," Mason chimed in. He smiled at Madison. "Since I've been a bad boy, I'll settle the check."

She did not bother to dignify his comment with a response.

Mason's eyes swept the group. "I take it we're all good."

Following the nodding of heads and a yes, he signaled to Tyler. "Bro, you're up."

"Gladly," Tyler said. "Let us pray."

CHAPTER 6

Madison smiled as she drove along the one-mile stretch towards the Rozene Bennady Performing Arts Academy. It was early afternoon, and she was always happy to be at the academy, one of her favorite places. It was named after her mother, and had been a gift from her grandparents to their daughter. Nevertheless, Madison had been integral in the running of the academy, so her mother had unofficially given it to her two years before she left for college.

Back then, it was the Rozene Bennady Performing Arts Center. Madison's smile widened as she recalled that at seven years old, she had begun teaching liturgical dance at the center on Saturdays.

As the number of students at the center grew, Madison convinced her mother to change the name from center to academy and expand the building. Her mother agreed, but also wanted to change the name to Madison Performing Arts Academy. Once again, Madison had to remind her that her grandparents might not be so appreciative of that. That discussion was put to rest.

Madison's smile widened as she pulled into her parking space beside Kelani's spot. She recalled the dance she'd done with her mother at the production before Tyler graduated. Their mother-daughter dance was the talk of the night. Albeit, she had to convince her mother for months to be her dance partner.

Madison was still beaming when she came face-to-face with Kelani, who was speaking with Megan McNeal, the receptionist in the awe-inspiring lobby of the academy. One wall was covered by floor-to-ceiling mirrors, the hallmark of any dance establishment. Several pictures lined the stark white walls—Misty Danielle Copeland, the first African American principal dancer for a major ballet company; Madison's grandparents and mother, and the academy's principal dancers.

The gold RBPAA logo featuring a ballet dancer holding a globe above her head, hung boldly on the wall behind the receptionist's circular desk.

Madison moved across the elegant black and white patterned floor and greeted Megan and Kelani. Soon, she and Kelani made their way to Madison's office on the third floor and spread out on the sofa.

"Did you make it to Estrina's?" Kelani asked, referring to Estrina's Children Home. The home had been one of Madison's charity projects, but based on the amount of time she spent there helping the children, anyone would think that she owned the facility. Some of the children who were interested in dance were enrolled at the academy.

"Yes, I sure did," Madison said smiling. "You'll be happy to know Malachi is up and running again."

Kelani beamed. "Thank God."

Madison grinned at Kelani. She had become attached to one-year-old Malachi. "He sure beat the flu. He was all teeth."

"All two of them." Kelani laughed aloud. "He's a sweet baby. I hope they find his parents. They will never be able to resist that toothy grin."

"No word on that yet," Madison said, while reaching into her work bag. She pulled out a paper folder and handed it to Kelani.

Kelani opened the folder and her eyes popped. "No changes."

"No. I love everything you are doing with this year's Christmas production."

"Thank you, Madam Chairwoman."

"Right back at you, our awesome COO."

With Madison's work schedule becoming hectic, two years ago, she decided that she needed a chief operating officer for the academy. Prayerfully, she began her search, interviewing ten highly recommended candidates; however, she did not hear a resounding yes in her spirit to any of the applicants.

One evening she attended "Praise Him", a stunning dance production that was staged by Victorious Christian Dance Center, with proceeds going to Estrina's Children Home. It was there that she saw Kelani worshipping the Lord in song and dance. Right there and then, she knew she had found the perfect COO for the academy.

It took two weeks to convince Kelani she was ideal for the job. Kelani did not feel she had the expertise and experience, even though she possessed the educational requirements. Madison assisted her with hands-on training and before long, Kelani was up to speed, and the two had become best friends.

"I can't believe you have nothing to add to the production," Kelani remarked.

"Believe it. I really love it. I'm glad you're taking it from before Mary conceived. It's about time we catch a glimpse of her courtship with Joseph."

"Me too. The team brainstormed and that idea came up."

"All good. On the program, I also liked where you placed the dance from Victorious Christian Dance Center."

"Thanks. Since they are our guest performer, the team thought the first half of the program was most appropriate."

Madison nodded her agreement. "Now, I know you're all hands-on, but make sure you delegate to the other instructors and managers. I refuse to carry you up the aisle."

Kelani laughed out. "That would be a sight to behold. I may test that."

"Please don't. Save your friend from becoming a public spectacle." Madison scrunched her brows. "I got your looooong list of things to do. I'm going to have to leave my day job to keep up."

Kelani grinned at her. "No such thing. The list only looks long. I know you'll have it covered."

"Like I have a choice," Madison teased. "Oh, before I forget, the Board has agreed to give Estrina's ten percent of the proceeds."

"Yeah!" Kelani clapped her hands. "I feel cartwheels coming on."

Madison grinned at her. "Errr, easy on the cartwheels."

"I think I'll just pop into one of the studios, since you fear for the office furniture."

"No, forget the office furniture. It's Mason I am trying to help, here."

Kelani smiled. "Yes, my boo thang would not be a happy camper. Me coming up the aisle on crutches." Suddenly, she squinted. "I'm drawing a blank."

"A blank?" Madison questioned.

"My, my, my. You never mentioned Tyler," Kelani accused playfully. "He is gorgeous, all chooooocolate. And what a great personality. We both have a thing for beautiful bearded men."

Madison refused to entertain her. "I don't know about all that, and there's nothing to mention."

"I'm hearing screeching brakes in my head. He referred to you as Em, the shortened version of your middle name. Sounds like there's a whole lot to mention."

"Trust me. That ship has sailed."

"I don't think so. Plus, you're holding on to it like a Grammy award. So, the question becomes—why aren't you in a relationship with him?"

Laughter bubbled up within Madison, but she refused to let it out. "Excuse me? And, you're asking the wrong question—the question is, why would I be?"

Madison could see the wheels turning in Kelani's head.

"Did he hurt you?" Kelani asked. "Do I need to do a drive-by or lay hands on him?"

A hollow laugh left Madison. "No. Please don't. Like I said, that ship has sailed."

"I beg to differ. You and Mason are all tight-lipped about it. Every now and then, he would mention talking with Tyler, his bro from college days. I figured one day, I would meet this Tyler. Now, I'm realizing it's a really big deal."

Madison sighed. "Mason and Tyler were friends back in college. Since college, once in a blue moon, Mason would mention Tyler, but I had no idea they were still in touch with each other."

"Hmm?" Kelani looked at her questioningly. "Well, all my antennas are up. And, I'm rooting for you guys."

"Don't waste your time," Madison said drily.

Kelani's neck rolled back. "I hear you."

"I don't think you heard me."

Kelani chuckled at the sarcasm in her voice. "I'm always rooting for love."

"Where are you heading now?" Madison asked, shifting their conversation.

Kelani let it go. "I am meeting with the director of Victorious Christian Dance Center, and then I'm heading home. Mason will be picking me up around five o'clock. We have counseling with Pastor Fotola."

"Ahhh, Pastor. That should be fun."

Pastor Robert Fotola was the minister-in-charge of the foot-stomping, hand-clapping, worship services and engaging Bible studies at their church.

"We're looking forward to meeting with him. This is our first meeting."

"Sounds good."

"What are you going to do?"

"Respond to my mails and emails, and then make my rounds with the staff. After that, I'll be on my way home for one of my Esther baths."

"Ooh, Esther bath! I see you're preparing for your wedding."

Madison cut her eyes at Kelani. "You best leave that alone."

"He was the hold-up, wasn't he?" Kelani rattled on. "Was he drunk, high, or out of his mind?" Suddenly, she stopped jesting and stared at Madison.

Madison tried not to squirm. "What?"

Kelani's mouth formed a silent O, before she quietly released, "You are still in love with him."

Her statement was so unexpected that Madison froze, blinking back tears as memories rushed in.

Thanks to Tyler, she had positioned herself for the worst kind of pain. A broken heart.

Unhinged, her love was suspended in an abyss of nothingness, and she had no choice but to begin the journey to get rid of the cruel mindset of feeling unlovable.

Unlovable. That was the strangest of feelings. Foreign to her, because all her life, she had only been surrounded by people who loved, motivated, and supported her.

For months, she couldn't pray. Couldn't hope. Couldn't see her way out. Sorrow crushed her soul as misery raged to and fro in her heart.

After six months of torture, she sought solace in the Scriptures. Even so, the days were hard and the nights long. And, the life she was living—mentally, emotionally, and physically—did not match the Scriptures she was reading.

In her season of sorrow, she had indulged in self-pity.

She broke down.

She cried out.

She wailed.

She screamed.

She hated.

She lashed out at herself...at her own stupidity.

She lashed out at God.

She prayed.

She found the pieces of her heart...all the pieces.

Then, she rose.

She rose a new woman, discovering a part of herself she didn't know existed. Survival mode. She never allowed herself the respite of daring to hope he would return to her one day. The only sure thing—she would never love like that again. Her heart was tainted forever.

"Madison." Kelani called out, gripping her hands.

Madison snapped back to life, tears running down her cheeks.

Kelani enveloped her in her arms.

They wept together.

Moments later, Kelani began praying.

CHAPTER 7

"Mom," Madison called out as she swept into the living room. She had left her mother and gone into her bedroom to change from stilettos to flip-flops. They had just returned from lunch at Tex Mexican Grill.

Rozene Kanate did not move from the spot where she was sprawled out on her back on Madison's sofa.

"Mom!" Madison called out again, chuckling.

A smile whipped across her mother's face before she pulled herself to a sitting position. "You know after lunch at a Mexican restaurant, I need a siesta."

Madison couldn't help the chuckle that burst from her lips. "Mom, you are funny."

"I was admiring your place and wondering when my home will ever look like this—neat. The twins are everywhere and exploring everything."

Her eyes traveled the living room, soaking in and admiring Madison's handiwork, once again. Against the dark hardwood floor, the white and light green color scheme created a luxurious atmosphere. The room popped through the subtle use of yellow, off-white, and green throw pillows. Huge glass windows supplied natural sunlight and a stunning visual view of the circular garden.

Elegant touches and upscale amenities—everything looked perfectly designed and well-placed in the living room, until Madison's guests encountered the outstanding yellow stone fireplace. A conversational piece.

Her mother sighed.

Madison flopped down beside her, telling her conspiratorially, "The twins are wearing you out. Admit it."

Rozene feigned ignorance. "My two princesses? Never."

Madison smiled at the replica of herself. "I know. They are perfect."

This time it was her mother who couldn't help the chuckle that burst from her lips.

Madison shook her head. "Last Saturday, they showed me how perfect they were when I picked them up for our movie date and sleepover."

Rozene laughed aloud. "I can tell. They came home on Sunday evening very happy. Heads up, they are planning for another outing with you, real soon."

Madison giggled. "I bet they are. Brittany swindled six outfits out of me at Macy's, three for Bri and three for herself. Mom, I don't know what you're going to do with that child. I'm not sure the world is ready for her."

"The world had better be ready."

"She has Dad—of all people—and Mason wrapped around her little finger. And she's skilled at it, too. Sometimes, I have to remind myself she's only seven years old."

"I've got her covered," Rozene assured her. "She's her father's child, and God has her in the palms of His hands."

"Well, alleluia!"

Her mother smiled happily. "God has all my children. They are my blessings."

"Awww, Mom."

Madison was quiet for a moment. "Brianna showed me one of the dances she will be doing for the Christmas production. She was making many mistakes, even though I think she should be able to master the choreography. That's unlike her. She was dancing to Michael W. Smith's 'Gloria' from his *Christmastime* album. Have you seen it?"

"No. I saw her dancing to 'O Holy Night' and she was a perfect little angel in it."

"Okay. When she's rehearsing at home, can you peek in? I'll ask Kelani to keep an eye on her during rehearsals."

"I will. I hope Bri is not feeling pressured. This is her third year as our prima ballerina."

"I don't think she is pressured. It seems like something else is going on. I tried to get it out of her, but you know Bri, you have to squeeze everything out of her."

"She reminds me of you," Rozene said quietly. "I'm not sure who you both got that from. Your dad and I are open books…just like Mason and Brittany. But, I have to admit, it's refreshing to be in the company of you and Brianna." She smiled at Madison, squeezing her hand.

Madison squeezed back. "Thanks, Mom."

"Speaking of dancing," her mother said, "I know you don't have the time to dance, but it would be nice for you to sing at the production. And when are you going to rejoin the praise team at church?"

"Mom, I really don't know."

"Madison, you are gifted. I know you have many things on your plate, but you need to find time to bless the church with your God-given talents. Don't forget, you have a double portion of the anointing that God has blessed me with, and to whom much is given, much is required."

Madison looked beyond her mother.

"Madison," her mother called for her attention, "it won't make you look any less strong if you talk about your emotions. We all go through stuff."

"Mom, if you're talking about Tyler, I'm—"

"Do you remember when you wanted me to do the mother-daughter dance with you?"

Madison was momentarily perplexed by the sudden change of subject, but in the next breath, she smiled. "Of course, Mom. Fond memories."

"I felt I couldn't, although truth be told I could," her mother confessed. "Something inside of me kept feeding me all kinds of excuses—you are forty-plus. You just had twins. You will make Madison look bad because you won't be able to keep up. Madison will have to simplify the choreography because of you. The list goes on. But you wouldn't let me give up because you saw in me what I could not see in my…" She paused to gather herself as her eyes watered.

Madison clutched her hands. "It's okay, Mom. I really wanted us to dance like old times."

"I know," her mother said. "You made a believer out of me. Not only that, but also your father and I were going through some stuff back then. That dance played a huge role in my healing process."

"I'm glad it helped, Mom."

Her mother watched her. "Talking about what happened with Tyler will liberate you."

Madison cringed. "What? Mom, no. Please don't think like that."

Her mother pressed on. "You gave me reason to think like that. I recall our conversation, back in the day. And I quote, 'I'm in love, but it's complicated.'"

Madison was stoic. She had hoped her mother would have forgotten that foolish conversation.

"That was a long time ago, Mom."

"Tyler was a younger man back then and probably unsure of himself. He and Mason popped by last week and he looks all grown up. I know you think Mason pressured him out of hiding—that's Mason's language—but I think Tyler was waiting for the right time."

Madison stayed silent.

"You are quite formidable in the boardroom." Her mother smiled at her. "That came from your father's side of the family. But in your personal life, you are also a rather tough young lady," she added.

"Tough?" Madison sighed.

"Yes," her mother confirmed. "Madison, sometimes, we do not understand the ways of the Lord, but I assure you He is always on time."

Madison remained quiet.

"By the way," her mother said, "Mason had mentioned that Tyler is the speaker for the youth convention at the church he attends. The convention is scheduled for some time in July… mid-July, I believe."

"Is that so? Mason never mentioned that. I know they had asked Mason to speak at the men's session. Anyway, I wasn't planning to attend the convention."

"Perhaps Tyler just confirmed." She eyed Madison.

"Mom, I'm not interested in Tyler." Madison raced on. "And contrary to popular belief, my breakup with Carlton had nothing to do with Tyler. I thought I loved Carl. It just never worked out. I had no pleasure saying no to him in front of all those people. You know he was trying to pull a fast one. I had already told him I was not ready for marriage."

"I know. But with Tyler, it was different for you. You fell in love with him. Baby, sometimes the road to finding and keeping love can be difficult, at best. You have to pray and press your way through. You have to believe that God is still in the midst of the situation."

"I see what you're saying, but honestly, I have taken myself out of that situation with Tyler and I have no intention of returning." Her brows jumped, creasing her forehead. "Right now, he makes me agitated and stirred up."

"I hear you." Her mother watched, expressionless. "So how is the wedding planning going?"

"Good." Madison paused, slightly surprised her mother let the subject go. "I think Mason and Lani are bringing their 'A' game. I have a meeting with Ty this evening, to pool ideas regarding our assigned duties." *Did I just say Ty? Lord, have mercy!*

Madison knew her mother heard her refer to Tyler by her special name for him but even so, her mother gave nothing away.

"I told him we could talk on the phone, but no, he insisted face-to-face would be better."

Her mom smiled at her. "I agree face-to-face would be better. Now make sure you look spanking hot, and please wear your hair down."

She landed her mother a blank stare. "Mom, this is not a date."

"Of course, it's not a date."

Madison brows furrowed. "Seriously, it's not a date."

CHAPTER 8

"He's waiting for you," the smiling hostess told Madison. "Please follow me."

"Thank you." Madison took a deep breath, hitched her small black purse higher on her shoulder, and glided behind the hostess.

Tyler had called begging to meet for dinner at Zilano Italian Restaurant, since he was desperately hungry. Thanks to Kelani, her cell phone number was on the contact list for the bridal party.

Dinner? Really? Like I have nothing else to do. I could have been....

Her thoughts were put to rest by the heart-warming smile on Tyler's handsome face when he spotted her. By the time she arrived at his table in a secluded part of the restaurant, he was on his feet.

She nodded her thanks to the hostess, who promptly left.

"Hello," he said, pulling out her chair. "Glad that you're here."

Well, that makes one of us. Madison reached down deep and conjured up her most civilized tone. "Hello." She took the seat he offered. "Thank you."

"Thanks for agreeing to dinner," he said, taking a seat across from her. "I got carried away with work."

"I understand," she replied in a flat tone. She slipped her purse from her shoulder and placed it on the chair beside her.

He took in her chili red, ruffled top blouse. Effortlessly, it shrugged off one shoulder and created a chic, elegant look.

"You look great," Tyler said smoothly.

She fought a yawn. "Thanks," she replied, like it was neither here nor there.

Her mom had said, 'Look spanking hot, and wear your hair down.' Well, she always made sure to obey her mother. Moreover, she knew that particular shade of red popped against her skin. Even so, she was not going to buy into his kill-her-with-sweetness mission.

"I really mean that, Em." His voice caught her attention and drew her in.

"I told you to call me Madison. And, I heard you, Tyler." *Now for some polite conversation.* "What—?"

Madison paused as a waitress approached them, and introduced herself as Careen. They inspected the menu and placed their orders.

"What were you going to ask me?" Tyler's low baritone caused her to pull her gaze from the beautiful skyline through the window.

"I was asking what you do for work."

"I serve as the Deputy Vice President of the project management division of Holt Architects & Engineers. Usually, I am stationed in Boston, but I pretty much go where the job takes me. I'm in Orlando because the Orvann Hotel construction project is way behind. The hotel is being built downtown."

"Yes. I've seen the sign." Curiosity replaced the boredom present in her eyes. "You're the fixer."

He smiled widely at her. "That's what they call me. Better than being called the company grouch."

That smile caused an erratic whip of emotion in her stomach. She almost forgot she was angry with him. She pulled herself together, noticing he was sporting a cleaner look. With no sideburns, she could clearly see the single dimple in his lean cheek. He always looked like he was in great shape, a constant glow on his chocolate complexion.

Annoyance gripped her when she realized she was checking him out. "What did you come up with for the bridal party?" she asked in a clipped tone.

"I'm sorry," he said quietly.

She gazed at him puzzled. "Sorry?"

"I am deeply sorry for what I did to our rela...friendship."

She was not in the mood for this...not now, not ever. Seven years in the making, she was primed. "I'm not here to rehash the past, Tyler," she countered, her expression devoid of emotion. "I'm here—"

She paused mid-sentence as Careen returned and placed their meals before them.

"Thank you," Tyler told the waitress before she left.

"Hold that thought," he said to Madison. "Let's pray."

Without saying a word, Madison closed her eyes.

"Father, thank You for being with us. We are grateful, Lord, that You have provided this meal for us. We ask that You bless the hands that prepared it. And, Lord, may this food nourish our bodies. In the name of Jesus Christ, we pray, amen."

"Amen," Madison added softly. She cleared her throat. "I would prefer if we didn't talk about what had happened between us. I am only in your company to play my role in Mason and Lani's wedding."

He ignored the flickers of bitterness in her eyes. "I hear you, Madison."

She wrapped her fingers around the glass of fruit punch. "Please don't give me any attitude, Tyler," she said before sipping.

"I won't." His stare grew serious and firm as they held hers. "I want my bro and his wife-to-be to have a great wedding. I will not be the one standing in the way of their happiness."

They ate in awkward silence.

"Congrats on the Women in Business award," Tyler said, breaking the silence. "I admire your work. You are excellent at what you do. You have something…special. A stroke of genius, even."

She sent him an eyebrow lift.

"Sometimes, Mason sends me articles of your success."

A retort was on her lips, but she quickly caught her bottom lip between her teeth. She attempted to be gracious. "Thank you." *Unimpressed…with both of you.*

"You are a leader in your industry. It's one thing to build a great hotel, but it is the interior design that really helps to set it apart."

Safe subject. Very good. "Thank you. I enjoy my job. In fact, it doesn't feel like a job. I have a great team, though. Once we come up with the concept, they are off running."

She waited for him to finish chewing his grilled salmon.

"Awesome," he smiled at her, but she looked away at the skyline once more. She could tell he was enjoying his meal, as usual. *As usual!* She all but cut her eyes at herself.

"This salmon is excellent," Tyler said, calling for her attention. "Have you tried it?"

"Yes, I have," she responded, returning her gaze to his. He was smiling at her, and immediately, her heart flipped. She decided to change the subject. "I thought you studied Civil and Environmental Engineering at MIT. How come you're doing architecture?"

He watched intently as she swirled pasta on her fork, before eating it.

What on earth! She decided to fix him with a questioning glare. That seemed to have jolted him back to the present.

He smiled at her. "You were always so good at that," he told her. "Remember you tried to teach me…"

Her pursed lips sent him a reminder.

"Right. My degree at MIT was a stepping-stone. Architecture was my goal. I wanted people to feel my passion through my work…to touch it. The buildings, that is. And, I wanted to be a part of something long after I am gone."

He adjusted his sitting position to lean forward. "In fact, all my professional experience before and while in college, was in architecture. Two years after MIT, I enrolled in the master's program in the School of Architecture and Engineering Technology at Florida Agricultural and Mechanical University in Tallahassee."

"Is that so? Good for you. Graduated top of your class again?"

"You know it." He watched her carefully. "I never meant to hurt you. I wish we could go back to the way we were."

She did not respond, but instead reached for her purse and pulled out her tablet. Not looking at him, she placed the device on the table and unlocked the screen.

"We have bridal party activities to plan." She glanced at Tyler. Not to worry, he was all ears, chewing on something, and by his expression, clearly enjoying it.

"I am not sure if Mason mentioned this—for the engagement party, we—me, you, Mason, and Lani—will go in one vehicle to Mom and Dad's home. Mason told me you live thirty minutes from our subdivision, so perhaps you can park by him. Lani will park by me and then you guys can pick us up. I told Mason he shouldn't drive his Crossfire so he's driving his SUV. Clear?"

"Very."

Madison swiped her tablet, her eyes searching the list. "The engagement party is formal. Mom told me she is going with the wedding colors, but we are under no obligation to wear the colors."

Tyler nodded, and then began to cut a piece of his salmon. Before long, he was chewing it with delight.

Madison looked at her tablet, attempting to keep focus. "Did Mason mention anything about you helping to select gifts for the groomsmen?"

"Yes. Any ideas? I know a little about Robert Taylor, but I just met Jayvis Shuler."

"They are both great guys. Rob and Mason have been friends since kindergarten. Same church, high school, and all—all of us. He's pretty cool, as you must have realized. He is a history professor at the University of Central Florida."

"Yes, he's cool," Tyler agreed.

"Jay is all right," Madison continued. "He and Mason hit it off from the day Mason started working at Goldman Investment Bank. They are both into investment banking, mergers, and acquisitions, though." She rolled her eyes. "I get so sick of them crunching numbers and talking about ROI. Well, that's when they're not pouring over negotiated mergers and reorganization agreements or preparing for a presentation."

"Mason is good at what he does. He has a good grasp of M and A accounting. He's driven to succeed. I'm proud of my brother."

Bromance in high gear. Madison wanted to laugh aloud. "Yes. Mason is Mason. He got a double portion of Daddy's drive."

"I can tell." Tyler smiled. "What are your gift suggestions for the guys?"

"Perhaps an antique watch or clock for Rob. Jay likes golfing, so golf clubs would probably make his day."

"Okay. Great."

"I am working on what the ladies will do during the week of the wedding." Suddenly she gulped. "I can't believe Mason and Kelani want to have a bridal party dance."

"Yes, I saw that. That's going to be interesting; even though they haven't decided on the song."

Madison grimaced. "I hope Lani knows what she's getting into. Mason has two left feet. Saying Mason and dance in one sentence sounds ridiculous in my ears. No. Just no."

Tyler laughed. "What? My bro doesn't have it together?"

"Pshhhh! You would cry if you saw him dance. In that regard, he's really an anomaly in our family."

Tyler chuckled. "You can't be talking about my bro like that. He's probably out of practice."

Madison pushed out a sigh. "Just guard yourself and don't dance near him. At least that's what I plan to do."

Laughter burst from Tyler's lips. "Good Lord. It's that bad? We need to start his dance class earlier than the rest of us."

"It's best to do that," she told him pointedly.

"I'll see to it as soon as they decide on the song." Tyler wiped his mouth with the white napkin and placed it on the table.

"Please do, for the sake of the rest of us." She laughed quietly. "They selected their wedding song, 'Endless Love' by Diana Ross and Lionel Richie."

"Hmm, good choice."

"Yes. I love that song. Good choice and fitting I believe."

"My endless love." Tyler softly sang a line from the song, gazing tenderly at her.

No, you didn't. Madison's mouth swiped to the side as she steeled herself against enjoying his offering. *He can hold a note!* She had to give him that. "Let's talk about the ladies of the bridal party."

Tyler smiled at her defense strategy, before asking, "When will I be meeting them?"

"Tomorrow. Lani called another dinner meeting with everyone. Albeit, I can't make it. I have a mission's team meeting at church."

"Okay." The disappointment in his voice was evident.

She ignored it.

"Well, the other two lovely ladies are Laurie-Ann Mento and Rebecca Shorter." Madison told him. "Laurie is like a sister to Lani. They grew up together. She's making a name for herself as Director of Training at Disney. Rebecca, aka Becky, is a sweet soul. She's one of the dance teachers at our dance academy."

"Right. I forgot about the academy. Is your mom still dancing?" He landed Madison a toothy grin. "That mother-daughter dance was awwwwesome."

Madison chuckled softly. "Thanks. Mom hasn't danced in a while."

"Actually, I saw your mom the other day when Mason decided to pop by her home. Unfortunately, the twins were not yet home from school. I can't wait to meet them. I hear they are a treat."

That brought on another chuckle from Madison. "They are a treat, alright. Quite delightful. Brit is unashamedly bold and Bri, her sidekick, is a stately whiz kid. And the world—"

"Is their oyster," Tyler finished. "All good. Your mom is still a strikingly beautiful woman of God."

He leaned back on the chair and studied her. "She reminds me of you," he said, flashing her a heart-stopping smile.

Madison was too stunned to respond.

But Tyler wasn't finished.

"You both have the same eye color and—"

Madison cut him off. "We need to think of more group activities for the week of the wedding."

Tyler gazed at her.

"Yes, we do," Madison insisted. She had to keep him on track.

He let it go.

"What are you thinking?" she asked.

"How about golf? Men versus ladies."

"Alright!"

She lifted a hand and he thought she was about to high-five him. He was on it. His hand ready and waiting. Oh boy, she didn't.

He sighed loudly with a comeback. "I believe the two words you're trying to find are—thank and you."

"Fine. Thank you."

"Now, that wasn't so hard, was it?"

She didn't respond, but as she moved to put her tablet in her purse, Careen arrived with their check.

"I have it covered," Tyler said, reaching for his wallet and handing the waitress a credit card.

"You didn't have to pay for my meal," Madison told him after Careen left.

"I want to."

She squared her shoulders. "Okay. Have it your way."

Momentarily, his eyes studied her. "Must everything be a fight?"

She pursed her lips to hold it together, and then finally breathed out, "No, Tyler."

When Careen returned, Tyler signed the check before he and Madison exited the restaurant.

"Enjoy the rest of your night," Tyler said, opening the driver's door of her black BMW.

She gazed at him and almost kicked herself when a tiny smile popped out. She quickly hopped into her car. "Thanks. You, too."

She attempted to pull the door shut but he held it, forcing her to look up at him again. She knitted her brows. "What?"

He watched her thoughtfully, then let out a satisfied smile. "Seriously, Em, I'm glad you stopped taking those ugly pills. You look great when you smile."

She attempted a stone face. "Am I supposed to be impressed? I suggest you start with flowers," she said cheekily. "'Night."

"'Night," he said, still smiling as he closed the door.

She backed out and kept an eye on him in her rearview mirror. He watched until she was out of sight.

Her face involuntarily blossomed into a smile.

She rolled her eyes...at herself.

CHAPTER 9

Madison looked at the many bridal magazines piled on the coffee table and on the floor. Since lunchtime, she and Kelani had been combing through the magazines to find a suitable wedding gown and bridesmaid dresses.

Madison kicked off her bronze sandals and allowed her feet to be enveloped by the thick, soft, pastel yellow rug in her living room. Yawning, she settled back on the sofa.

"Did he make you clutch your pearls?" Kelani asked.

Madison laughed out. "What are you talking about?"

"Ahhh, he did."

Kelani poked Madison on her side and she hollered.

"Girl, stop the madness," Madison said, marking an apple-red gown with a piece of Post-it.

"You need to stop."

Madison dragged her eyes to Kelani's. "What do you mean?"

"You had dinner with Tyler and not a word. Nothing. You're keeping more secrets from your bestie."

With a determined headshake, Madison replied, "Nothing to tell. We met and discussed stuff for you and your boo's wedding."

"I'm not interested in that," Kelani teased. "I want to know about the fiiiireworks between you two."

Madison shook her head. "None of that."

"Whatever you say." Kelani scrutinized her with disbelieving eyes. "Anyway, I noticed how much he and Mason like each other. We are going to have him around for a looong time. Is it my imagination, or do Tyler and Mason walk with the same kind of swagger—not too much, just enough? You know how we glide when we walk? They walk as if they are always in purpose. I love it."

"Okay then," Madison responded. *Next.*

Kelani laughed out. "You better pay attention. I'm trying to help you out. Anyway, this is what I want to know—are you guys going to date each other, while we are still young?"

"I don't know what you're talking about. I already told you that I'm not interested."

"You can pretend all you want, but, the writing is on the wall."

"I hear you."

Kelani looked at her as she began leafing through the magazine on her lap. "Remember what Pastor Fotola said at Bible study last night—sometimes God shows us our future and then moves us towards it. The thing is, we don't always know all we have to go through to get it. Just like Joseph."

Madison remained silent.

"I understand how hard it is to put your heart out there, again," Kelani consoled her. "But you know I have plenty of experience where that is concerned."

Madison smiled at her. "I'm glad you found the love of your life."

"I sure did," Kelani said, returning her smile. "But before all of that," she said dramatically, "you witnessed me running away from my feelings for Mason for three whole months. Running from him and his handsome self." She laughed. "The day I walked out of your kitchen and saw him, instinctively, I knew it was the beginning of the end of my I-don't-need-a-relationship conversations. Girl, I took one look—hazel-colored eyes; wavy, dark-brown hair; chiseled jawline, and honey-brown skin—and I felt myself swooning. Ooh-lalaa!"

"Ouch, do I know him?" Madison laughed. "I'm going to have to take your word for it."

"Yes, you can," Kelani laughed, too. "He's your brother, so you won't see him quite like that."

Madison shook her head. "Nope. He's just a pain in my life, but I love him."

"And he loves you, too. It must be nice to have a big brother."

Madison waved her away. "Don't join Mason. He needs to stop that foolishness. For all you know, I arrived in this world before him." Her head jerked upward. "I need to see his birth certificate."

Kelani doubled over. "You two are good for me," she said, when she got her laughter under control. "Anyway, I believe my boo—he's your big brother."

"Why am I not surprised?"

"Well, he kind of earned it." She clutched the arm of the sofa. "I am thankful he's a praying man. Super thankful he followed his heart and stayed the course of pursuing me. Now I can't see myself living without him." She smiled, a pensive expression covering her face. "In fact, my prayer is that I'll never know what that feels like. He's a good man, and I will be glad to call him my husband."

Madison smiled at her. "Mm-hmm. And you both make me lovesick."

"*You both make me lovesick,*" Kelani mimicked. "That will be you and Tyler soon."

"Pshhhh! You're seeing things."

"Of course, I'm seeing things."

"Ouch! I walked right into that one, with both eyes open."

"What happened between you guys?" Kelani asked quietly.

Nothing came from Madison, but she was staring ahead.

"You already know my story," Kelani said. "I'm no stranger to heartbreak. Here I am, still wishing to meet my father one day."

"Lani—"

Kelani rolled on. "You know I spent most of my childhood at Estrina's because my mother died during childbirth, only for me to be adopted by a horrible couple who treated me like...like Cinderella."

She paused, choked up, and Madison moved over and clutched her hands.

"Lani, please stop."

"No. I need you to understand that I understand your heart breaking over Tyler."

"I get it."

Kelani wiped her eyes. "That's not where it ended. I never mentioned this to you, but I think the time is right. After all the abuse I had suffered, I had decided in my heart to remain single so I did not date..."

Madison gently squeezed her hands, and Kelani glanced at her before continuing. "I did not date at all. Two years into college, I met Tre...Trevor Miller at my roommate's birthday party. He pursued me relentlessly, and after a while, I gave in and we started seeing each other. After I graduated, he proposed. Of course, I said yes. So when he asked me to move in with him, I said yes, since in my silly head, we were going to be married anyway. Yep, I agreed to move all the way to California. That's where he's originally from."

"What happened?"

"We were okay for a month, give or take, and then the verbal abuse started. I went into shock for a while, Madison. I didn't know what to do. Three months later, I got up the courage and called Mrs. Clarkson. She and her husband were no longer managing Estrina's but she said I could use her guest room until I sorted myself out. That was a great relief, because Trevor was about to put me out anyway."

"I'm sorry, Lani." Madison eyes filled with tears. "My heart is rejoicing you survived and are literally thriving right now."

Kelani mopped her eyes. "I gave my heart to the Lord while I was staying with the Clarksons. My life took off after that. Mrs. Clarkson knew the owner of Victorious Christian Dance Center, and for six months, we worked on that stunning dance production you saw." She smiled at Madison. "The rest is history, as they say."

"Thank You, Lord," Madison rejoiced.

Kelani let out a sigh of relief. "I told Mason." She lifted a hand. "Thank God, my beautiful bearded man took the news well."

Madison smiled at her. "He loves you, you know."

Kelani returned her smile, blinking back tears. "I know."

They were both silent until Kelani spoke.

"Madison, you told me about the love of God. Better still, you and your family showed me the love of God by pouring into me, the love that I had been missing all my life. You are…" Kelani began sobbing, and Madison pulled her closer and hugged her.

"Shhh. Shhh. It's alright," Madison consoled her. "We all love you, and I could never have asked for a better sister and friend."

They wept together.

"We are a mess," Kelani said, some fifteen minutes later.

"It was necessary," Madison said smiling through her tears. "I still remember…"

Kelani waited, watching Madison struggle to get her story out.

"I loved him, deeply. And oh, the rush of newly discovered romantic love. No word, Lani, no word to express it. My nineteen-year-old self had found the man of her dreams." Madison looked at Kelani. "For almost two years, it was always Ty and Madison. We were on every ministry team and trip together. Girl, I was all charged up. So much so, I had built up false expectations concerning him."

"Weren't you guys in a relationship?"

Tears filled Madison's eyes. "He never asked, but I knew he had feelings for me."

"You confronted him?"

"Yes, after dropping subtle hints. I was feeling anxious, especially when I realized he was about to graduate."

"What did he say?"

Madison's eyes burnt from unshed tears and she blinked rapidly before wiping them away. "He was picking me up so we could attend his graduation dinner. He was popular, so he had a few graduation events. But this particular event was being held by our church at a local hotel in Boston. His parents, Pastor Daniel Bradshaw and his wife, the lovely Elder Paulette Bradshaw, were the pastors for the church we all attended."

"When Tyler came to pick me up, I asked him to come in. During that time, I had my own apartment off-campus. We sat on the sofa in the living room and I asked him what would happen with us after he graduated. He said we would still remain," she air-quoted, "friends."

Madison sighed. "Friends. I was sure a thunderbolt had hit me. I tried to recover quickly, but I couldn't. He must have seen the shock in my eyes, because he reached for my hand, but I pulled it away."

Madison wiped her eyes. "He told me that he would still be in Boston, since that's the job he had lined up."

Madison looked directly at Kelani. "There's more. My secret shame—I tried again. I told him that I thought we would be moving toward something more permanent since I loved him." She looked cross-eyed. "Yes, I really told him that."

"What did he say?" Kelani asked quietly.

"He looked crazy, like he wanted to be anywhere but where he was sitting. Then he said that he was sorry, he didn't think he would be a suitable person for me to be in a relationship with."

"Did you ask why?"

"Er, no. I had a little pride left and I decided to keep it. I told him that I would drive myself to the dinner. He left after that, still looking crazy."

"Maybe something else was going on with him. Did Mason say anything?"

"No. He doesn't know what went down. In any case, Tyler was always cagey about his life."

"Really?"

"After the fiasco with Tyler, we left the church. I haven't had any contact with him since then."

"This is strange. It's just not adding up."

"Listen, I'm not putting myself back in that situation. He was my hardest goodbye. I think a piece of my heart is still dead," Madison confessed. "Thank God for Jesus. He restored my soul."

"This calls for much prayer."

"No need, Lani. That was too painful. I ca-can't handle another heartbreak from Ty. And, I hate to tell you this but the little pride I had left, I used it, too. I didn't attend his graduation event, so in the evening, I decided to drive over to his apartment to give him the gift I had bought for him. I parked and climbed the patio stairs, and was a bit surprised to see the door to his apartment open. Girrrl, as I reached the door, who did I see but Camela Caine, dressed in her worldly attire, and putting her moves on Tyler. And Tyler, mesmerized—gaping into her lust-filled eyes as she enticed him with her words. Before I could blink, they were in a tight embrace."

Madison shook her head. "That girl has been after him for years, and Tyler knew about her colorful history…everyone knew, because she'd testified about it at youth service one Friday evening."

"Sorry you had to see that," Kelani said quietly.

"Your girl here ran for her life, and her heart. I heard him calling as I pulled away, but I didn't stop. He called and left the usual sorry-I-hurt-you messages, but I didn't return any of his calls. I filed him away, and with God's help I stayed sane. Trust me. I am over it. All. Of. It."

Kelani was thoughtful. "Madison, that was seven years ago. Sometimes, when we are young we do silly things."

"I beg your pardon, but Tyler is a Christian. A serious Christian at that. He—"

"Does that mean he's perfect?"

"Of course not, but he must have known what he was doing when he was ripping my heart to pieces…when he was all up on Camela Caine, and she was on him like a well-trained Jezebel. The good Lord rescued me. For that, I am grateful."

"I feel like something is amiss. If you stop fighting, maybe you will realize a piece of the puzzle is still missing. God does not make mistakes. Tyler is back in your life."

"Tyler isn't here for me. He's here on business."

"You better get it together. You *are* his business. I know that because I see the way he looks at you." She giggled, playfully punching Madison. "That hot, hooded, simmering gaze. It's game on."

Madison gave her a blank stare, adding a dry, "Okay."

"I'm serious, Madison. I think he is back to claim what he knew the Lord gave him. He may not have been able to handle the magnitude of you back then, but sister, he's ready now." Kelani smiled. "He's got the look we teased Mason about—the one that says something big is about to go down. Those two are cut from the same cloth, only your Ty is a silent weapon. Mason will come in hot and heavy, but not Tyler. He will wear you down slowly. I'll be praying."

"You and me."

Kelani laughed. "That doesn't sound right."

CHAPTER 10

"Man, I'm beat. I'll probably sleep through the basketball game," Mason muttered. He watched Tyler move about in the U-shaped eat-in kitchen, which combined style and functionality in equal measure for a luxurious vibe.

Tyler chuckled. "Bro, you couldn't be tired because you moved the food from the kitchen to the dining room. What you need to do is go to bed at night and leave Kelani alone."

"You better be glad I like your cooking," Mason grumbled. "If that's it, I'm going to sit in the living room."

"Go ahead, you deserve a seat," Tyler playfully told him while placing the large bowl of vegetables on the granite-top island and covering it with Saran wrap. "After all, you were here all afternoon, making these tasty dishes," he waved a hand dramatically, "in my timeless kitchen."

Mason laughed. "Whatever, man, I am hungry."

"Do you want me to put some food on a plate for you?"

Mason grinned, knowing he was being flippant. "I'll just wait until Rob and Jay get here."

"Your taste buds will not thank you."

"I agree. And I also agree that your kitchen is timeless."

He seemingly admired the architectural details, light gray walls, gray-blue cabinets with glass insets and brass pull handles, granite countertops, dark hardwood floors, and sleek stainless-steel appliances.

"Come to think of it," Mason added, "Madison would like your kitchen."

Tyler paused briefly before continuing to wrap the dish. "She would?"

"Yes. Listen, bro, now that you are back in the picture, don't let me have to hurt you for my sister. I've been witnessing the joy returning to her, since you've been back."

"Could you bring the excitement all the way down?" Tyler said, dropping onto one of the stools around the island. "She hates me."

Mason moved closer and took a seat. "That's no way for a preacher to talk."

Tyler sighed.

"You did a great thing, taking her to dinner," Mason encouraged. "Sneaky, but great."

"Sneaky? I don't know what you're talking about."

"How did it go?" Mason pointedly ignored Tyler's comment.

"Did you ask her?"

"Of course not. I don't want to be accused of matchmaking."

"It went okay. A victory, I would say."

He had to count it as a victory because in the parking lot, he had seen the touch of a smile that had ghosted her lips when he'd said he was glad she'd stopped taking ugly pills.

"A victory sounds great, bro," Mason said. "Good for you."

"True," Tyler respond, "if I'm not counting her disdain when I tried to compliment her or a high-five that didn't happen."

A loud chuckle burst from Mason. "A high-five that didn't happen?"

"Bro, she moved her hands and I thought a high-five was coming. My hand was in the air—ready."

Mason was hollering. "No, you didn't."

"She left me hanging. It was crazy."

Mason doubled over laughing.

"I brought my A-game, so I played it off." Tyler chuckled. "But, good Lord, that was a mortal blow to my already fragile ego. Anyway, I didn't think she really wanted to be at the dinner. She did it because of you and Kelani. There were moments when I thought she would set off the smoke detectors."

"No way."

Tyler shook his head in defeat. "I have a lot of work to do to regain her trust."

"I hear you. So, you're moving to plan B."

"Plan B?"

"Yes. Your plan A is not working."

"There's no plan B."

"Come on, man!" Mason said in a get-it-together tone. "I know you're fasting tomorrow about the youth convention. I will join you. Let's put our wives-to-be before the Lord."

"I like that."

"You should invite Madison to the convention."

"Great idea, but if it's not the wedding, she's not inclined to be anywhere with me."

"We will have to talk with the Lord about that. Break up that fallow ground. July is not around the corner, but I would invite her as soon as possible. You know she's out there saving the world."

"Agreed. But, bro, I love that about her. She's doing outreach—giving a helping hand." He smiled. "Allow me to climb on my soapbox. History is created by those who dare to make a difference, those who dare to stand up and do something, and by those who are bold enough to go against the status quo or accepted norms."

"Amen to all that, bro. What Madison is doing is a great thing," Mason agreed. "I just don't want her to use doing missions as an excuse for not forming a healthy relationship."

"I hear you. Let's move to the living room so I can stretch out. I'm feeling as tired as you."

Mason chuckled. "Are you going to ever let that go?"

"Of course," Tyler responded, following him out of the kitchen and into the passageway.

Mason threw him a backward glance. "Remember, we let it go last week—when you liked all the cake samples, yet had no favorite."

Tyler's eyebrows shot upward. "What can I say, they were all tasty."

"We could tell. You better thank God you workout every day."

Tyler laughed. "Yes. All day. Every day."

They entered Tyler's open-concept, contemporary living room with its great layout for practical everyday living. The light gray walls deployed in the living room drew the eyes toward the beautiful, vaulted ceiling. Evidently, the decorator went for a monochromatic color scheme, with the splashes of fun blue and gray accents to add the perfect touch.

Mason paused next to the light gray center table. "At least, you were helpful with the selection of the suits."

"Glad to chip in," Tyler remarked, slipping around him and spreading out on his stomach on the plush gray-toned sofa. "Ahhh, rest."

"Take all the time you need. The guys won't be here for another half an hour."

Mason dropped onto the smaller sofa next to him, stretching out his long legs so they rested on the dark gray area rug. He reached for the TV remote to turn on the sixty-inch flat screen TV that was hanging from the wall in from of him, above a silver-toned rectangular fireplace.

"Bro, you're too quiet," Tyler said, flopping over onto his back.

Mason placed the remote on the coffee table. "I was about to turn the TV on, but now I'm thinking I should kick back." He threw his hands open, chuckling. "And take all of this in."

"I wonder why Kelani asked Madison to help decorate your new home." Tyler rested on his elbows and considered Mason. "I know. She saw your bachelor pad."

Mason sat upright. "Bro, I told you that in confidence. My place was designed for a single man."

"Right? Either way, the sister is trying to save herself. And Madison heard her cry."

"It's like that now."

"Yup. Now, I'm going to help you out. Madison told me that there will be a bridal party dance. What's up with that?"

"What do you mean? We're all going to dance. Kel and I are checking out songs, so we'll let you all know what we selected."

Tyler looked at him carefully.

"What did I miss?" Mason asked, landing Tyler a wide-eyed stare.

Tyler swung his legs off the floor and prepared to make an all-important speech. "Bro," he started slowly, "I understand that you're not going to win any awards for dancing. I can help. We need to get the song as soon as possible so we can get rehearsal going."

Mason chuckled. "I see Madison has been talking, after all. I've got my moves together, but I'll take your help."

"Spoken like a true gentleman."

"Always."

"For gifts, Madison is suggesting an antique watch for Rob and golf clubs for Jay. What do you think?"

"Great choices."

"It's settled then. I'll start the hunt for them."

"And Madison will be helping you," Mason teased. "Do you know how many times you said Madison's name in the last few minutes?"

"I am giving you competition. 'Kel said this. Kel said that.'"

"So..."

The vibrating of his cell phone distracted Mason. He unclipped it from his belt and checked it.

"And speaking of Madison...." Mason paused to check the text from her. A wide grin covered his face. She had sent a photo of Kelani sleeping on a sofa with Malachi in her arms.

Another beep drew his attention, and another message popped on his phone.

Madison: *She is going to make a wonderful mother. Check that off your list.* ☺

Mason: *I know.* ☺ *Already checked off.*

Madison: *Awesome!*

"Check this out," Mason said, handing his phone to Tyler.

Tyler took it and gazed at the photo. "Nice," he said, handing the phone back to Mason. "Where are they?"

"Estrina's. A home for children. Kel..."

Suddenly, Tyler zoned out, looking beyond Mason.

"You okay, bro?" Mason asked tentatively. "You were gone for a moment."

Tyler reached for the TV remote. "I'm good. What are they...?"

"The home is downtown. It is one of Madison's save-the-world projects. Kel has it bad for one-year-old Malachi. He was left at the door of our church and that's how he ended up at the home. In fact, it's the same home where Kel spent most of her years."

Dumbfounded, Tyler blinked as moisture filled his eyes.

"Yes. Kel grew up there," Mason confirmed. "She's a rock star in my eyes to have survived a life as difficult as hers and become a jewel in the Kingdom of God."

Tyler puffed out a breath. "Bro, you never told me."

Mason smiled at him. "I'm going to need you to hold it together," he teased. "Kel is fine. You know what the Word says: '...all things work together for good to them that love God, to them who are called according to His purpose.' I'm thankful to God for blessing me with her. I love her, bro."

"I know you do. That's a good thing. A really good thing."

Mason nodded in the affirmative.

Just then, the doorbell sounded.

"The guys are here," Tyler announced.

"Jay, I bet," Mason said.

Tyler glanced at him as he moved towards the door.

"I'm right," Mason remarked self-assuredly.

"We'll see."

Shortly thereafter, Tyler shouted. "You're right on the money."

CHAPTER 11

Tyler gazed at Madison as she hugged the back door while staring out the window. Her red Michael Kors purse and black jacket sat between them like the Great Divide. He exhaled quietly, thinking, *It's going to be that kind of trip, huh?*

Madison moved slightly and as he was about to look away, he caught sight of Mason watching through the rearview mirror. The twinkle in Mason's eyes warned him trouble was coming.

"Everything good back there?" Mason asked, throwing a glance towards the back of his silver BMW X5 SUV. "You're all so quiet."

Bro, cut me some slack, was all Tyler could think.

When no response came, Mason rolled on. "Let me see your hands."

Kelani let out a low chuckle. "Boo, you are a trouble maker."

Tyler piped up. "We're good. Madison is wearing her save-the-world look, like she's still holding the universe together, and I," he shot Madison a toothy grin, "I'm playing the role of a happy passenger."

Madison tore her gaze from sightseeing and pierced holes in the back of Mason's head. "You're one vote away from being kicked out of this SUV pool."

"Me? Voted out?" Mason chuckled loudly. "To borrow your expression—pshhhh! My Kel would never do that, and bro has me covered. Plus, I am the driver." He held up a hand. "I rest my case."

"Such confidence," Madison countered. "You know what they say about assuming." She paused for effect. "I rest my case."

"She scores!" Tyler jumped in enthusiastically.

"No allegiance," Mason accused him.

"I got you, bro."

"There was a time when I could say without reservation—Tyler will make sure I come out on top," Mason said. "Now, I'm not so sure, but I am going to stay positive. You've got my back. It has been like that from day one—when we met in the hall at church. I remember it clearly—you with that lost look in your eyes. Right there and then, I said to myself—he needs a friend."

Laughter broke out in the car.

"Man, please," Tyler countered, still chuckling. "After youth service that Friday evening, I was making my rounds when I came upon you. And right there and then, I said to myself—he needs a friend. We started talking, and I told myself—he's kind of cool, and there began a friendship for the ages."

"Are you done?" Mason asked.

"I have more, but I'm going to hold back," Tyler said confidently.

"I can't with you two," Madison said in a bored voice.

"I know, right?" Kelani quipped. "We only have twenty minutes left to endure more of their shenanigans."

"Right?" Mason replied. "Like you're both not enjoying it."

"I know I am," Kelani stated, grinning, "but I'm sure Madison can't wait to get to The Kanate."

"I can handle the shenanigans," Madison said, "but of course, it's always a pleasure to see Mom and Dad."

"How did you and Mason end up at that church?" Kelani asked.

Before Madison could respond, Mason spoke up. "Madison and I were scouting around for a church to attend. We visited a handful of churches, and Trinity Baptist was the last one on our list. That Sunday, the worship service at Trinity was impactful. Pastor Daniel

Bradshaw preached the Word, and we were blessed by it. It was collegiate Sunday, so other college students attended, and Pastor Bradshaw invited us to youth service that coming Friday. After the youth service, we gathered to eat in the church hall, and that's when we met Tyler. Later, we found out Pastor Bradshaw was Tyler's father. Since Tyler was living with a godly man, I figured he couldn't be that bad." Mason chuckled, finding himself funny.

"This is unending," Tyler quipped.

Kelani threw a pleasant glance Tyler's way. "I see you were right, Boo, because you guys have remained friends."

"Yes," Tyler said. "I decided to keep him."

"Strange, I decided to keep you, too," Mason said, still chuckling.

"Awww! How sweet," Kelani teased them. "A bromance."

"Stop the foolishness, Kel," Mason said quickly.

"Yes, stop the foolishness, Kelani," Tyler echoed.

Kelani guffawed at the horror in their voices, while Madison let out a short snort.

Mason grimaced, quickly changing the subject. "Now, I can't wait to see Mom and Dad. And Brit and Bri." He exhaled noisily. "I'm glad Mom didn't listen to me back in the day." He explained. "Before the twins were born, I kept telling her not to bring more babies in our home."

"You didn't!" Tyler's eyes widened.

"I would believe it," Kelani snickered.

Madison hollered. "You all should have seen Mom's face the first time Mason said it. She was stunned for a hot minute. I laughed so hard that day; I was literally bowled over. Even Dad let out a loud chuckle."

"Bro, you are one brave soul," Tyler said.

"Yes, that was my bad," Mason responded. "Mom threatened to put me on time-out. But I wowed her with my love."

"I won't tell Brit and Bri that you were a deterrent to their conception," Madison said. "I bet their hero worship of you would cease immediately."

"Ouch!" Mason let out. "Madison, I will pay you in gold to keep quiet."

Everyone laughed.

"I'll have my lawyer call your lawyer," Madison quipped.

"Lord, have mercy," Kelani said. "I'll be on my knees...a lot."

"You and me, baby," Mason told her, smiling.

"Being on your knees is a great thing," Tyler chimed in.

No sympathy came from Madison. "You'll both be fine."

"We're here," Mason announced shortly thereafter, opening the electronic gate to the haven of tranquility. The Kanate was an impressive two-story home, which was elegantly nestled in the midst of a tapestry of trees, well-manicured lawns, and beautiful gardens. *A thing of grace and beauty* was a phrase that aptly described its French design, which captured the allure of past and present times. The classical theme was obvious in the structure—from its gray-blue tiled roof and stone exterior to its magnificent arches, columns, and curved windows. Adding to its appeal, deep contrasts of lights played over the structure, making a strong yet refined statement.

"It's always great to be here," Kelani murmured as Mason pulled up on the circular driveway at the front of the luxurious mansion. Mason moved slowly past his father's new red Audi S5 coupe and parked near the front patio.

"You want to take that off your father's hands, don't you?" Kelani teased.

"Yes, I do." Mason said, smiling as he turned off the ignition. "Alrighty, no need to thank me. Just remember to leave your fares on the seat."

"Sure," Madison said drily, while Kelani sniggered.

"Sure thing, bro," Tyler said, slipping out of the SUV. He quickly walked to Madison's door and opened it.

She grabbed her jacket and purse before sliding both legs from the vehicle and making her exit.

Tyler boxed her in between the door and his body as she straightened her form and stood before him.

"Hmm," he murmured softly, gazing at her. Even in the red heels she had on, she only reached his shoulders. He resisted the urged to wrap his arms around her waist.

She caught his hot gaze as he studied her face. "Are you going to move?" she asked.

"I don't want to." His dark-brown eyes pinned her in place. "But I will."

He allowed her to escape and closed the door behind her. He noticed Mason and Kelani had still not exited. *My bro has me covered.*

His gaze swung to Madison, who was standing near the rear of the SUV. He walked towards her. "You always look great," he told her.

Her eyes narrowed. "Thank you," she said drily.

He decided to ignore it, wowing her with a smile instead. "You're welcome."

"You don't have to pretend we are friends," she informed him.

"Pretend?" He smiled at her. "We're more than…friends."

She cut her eyes at him before knocking on the trunk of the SUV.

The trunk popped open, Mason and Kelani exited the vehicle.

Before long, Tyler and Mason removed the suitcases from the trunk and Mason locked the SUV.

They walked to the huge patio, and Mason was about to open the front door when it opened and squeals of delight filled the air. They were greeted by Armela Copola, head of the household staff. Armela had been with the family since Mason and Madison started middle school.

"Come on in!" she exclaimed. "Everyone's waiting in the living room."

Mason closed the front door and Armela steered them through the oval entryway and towards the handcrafted, vintage French oak flooring in the formal living room.

Mason and Tyler placed the suitcases near the grand double door, and Armela pushed it open to reveal the beautifully decorated room. The entire home whispered elegance yet comfort through its exquisite artwork, handcrafted furniture, unique decor, and all the latest amenities of modern life.

High-pitched squeals and screams echoed everywhere as the group greeted Larry and Rozene Kanate and the adorable twins.

Tyler watched as the twins hugged Mason's waist, smiling with joy, which highlighted their dimpled cheeks. They had inherited the prominent Bennady features—curly, honey-brown hair and hazel-colored eyes.

Tyler did not miss Kelani's ecstatic expression as she watched the girls hero-worshipping Mason. His eyes shifted to Madison, who was beaming while she spoke with her parents.

A quiet sigh left him.

Everything he had ever wanted was here.

Love.

Family.
Home.
Everything.

CHAPTER 12

Madison exited her room and moved swiftly along the softly-lit passageway on the second floor. She was on a mission.

She smiled, thinking it was odd to be on this side of the house. Before the birth of the twins, she and Mason had occupied rooms a few doors down from their parents' master suite. Now they were occupying two of the four available guest rooms. The twins had moved into their old rooms.

Notwithstanding, it was always great to be home. The group had arrived earlier in the day, eaten, and settled into their rooms. Her mom had announced dinner would be served at 6:30 p.m. and Madison was deliberately early because she wanted to have a quiet word with her father. She had seen him subtly watching Tyler, who was using every opportunity to gain her attention.

Well, she didn't care how much attention Tyler was loading on her. Neither did she care for the way he was smiling lovingly at her every chance he got. She would fix him later. Right now, she needed to calm her father's fear, not to mention put an end to his surveillance scheme.

Gritting her teeth, she moved across the elegantly decorated circular landing and accessed the grand double staircase leading to the ground floor.

"You're looking gorgeous, as usual," Armela said, from the bottom of the stairs.

"Thank you." Madison smiled as she descended the staircase.

Armela gazed at Madison as she came closer. "Fabulous!" She smiled, taking in Madison's sleeveless burgundy V-neck maxi dress with a side slit. The georgette fabric draped and enhanced the maxi skirt flowing from a banded waist. A fantastic finish with an air of romance. "You look like a goddess."

Madison grinned at her. "Thank you, lovely lady."

"I like him," Armela said.

Astounded, Madison paused slightly before joining her at the bottom of the stairs. "Like who?"

"Just stop." Armela laced their arms and moved them towards the living room. "You know who. Tyler."

"Good for you," Madison teased.

"Ooh, my dear, it's good for *you*."

"Me? Noooo. We are not like that. We're not even friends."

"Deny. Deny. He's got it bad for you."

Madison chuckled. "I doubt that strongly."

They paused at the living room door and stood before each other. "Trust me, he'll be good for you," Armela encouraged.

"I see what this is. You enjoyed Aisha's wedding so much, you decided you need two more weddings. Not to worry, Mason and Lani's wedding is coming up. Hate to disappoint you, but don't keep your hopes up about me. At least, not yet."

A brilliant smile popped onto Armela's face. "Of course, I enjoyed my beautiful granddaughter's wedding last year. I'm happy for Mason and Kelani, too. But that's not it. I have always been honest with you. Remember, I told you Carlton was not the one. He was okay, but why settle for less than God's best for you? I will be praying for you."

"I hear you." Madison patted Armela's hand. "Thanks, my second mother."

"You better stop," Armela teased, grinning. "Your parents are on the back patio. I know what you are up to."

Madison smiled. "And what would that be?"

"Bad Daddy. Do I need to say more?"

They both laughed loudly.

"You're the best," Madison said, still chuckling. "I'm off and running to declare my independence."

"That's what I'm talking about."

A smiling Madison moved through the living room into a large circular lounge, and then veered left to pass through the formal dining area, which was set for dinner. She was not surprised, although as a family, they ate in the nook between the kitchen and the formal dining room or on the huge patio outside the kitchen.

Madison greeted the kitchen staff as she passed through to access the patio. As she opened the patio door, she caught sight of her parents. A smile crept up her face as she watched them leaning against the patio rail. They were oozing love.

Her father reached out a hand to pull on her mother's curly light-brown hair.

Her mother all but licked her lips as her eyes roamed her husband's face.

Madison smiled as she recalled a few of the dancers' parents exclaiming that her father was a 'fine-looking fifty-two-year-old man'. She wished she'd inherited his bold personality and freedom of spirit. He always seemed indomitable and comfortable in any environment.

Madison chuckled, thinking that Kelani had better ask her mother for tips regarding the storm called Mason. Not only was he the spitting image of his father, but they definitely operated in the same mode...logical to a fault.

"Your father is a strong man," her mother had said. "He is self-assured but not cocky, certain of his God-given ability and authority, and the correctness of his path." All this, when Madison had come begging her mother to talk with her father about allowing her and Mason to be a part of their high school trip to Venezuela. Since neither her mother nor father could accompany them as a chaperone, their father was not inclined to sign the permission slips for the trip.

She couldn't agree more with her mother's statement.

"Mom, Dad," Madison called out.

Their gazes swung towards her.

"Here she comes," her father hollered. "Beautiful."

"You look great," her mother said, exposing her perfect white teeth.

"Thank you, Mom and Dad. I think I'm going to keep you after all."

"You better," her mother teased.

"I like that," her father said, as they group-hugged her. "We've decided to keep you, too."

"Awww, Dad. Thanks."

He pierced her with his gaze. "Are you good? I can make him disappear." He snapped his fingers. "Just like that."

"Tyler?" Madison gave her best nonchalant expression. "He's alright. We're making it happen for Mason and Kelani."

Her father's eyes twinkled. "For Mason and Kelani, huh?"

"Yes, Dad," she responded with firmness. "So, you don't need to rescue your first daughter."

"Got it," he smiled. "I will keep an eye on him, though. Closely. Deliberately. Ready to strike anytime."

Her mother laughed loudly. "Closely. Deliberately. Ready to strike anytime. Honey, please put down your binoculars." She looked at Madison. "I'll make sure he behaves himself."

"Me?" Her father feigned shock. "You know I will."

"Yes, you." Her mother touched his cheeks playfully.

"Mom, Dad, come on!" Mason's voice echoed loudly as he walked towards them. "You need to cut all that out. This family is already too large."

"You're just jealous," his father teased as Mason arrived before them.

Mason grinned at him. "Just a little, but I have my special lady now."

"You're a fine one to comment," Madison argued, and then she imitated Kelani's voice, "Boo thang. Boo-boo."

They all laughed.

Mason slung an arm around Madison's shoulder. "Your day will come." He waved a hand out front. "I can see it."

"I'm sure you do," Madison replied.

Their parents watched their exchange.

"Mom and Dad," Madison said, "I want you to break the news to Mason."

Her parents looked puzzled, then her mother asked, "What news?"

"The news that I was born first so he's my baby brother."

Laughter erupted from her parents before her father said, "How did you find out? We thought we covered our tracks."

"Not well enough," Madison said in all seriousness. "I'm tired of all this baby sis stuff, so I decided to check out the facts."

Mason held her at arm's length, dramatically telling her, "I am devastated. Didn't you see my distress signal—the wink-wink we did as kids?"

"That signal is supposed to be a secret." Madison cut her eyes at his antics. "Anyway, I have no doubt you would be on somebody's couch, if it was true."

"Ah, come on, baby sis!" Mason exclaimed. "I am not that shallow. Nevertheless, I enjoy having a baby sister. Well, now I have three, since—" he shook his head from side to side, "—two people could not behave themselves."

Their parents laughed loudly.

"I hate to break it to you—we're not done yet," their father gallantly declared.

Mason grabbed his head. "Make me un-hear that."

Their mother laughed even more, playfully telling him, "Just the kind of enthusiasm we need."

Madison laughed, too, slapping Mason on his shoulder. "You'll be alright. More princesses to adore you."

A smile burst on Mason's face. "Yes. Great trade-off."

"I knew you would come around," their father said joyfully while hugging his wife.

"We better get inside before the princesses miss us," Madison said.

"On that note," their mother said, "they'll be home for two days next week, please pray for my groceries."

Madison couldn't help the laughter that burst from her lips.

Shortly thereafter, they stood near the dinner table in the formal dining room and awaited the arrival of the twins.

Armela pushed her head through the door, and proclaimed, "Announcing the arrival of Ms. Brianna Kanate, daughter of Larry and Rozene Kanate."

They all clapped as Brianna, dressed in a pink dress, took her bow. Her father moved quickly to pull out her chair and made sure she was seated.

"Announcing the arrival of Ms. Brittany Kanate, daughter of Larry and Rozene Kanate."

Brittany entered, adding, "Favorite daughter."

That brought many chuckles to an already celebratory atmosphere.

Brianna would not be outdone. "You wish," she told Brittany.

"Okay, girls," Larry said, escorting Brittany to sit across from Brianna. She looked cute in her long royal blue dress.

Larry seated his wife next to Brittany.

"Where is my first daughter?" Larry asked, loud and proud. He pulled out a chair across from Rozene.

"Here I am," Madison said. Somewhat relieved, she accepted the seat near to her father at the head of the table. After arranging herself on the chair, she glanced up to see Mason throwing her an annoyed expression. He seated Kelani and sat beside her, while Tyler sat next to Brianna.

After Larry prayed, they dived in.

"You two certainly took your time getting here," Madison teased the twins. "I'm surprised you're not wearing your tiaras."

"I wanted to," Brittany said, "but Bri insisted that this was not the occasion for it."

"And what did you think about that?" Larry asked.

"Oh, Daddy, I wanted to wear my tiara. You said that I'm a princess all day, every day."

Larry smiled at her. "Yes, you are a princess all day, but what did you think about not wearing your tiara for this occasion?"

Brittany relented. "I agree with Bri. It may have been a bit much." She grinned cheekily. "But guess what, Daddy? I see the world is still turning, even without me wearing my tiara."

Smiling, Madison declared, "I think Brit could argue with a wall and win."

Brittany clutched her chest, her eyes widening. "Madison, you're hurting my feelings."

"Poor baby," Rozene said, hugging her shoulders.

"Awww, Brit, it was not intentional," Madison added, "but you know it's the truth."

"That's okay, Madison," Brittany said in a childish tone. "Honestly, I agree with Bri about not wearing our tiaras. She's really smart." She chuckled mischievously. "But I won't tell her."

Laughter broke out in the room.

"That's okay, Brit," Brianna remarked. "I think Bri already knows."

"Mom and Dad," Mason called for their attention, "what are you feeding these two? Whatever it is, you need to stop. They think they're the smartest people in every room." He chuckled, placing a piece of grilled chicken into his mouth.

"Thanks, big brother," Brittany said, eyeing Brianna. "That's why we love you."

Mason looked from one to the other.

"Yes, thank for always lifting our confidence," Brianna told him. "We're glad you think we're the smartest people in the room."

Chuckles broke out again.

"You two are the best," Mason teased them. "I said that you *think* you're the smartest people in the room."

Brittany and Brianna grinned at him.

An hour later, conversation dwindled and the twins hugged everyone and bid them goodnight.

"Please keep her out of trouble," Larry said as the twins made their way to the door with Armela.

"I sure will, Daddy," Brianna responded.

"Brianna, I was asking Brittany to do that."

106

A look of horror shrouded Brianna's face, causing pockets of snickering to echo in the room.

As the laughter died, Madison caught Tyler's soft gaze only to see it suddenly die. She whipped her head to the right to see her father shifting his gaze from Tyler's direction.

Her mother jumped to the rescue. "We have our action plan for tomorrow. I hope everyone saw the email. Breakfast will be served at seven o'clock. Any questions?"

Silence.

"Seems like we're all good. Have a good night, everyone," Larry said, rising and then helping his wife to her feet."

"Good night," rang out from the group.

As everyone filed out, Madison waited by the door to leave with Mason, Kelani, and Tyler.

As her eyes landed on Tyler, she heard her father's voice.

"Madison, could you please stay with us? We need to see you."

CHAPTER 13

"Twenty-seven. Twenty-eight. Twenty-nine..." Tyler counted pushups in an attempt to keep his morning ritual. He groaned and stood, he'd lost count. Just as well; pushups were the last thing on his mind. Anyway, he doubted he would do enough for his muscles to be sore.

He began pacing. Thinking. Pacing. *Forever came too early and ended early,* he concluded, scouring the recesses of his mind for a strategy to win back Madison's love.

Panic welled up within him, so he dropped to his knees at his bedside in the Kanate home and prayed, "Lord, You are God and beside You, there is none else. I trust You, Lord.

"I pray You will grant me the courage and freedom I need at this stage of my life. I have suppressed my feelings for Madison for so long, it feels unnatural to express my love for her. Lord, her spirit is hard and unyielding, and just looking at her zaps my energy, making me feel powerless.

"Lord, I pray for strength. Fortify me by Your Spirit. And, Lord, deliver me from any attitude and actions that hinder a healthy relationship with her. Help me to live a life of integrity and authenticity so Madison will see You in me. Help me, Lord, to be steadfast, immoveable, and always abounding in Your works and Your Word."

"Thank You for Your Word— '...My grace is sufficient for you, for My strength is made perfect in weakness. Therefore, most gladly I will rather boast in my infirmities, that the power of Christ may rest upon me.'

"Lord, my soul waits on You, for my expectation comes from You. In the name of Jesus I pray, amen."

He rose feeling strengthened.

Water. He was thirsty after his early morning workout. He had half an hour before breakfast, so he made his way to the kitchen.

After acknowledging the kitchen staff, he took a bottled water from the refrigerator and headed through the door to the back patio. He uncorked the bottle and drank slowly.

Madison. Madison. Madison. His mind was constantly on her…every opportunity he got. This Saturday morning was no different. He missed their relationship. It had been a natural alliance.

He stopped drinking and moved closer to the rail. Spontaneous praise broke out in his heart as his eyes swept the backyard from right to left. The lush landscape pulled him in—the beautiful colors and hues in the backyard.

He was moving towards the steps to take a closer look when he heard footsteps and paused. A book in hand, Madison appeared from the left side of the garden and made her way towards the gazebo in the distance.

His body perked up and he was set to call out to her when she stopped, her back to him. He shifted to see what she was looking at, but couldn't. When she moved on, he noticed the morning sunlight had created a fiery glow on her honey-brown hair.

He inhaled deeply, taking a few minutes to tamp down the attraction he felt for her before moving with speed towards the gazebo. He found Madison stretched out and reading a book.

He leaned against the column.

Sensing his presence, he saw her twitching to be rude, but she made an effort to restrain herself. Clearly, she resented his intrusion in what looked to be her private time.

"Good morning," he drawled, smiling.

"Good morning." She painted on a smile.

"You're up pretty early."

"I went for a run." She pulled herself to a sitting position and then threw her feet on the ground.

"Why didn't you call me? I would have gotten up to take that run with you."

"Right."

"I would have. I still exercise early morning."

"Okay." She all but yawned.

"So much ugliness in the air."

She cut her eyes at him.

He glanced at the book—*Our Secret Place*—that was now resting on the chair beside her.

"Is that your second or third read?" he asked, taking a seat across from her. He remembered that she was an avid reader, and she would sometimes re-read the books she loved.

Surprise lit Madison's eyes for a brief second before she quickly quelled it. "My second."

"Good read, huh?"

"Yes, it is."

"I didn't mean to disturb you, but since you refuse to give me the time of day, I have to catch you when I can."

He watched her pushing back retort after retort before coming up with, "I think you should spend your time doing something that will move you forward."

"That's exactly what I am doing." He smiled at her. "You are allowed to show your pleasure."

Her lips curved into a tiny smile. "I walked into that, didn't I?"

"I'm glad you did. I like this new wild side."

A chuckle escaped from her lips. "Man, please."

"Anyway, your dad," He lowered his voice to a conspiratorial whisper. "seems bent on not letting me anywhere near you."

"Dad is…." Her words trailed off.

"I know. He's a loving, overprotective father. Can you please tell him you've got this?"

"Dad will be Dad. He's just like…"

He gazed at her for a moment. "He's just like me," he finished.

She relented. "In some ways."

"Good ways?"

"Good ways, too, but you both can be hard-headed. Not knowing when to quit."

"It's hard to quit when you care for someone."

"That season has passed, Tyler," she spat sarcastically. "I wish you would let it go."

He pressed on regardless. "I can't. I miss us."

She waved him off. "You are seven years too late. I have moved on."

"I don't think you have."

Her head jerked up. "You can think whatever you like. That's your prerogative"

He softened his tone. "Madison, give us a chance. Why not pray about it, and let the Lord lead you?"

The hardness in her eyes met the softness in his gaze. "There's no need for that. I'm not interested. And on that note, stop looking at me like that."

"Like what?"

"You know—like you're trying to melt me with your eyes."

He tapped the side of his face then displayed an arresting smile. "I can't help it. You're at fault, looking gorgeous all the time."

She shifted uncomfortably, unsure how to respond. "Well, don't expect me to come running and throwing myself at you."

"Please do." He threw up his hands in mock surrender. "Like I said, I really like this new wild side."

"Ugh!" She cut her eyes at him. "I see you haven't heard a word I said."

"I have, but I still miss us."

"Well, enjoy as much of *us* as you can, because after this wedding you're getting a cease-and-desist order."

"You don't mean that. You know that I would never hurt you."

She thrust out her chin. "I used to think so, until I found you locked in Camela Caine's arms. You didn't have the decency to let me know you were in a relationship with her."

"There's not a kernel of truth in what you just said. I was not in a relationship with Camela. Why would you even think that?"

She blinked at him in surprise then recovered. "Don't pretend that you didn't know she had the hots for you. Everyone knew." She gave a little laugh. "At least, all the ladies did."

"Don't exaggerate. My role in the church caused me to be in contact with a lot of people."

She eyeballed him with barely-held contempt. "I can tell."

It was hard to miss the double meaning in her response. Perhaps, at any other time, Tyler would have laughed wildly, but he held himself together.

"Camela and I were never in a relationship. Her father had died. She had just visited when you saw us. But if you had stayed, you would have seen that I made her sit on the sofa. *By herself.* After that, I called the college chaplain and Mom to attend to her."

A heavy silence fell between them.

"You can't judge a book by its cover, Madison," Tyler warned. "Maybe you didn't notice that Camela was no longer in college. She is an only child and her dad had sole responsibility for her. Dad and Mom kept in touch

112

with her, to make sure she was okay. I believe Mom said that she got married...around three years ago."

Madison looked beyond him, before holding his gaze. "I'm sorry I judged you and the situation," she told him. "Thanks for clearing that up."

"I know that I hurt you Madison. Please—"

"Please put myself out there so you can hurt me again? I'll pass."

"I'm not saying—"

"I'll pass, Tyler," she repeated emphatically. "Been there and done that. Not returning. I humbly suggest you move on."

Tyler was about to speak, when Mason yelled from the patio, "Breakfast is ready!"

Madison sprang to her feet as if she had been caught doing something dubious.

"We'll pick up," Tyler said, rising.

Madison did not respond, and they walked in silence towards Mason.

Mason grinned as they approached. "Well, hello, early risers."

Madison avoided his gaze as she climbed the steps with Tyler on her heels.

"Hey, bro," Tyler said.

Mason did not respond; he was busy observing Madison. "You look fresh and...blushing," he whispered to her as she hurriedly slipped by him.

Madison cut her eyes at him before disappearing through the door.

Mason was not daunted; he was ready for Tyler. "Happy Saturday, isn't it?"

Tyler was ready, too. "Thanks, Captain Vigilant."

Mason chuckled softly.

Almost an hour later, after a healthy breakfast, they gathered in the kitchen—Madison and Kelani washing dishes, and Mason and Tyler drying. Madison had insisted that they give the kitchen staff a break.

Soft giggles caused them to turn.

Larry was landing soft kisses on Rozene's cheek as he trapped her with his hands against the island.

Madison and Kelani laughed quietly, their hands covered in soap at the sink.

Tyler's eyes bulged as he looked at Mason before turning back to the task at hand.

Mason couldn't help himself. "Mom! Dad!" he called out. "Good Lord, make me un-see it."

"Come on, cut me some slack," Larry said, as his wife buried her head in his chest, chuckling quietly.

"That we can do," Mason said, adopting a serious tone, "but promise me, no more children. This has got to stop somewhere."

That brought laughter all around.

Soon, the dishes were stacked and Rozene made sure that everyone knew the schedule for the day.

The men disappeared to do their own thing, and the women agreed to meet in the living room in fifteen minutes to head to the hairdresser. The ladies intended to doll-up for the engagement party.

******

"You two are looking great," Rozene told Madison and Kelani. "Are you sure you're only going to the hairdresser."

"Thanks, Mom. Only to the hairdresser," Madison responded, smiling while taking in her mother's flattering figure, wrapped in an ankle-length floral dress. "You're looking your supermodel-self, too."

Her mother grinned back at her. "You know I try."

A strangled sound came from Kelani, and both Rozene and Madison glanced her way. A tearful Kelani was watching them.

Madison hugged her shoulder. "Lani, what's going on?"

Kelani was quiet for a moment then she spoke. "I know you had said you would help me select a wedding dress, but," she looked at Rozene, "Mrs. Kanate, I would be grateful for your help, too."

"Of course," Rozene told her happily. "I would be honored."

As if she didn't hear Rozene, Kelani tried to make her case. "I know you're busy and—"

"Kelani," Rozene touched her shoulder. "Yes. Yeeeees. I will gladly help you find your perfect dress."

Smiling, Madison gently teased Kelani. "Mom is super busy, but she has been known to pull off more than a few miracles."

Tears ran down Kelani's cheeks, and Rozene pulled her into her arms. "I've got you." She kissed the top of Kelani's head. "You can call me any time to run your plans by me, okay?"

Kelani clung to her, mumbling a tearful "Thanks."

CHAPTER 14

Later that day, Madison sat beside Kelani in one of the limousines whose drivers were being greeted by Cedrick Somack, the chief security officer at the electronic entrance gate to the super exclusive Abella. Benson, a cousin to her father, owned this French restaurant and lounge. Madison and Mason affectionately referred to him as Uncle Benson.

The prestigious restaurant offered a unique contemporary French dining experience that tantalized the taste buds, leaving memories that would linger forever…well, that's if you could get a table in the first place.

It was Kelani's first time at Abella, but Madison recalled dining there with her parents more than a few times. "An investment in yourself that just won't ever dissatisfy," Uncle Benson would tell them every chance he got. And the restaurant did live up to the hype from all the great reviews in top chef magazines and on social media.

Madison couldn't help the smile that climbed her face as the driver slowly moved forward through the gate before proceeding through another entrance into the heart of the breathtaking location. Marked by elegance and luxury, the magnificent off-white and gold building borrowed generously from modern French architecture.

She remembered her father telling her about the origins of Abella.

Benson had met his wife, Abella, some twenty years ago while he was studying French cuisine in Paris. He was so taken by her beauty that he named his new restaurant after her. When she told him that her name meant *breath*, Uncle Benson did not skimp on cost, for he was determined that every detail—even the minute features of the restaurant—would be designed to 'take your breath away'.

And that it did. This stylish playground, which the rich and famous frequented for private parties and events, had become a hot spot. Filled with unimaginable treats, this exclusive setting was the perfect place for many celebrities to enjoy relaxing moments while sipping aperitifs before dinner.

The limousine came to a stop and Madison dramatically asked Kelani. "Are you ready to roll?"

A chuckle burst from Kelani's lips. "That was unexpected. I can't play with you this evening."

"That was my bad. My inner Amazon woman came at you, just like that." Madison's face squeezed into a huge grin. "She's back in hiding. Hopefully, for the rest of tonight." Madison whispered. "I told her she can't be out with me wearing this gorgeous royal blue Valentino gown."

Kelani chuckled. "Thanks for helping me to relax. That blue brings out the colors of your eyes. I really don't know how Mr. Chocolate is going to resist you."

"He'll be alright. Plus, I don't bite."

"Yes, right?" Kelani said drily. "By the end of the night he will be tattered."

"Tattered?" Madison clutched her chest as she pretended to be shocked, then grinned wickedly. "At least, he'll be alive."

"Shameful," Kelani admonished her, rolling her lips to the side.

Before Madison could respond, the doors opened on both sides to reveal two dashing men—booted and suited in black tuxedos.

Madison and Kelani glanced at each other before accepting the hands that were offered by Mason and Tyler.

"You look stunning," a smiling Tyler told Madison as they waited for Mason and Kelani to join them. His eyes roamed her body before settling on her face.

His outpouring of admiration startled her at first before the sides of her mouth twitched into a smile. "Thank you," she responded breathlessly, stifling the wild beating of her heart.

She turned to Mason and Kelani, who were still on the other side of the vehicle. "Are you two...?" She shook her head as she saw Mason flashing Kelani a rakish smile while admiring her fitted bodice, sleeveless, red sequined Valentino gown.

Sensing their stares, Mason and Kelani looked towards her and Tyler.

"Shameful," Madison teased mercilessly.

"Don't be a hater," Mason told her playfully, without a hint of shame.

Madison pivoted gracefully back to Tyler, her tiny side smile meeting his full-blown grin before blossoming widely. Her heart rate sped up as she witnessed the hint of desire in his eyes. She liked it.

He cocked his head to the side. "Did I tell you how amazing you look?" he asked softly.

Madison swallowed hard, opening her mouth to speak, but nothing came out. She cleared her throat. "Yes, you did."

"Are you two coming?" Mason's teasing voice reached them.

"Of course," Madison said, desperately trying to pull it together. *It must be the atmosphere*, she hastily concluded, accepting Tyler's arm.

They walked up the steps to the lobby. The glass doors to the lobby swung open, and a receptionist in a trendy black suit greeted and ushered them into the foyer.

A minute later, Susan Bowen, the wedding planner from All Things Divine, joined them. She was decked out in a navy blue pantsuit highlighting her mocha complexion. She smiled confidently at them with a set of even white teeth. "Good evening. It's a pleasure to have you here for this wonderful occasion."

While they all smiled their appreciation, Mason took the lead. "Thanks, Susan."

"Please come with me. I'll take you to a waiting area until it's time for you to make your entrance."

"Sure," Mason responded.

They followed Susan through the lobby, oblivious to the heads turning in their direction.

As Madison recalled, the lobby was gorgeous. Just perfect—open, immaculate, and welcoming. Beautiful arrangements of fresh flowers were intricately incorporated and the pleasing fragrances they emitted delighted her senses. A luxurious marble floor and radiant chandeliers grabbed their attention as they moved from the lobby to a bank of elevators that took them to a private room.

Madison briefly glanced around the cozy, yet quietly sophisticated room.

"Please make yourself comfortable," Susan said, smiling widely.

Mason spoke up. "Thanks, Susan. We will."

"You are most welcome. Everything is in place and we will proceed once your parents give permission to do so. I will be back shortly."

Murmurs of "Okay" filled the room.

Smiling, Susan made her exit.

The group walked further into the spacious room and reclined on the overstuffed white leather sofas, which were set around a coffee table with a tall floral arrangement, two gold trays with gold-rimmed glasses, and a selection of cold beverages.

Madison smiled at Kelani and Mason, who were sitting across from her and Tyler. "Are you both ready?"

Mason hugged Kelani shoulders. "Of course! Kelani got this. I plan to follow her lead."

Kelani nervously grinned up at him. "Boo, don't be saying all of that. I'm planning to follow *your* lead."

"Baby, you'll be okay," Mason reassured her, tenderly brushing his fingers across her cheeks. "I've got you covered."

Kelani's grin widened. "I know you do."

"Well, now that's settled," Tyler teased. "It's going to be great."

"Yes," Mason agreed. His eyes twinkled as he watched Madison. "And look, Madison is not wearing her save-the-world look."

That brought chuckles all around, and even Madison had to smile.

"You look great, my sister," Mason added. "But, I'm sure you were already told that." Mason's gaze shifted to Tyler.

"Boo," Kelani raced to their rescue. "Don't be upsetting them. We need them happy for our engagement party and wedding."

When Tyler and Madison would not dignify his comments with a remark, Mason chuckled. "You are truly two of a kind. I see you—wearing your perfected blank expressions."

Before Tyler or Madison could respond, a gentle knock on the door drew their attention.

"Come in," Mason called out.

The door opened and Susan entered, followed by joyful greetings from the rest of the bridal party—Laurie-Ann Mento, Rebecca Shorter, Robert Taylor, and Jayvis Shuler.

Susan looked towards Mason after the noise died down. "Mr. and Mrs. Kanate and your grandparents are all in place. Your uncles—Zane, Zadan, and Michel—are here, too." She zeroed in on Kelani. "And your parents are here."

She referred to Thomas and Edna Clarkson, who were operating as the bride's 'guardians'.

"Thank you," Kelani responded.

"So, ready when you are," Susan added, her eye trained on Mason.

"We need a few minutes," Mason told her, before looking at Tyler. "Let us pray. Pastor Tyler, can you do us the honor?"

"Sure," Tyler said, signaling for them to join hands in a circle.

"Father, it is in the name of Jesus Christ that we come to You," Tyler prayed. "Your Word said that where two or three are gathered, You will be in the midst of them. So, Lord, we are thankful that You are here with us. We thank You for this awesome occasion where we get a chance to celebrate Mason and Kelani's engagement.

"God, we call forth Your original plan and purpose for their lives. We speak Your anointing and divine success over their marriage. We pray everything will operate in accordance with Your timetable and that they will be daily loaded with benefits.

"Thank You, Lord, for allowing the rest of us to be a part of their wedding and this celebration. Remind us to continue praying for them, and to be a source of help, especially when they need it most.

"We pray everything concerning this celebration will be done decently and in order, and that we will have a great time. In the name of Jesus Christ we pray, amen."

A satisfying chorus of "Amens" and cheers filled the room.

Mason clutched Kelani to his side as his smile swept the group. "Let's get this party started."

CHAPTER 15

A seamless blend of classic sophistication and luxury, Madison thought two hours later. After much pomp and circumstance, her eyes still wandered around the ballroom, taking in its splendor—sparkling Swarovski crystal chandeliers adorned the beautifully decorated high gold-detailed ceilings and walls of the stunning six thousand square foot space with a capacity to seat almost five hundred guests. The apple-red, green, and gold decorations highlighted the cool off-white walls and plush cream-colored carpet. Floor-to-ceiling windows, even though curtain-dressed, drew guests to the awe-inspiring views of the lighted gardens.

Thanks to Susan, this celebration had everything that was expected at an engagement party and suited Mason and Kelani's warm personalities.

The moderator called for Mason with fanfare. He whispered to his fiancée, and then helped her out of her seat. Smiling, they strolled to the podium to cheers and heartfelt applause.

"Good evening, everyone," Mason said exuberantly, with a smiling Kelani by his side. "Thank you for joining us on this very momentous occasion."

The crowd continued clapping and cheering.

"Yeeeessss. It is a cause for celebration," Mason said, smiling. "I hate to sound cliché, but I never knew this day would come. I'm glad it's here."

"You'll be even happier when your wedding day comes!" Jayvis shouted from the bridal party table that was set at the forefront of the ballroom.

"Yes, Lord!" Mason put on his game face. "You feel me, my brother."

That brought more laughter to an already joyful occasion.

Mason waved a hand in the air. "But, we digress."

"That's alright!" someone shouted from the back of the room.

"Indeed," Mason said, glancing at Kelani. "You look beautiful, my fiancée."

A blushing Kelani grinned up at him, mouthing, "Thank you."

Mason looked at his parents, who were sitting with his grandparents, uncles, and Mr. and Mrs. Clarkson at a table next to the bridal party table.

"My dream was to have a love similar to what my parents share," Mason said, smiling.

"Awww," came from the guests.

His mother smiled widely with her hand on her chest, while his father wore a proud that's-my-son look.

"Folks," Mason continued, "my parents are exemplary, but honest to God, I thought we would have many, many, *many* more little Kanates running around here." He chuckled. "But God! The good Lord heard my cries."

Pockets of snickering broke out and some of the guests started to beat on tables, making the atmosphere even more euphoric.

"I digress," he admonished himself. "Thanks, Mom and Dad, for setting a great example for us to follow."

The guests cheered.

"Now, Kelani Andria Norwood, my fiancée, my love, my wife-to-be," Mason said proudly, "I have not stopped giving thanks for you, remembering you in my prayers." He paused to pull himself together, then continued.

"If finding the love of your life means finding someone you can always count on, no matter what—then, I am in love with you.

"If finding the love of your life means having someone who understands your heart—I am in love with you."

He kissed her cheek and Kelani buried her head in his chest. Mason held her for a moment whispering quietly in her ears in a bid to calm her.

Moments later, she lifted her head with tear-stained cheeks and he gently wiped her cheeks with his fingers.

He flashed her a smile and teasingly asked, "Can I continue now?"

"Yes," Kelani said softly. "I promise I have it together now."

More choruses of "Awww" filled the room.

Mason gazed at Kelani.

"If finding the love of your life means having someone to pray with—I am in love with you.

"If finding the love of your life means having someone who makes your heart skip a beat with just a smile—I am in love with you.

"If finding the love of your life means finding someone who loves you just for being you—I am blessed and highly favored to have found that perfect someone in you."

"Thank you." Kelani beamed at him and then kissed his cheek. She reached for the microphone.

Mason chuckled, moving the microphone out of her reach. "Wife-to-be, I'm not finished."

Kelani's mouth opened in a perfect 'O', bringing more laughter to the room.

"I have it together," Kelani said, chuckling loudly.

"See, that's why I love you," Mason declared. "I love the way you're wise and perceptive. The way you trust your intuition and your consistent commitment to all that you do. I am encouraged by the strength of your character, by your drive to succeed, and by your resilience to bounce back even stronger when things don't go according to plan.

"No matter what may come our way, I will always find the courage to smile by thinking thoughts of you.

"On this special day, I pledge to you my love. You are my wife-to-be, my friend, my love —" he paused to gather himself, and as his eyes swept the gathering then landed on Kelani, he choked back tears, "—my heart. For with you, I have found where my heart belongs. Thank you for your unending love. I love you."

A hush fell on the room as they hugged.

When they broke apart, Kelani reached for the microphone that was resting on the podium.

She wiped her eyes with her fingertips. "I love you, Mason Shane Kanate," she told him, smiling. "I love sooo many things about you. With you, I've found someone I can be myself with; someone I can pray with; someone I can laugh with. With you, I've found someone I always like to be around, no matter what we are doing. With you, I've discovered someone that I can share just about anything with—my hopes, my vision, my dreams, the good times, and the bad times."

She grinned at a mystified Mason. "With you, I've found a love beyond my imagination. Your warmth, thoughtfulness, understanding, and depth of care have touched my heart more than you know. With you, I have found exactly where my heart belongs.

"I thank God every day for blessing me with you. For with you, I've found the love of my life and my best friend, wrapped in one package. Thank you for helping me to be the best version of myself."

Kelani paused, obviously tamping down her emotions.

The silence in the room was deafening as the guests gave her time to recover.

Mason hugged her to his side, brushing his lips across her forehead. When she was ready, he released her.

She gazed up at him. "You are everything I have always wanted in a husband and so much more. Thank you for your unending love. I love you."

She threw her arms around Mason's waist and gave him a tight squeeze. He held her even tighter.

"What about us?" Someone yelled from the back.

Kelani released Mason and he took the microphone from her.

"You'll have to wait your turn," Mason said, chuckling. "Thank you for bearing with us. As some of you may know, our coming together was a journey, and I will add—perfectly orchestrated by our Almighty God."

Loud applause reverberated in the room.

"Thank you! We thank God for His unending love towards us." Mason paused, distracted by a beaming Kelani, who then nudged him back to reality.

Pockets of snickering broke out in the room.

"Your day will come," Mason warned, smiling. "It is great to know there are people in our lives who take such pleasure in doing special things and making us feel great. Thank you to my parents—Larry and Rozene Kanate—for not only being an awesome example for us, but for putting on this grand occasion for us to celebrate our engagement."

He smiled at his parents. "Mom and Dad, please stand."

The guests cheered and beat the tables as his father rose and helped his wife to her feet.

"Beautiful and handsome. Brave and strong. Spirit-filled and loving." Mason threw compliments their way.

His parents smiled, waving at him and Kelani before taking their seats.

"So now you know where I got my fine features," Mason drawled.

Chuckles erupted in the room.

"But, enough about me," he said, clearly enjoying himself. "Extra special thanks to my very young grandparents—Benjamin and Elizabeth Bennady. They are my mother's parents," he explained. "Grandma Liz, you are beautiful. Folks, now you see where Mom got her great features."

"Ahem. Ahem," came from Grandpa Ben, and pockets of laughter broke out.

Mason laughed out. "My bad, Grandpa Ben. Mom definitely has some of your features."

"Now you tell me!" Grandpa Ben yelled, causing more laughter.

"Better late than never," Mason told him, playfully. "Please wave your hands, Grandpa Ben and Grandma Liz, for those who don't know you."

Smiling and wearing a proud look, his grandparents waved their hands.

"Yes, folks," Mason chuckled, "the Bennady look is undeniable."

The guests cheered.

"Special thanks, too, to my one living grandparent on my father's side. Shout out to this special lady—our beautiful prayer warrior, Grandma Darlene. Make some noise for Grandma Darlene as she waves a hand."

When the noise died, Mason continued. "I cannot go any further without mentioning Thomas and Edna Clarkson, the guardians of my dear wife-to-be. Thank you, Mr. and Mrs. Clarkson for loving and nurturing Kelani into the marvelous woman of God that she has become. I am forever indebted to you. And, just in case I had forgotten to tell you, always remember that you are family. I love and appreciate you."

Deafening applause and cheers went up.

Smiling, Thomas and Edna Clarkson waved at Mason. He smiled at them, and then rested the microphone on the podium and began to clap, too.

Soon, Mason picked up the microphone, and begun speaking again. "Thanks to my aunt Alexandria, and my uncles Zane and Zadan—all on my father's side. Also, thanks to Uncle Michel, on my mom's side of the family. Thank you to Uncle Benson and his beautiful wife, aunt Abella. Thank you, everyone for coming out to celebrate with us. Feel free to dance the night away."

"Yessss!" came from some of their guests, causing spluttering of laughter.

Mason smiled at Kelani, then told their guests, "I'm so glad my wife-to-be is a dancer." He chuckled. "I was not gifted in that area. Without further ado, please join us on the dance floor."

He held Kelani's hand and led her to the center of the room.

CHAPTER 16

Madison wandered back to the ballroom and saw that many of the guests had left, while others were milling around—chatting and eating. She caught sight of Mason and Kelani near the front of the room, talking with Pastor Fotola.

She'd managed to escape to the balcony over half an hour ago, after rejecting several invitations to dance as she tried to slip away. The pressure of being in Tyler's presence had been a lot to handle. He was awakening feelings in her that had lain dormant for years.

Dormant.

She wished!

Her desire for him had fizzed its way to the top of her heart.

And despite its sudden appearance, it refused to go away. Still, there was no denying the attraction that she felt for him.

This setting is to be blamed, she concluded, meandering to the area where they were serving drinks.

Smiling politely, she nodded at two ladies who were sitting at a table nearby.

"May I have a glass of water, please?" Madison asked the server.

He smiled at her. "Sure, Ms. Kanate, I can take it to your table, if you'd like."

"That's alright. I'll wait," Madison told him.

"Just a minute, please," he responded.

Madison's mind drifted until she was distracted by the conversation of the ladies at the table.

"Yes. Yes. Yes. I hear him calling my name," one said. "Yeesss! I'll take that cupcake anytime!"

The other woman giggled foolishly. "Me first. He's super yummy."

With arched brows, Madison turned to see whom the gush fest was about. Her heart began a crazy dance when her eyes landed on Tyler strutting towards her.

"Ladies," Tyler greeted the women as he rolled by them.

"Heeeey," they cooed.

But Tyler wasn't taking them up on their obvious offer. He smiled widely at Madison, moving into her personal space. "Thank God I've found you. I've been looking all over for you. Where did you go?"

Oh wow! She watched as Tyler's eyes traveled her evening gown, which she knew accentuated her figure before cascading to the floor.

"Errr...." The intensity of his gaze caused her to forget what she intended to say.

"Your water, Ms. Kanate," the server interrupted them, his gaze swinging between them.

Tyler took the glass of water and offered his arm to her.

Madison took it.

"Come now, tell me where we are off to?" Tyler asked conspiratorially.

A surprise giggle escaped Madison. *Lord, have mercy!* "We?" she asked.

Tyler wiggled his eyebrows. "Yes, we."

"The balcony. That's where I was camping out after the reception," she said, grinning up at him. "I hope we can make it there without being seen."

"Which exit?"

"Side door, on the left."

That was all Tyler needed to hear. Subtly, he moved them through the room and out the side door.

The huge frosted glass door swooshed shut behind them and laughter bubbled through their mouths.

"We made it. Where to?" Tyler asked with great urgency.

"It's through the glass door," Madison said, still chuckling as she pointed to a double door with a male security officer standing by it.

They walked towards it and Madison greeted the officer, who let them through.

"I can see why you ran away and stayed here," Tyler said, as he moved Madison across the huge balcony towards wooden rails.

"Gorgeous, right?" Madison said, watching as Tyler took in the awe-inspiring view of the city lights.

"For sure," Tyler said, handing her the glass of water.

She barely drank any, since he was staring at her so intently. She needed to back away from him. He was way too close.

As if sensing her deliberations, he stepped slightly away from her, but still kept his eyes on her.

What is he looking at? Gosh! She stopped drinking and glanced around to avoid looking at him.

When she looked back at him, he was still piercing her with his gaze.

"Will you stop that," she said, eyeing him. His gaze was unbearably intimate.

"Stop what?"

She felt her temperature shoot up several notches. "You know what, Tyler," she said, blushing.

He took the glass from her stiff fingers and rested it on the narrow ledge nearby.

"I believe you know I can't help it."

His voice was like a sweet caress, so Madison busied herself with an intelligent look as she prepared to engage him. "I'm not following your line of reasoning," she said, and then almost winched. It sounded like—*Tell me more. I'm all yours.*

His all-knowing smile and the mirth in his eyes told her he didn't buy it. "I have always had difficulty keeping my eyes off you," he said, moving closer.

His words felt like a jolt. She was all over the place—infuriated and mesmerized in the same breath.

"It was hard watching all your fawning suitors making a beeline for you every chance they got." He chuckled softly, caressing her cheek with the back of his hand.

"Hmm!" Madison held back a moan as fire leapt through her veins at his touch. *Step away*, her mind begged him, even though she didn't want him to stop.

He moved his hand from her cheeks but continued to watch her. There was no apology in his stare.

He stared at her. Fixated, the same way he'd been the first time he'd glanced to his right and caught her gaze across the hall at Trinity Baptist Church.

She almost swallowed her tongue when he leaned in. *Oh God.* Her heart thumped against her ribcage and she all but lost her senses as the woodsy scent of his cologne filled her nostrils.

"How do you do it?" he asked, his expression puzzled as if he couldn't understand something monumental.

"What?" she puffed out.

"Look elegant all the time, like the world is your oyster."

Adrenaline rushed between them.

It was electric.

He pulled her against him, and she melted against his rock-hard abs.

Their breaths whirled together as he gazed down at her. "You are so beautiful," he said lifting her chin so that she could look at him.

She flashed him a toothy smile.

"From the first day that I met you," Tyler said, his voice was above a whisper. "I've been in love—"

"Madison."

Immediately, Madison felt Tyler's hand drop from her waist as they both turned towards the door and saw the look of displeasure on her father's face.

Heat rushed to her cheeks as she stared at Tyler, then back at her father.

She pulled away. "Did you need something, Dad?" she asked, looking beyond her father.

"Your mother wanted to speak with you. We're about to leave."

After a hard stare at Tyler, her father went through the door.

The silence was deafening as they both stared after him.

"Good night," Madison puffed out as she moved to follow her father.

Tyler touched her shoulder, but she shrugged him off.

"Why are you mad at me?" he asked.

"That's what you do all the time—think about yourself. And let's pretend that didn't just happen," she spat at him over her shoulder.

"What are you talking about?"

She felt her defenses climbing as she swung around. "You know what I mean." She paused long enough to watch the spark die in his eyes before walking away.

CHAPTER 17

"Oh, boy." Madison cringed as she pressed the button to open the entrance gate to her home. She knew sooner or later it would come down to this—a visit from Kelani. She had been avoiding a face-to-face with her best friend.

Hiding.

That's what she'd been doing.

Anything not to see Tyler.

She had not traveled back with the group after the engagement party. She couldn't even muster up the courage to see the group off. She'd texted them to say that her father wanted her assistance on a project, so she would be staying behind to get details. Further, she was feeling oh-so-tired, and she would definitely be sleeping in.

Tired. Now that was the truth.

She barely slept because of her impromptu rendezvous with Tyler. Thanks to him, a verse from Song of Solomon—*"Let him kiss me with the kisses of his mouth: for thy love is better than wine"*—kept playing in her head.

Her every waking moment was spent arguing with herself for almost allowing him to kiss her. Worst, she had really wanted him to. *Wow! Oh, wow! Slay me now.*

Her train of thought caused her to greet Kelani with crumpled eyebrows.

"Whoa," Kelani said, walking through the door. "You are not a sight for sore eyes. What's up with that hard stare? Did someone hurt you? Do I need to do a drive-by?"

Chuckling, Madison closed the door and then hugged her shoulder. "Noooo. I was just thinking," she said, leading her into the living room.

"I can see that. I hope it wasn't about me or I may have to call for back-up."

Madison chuckled even louder, dropping on the sofa. "Stop. Just stop."

Kelani studied her. "I know you are trying to avoid Tyler, but what's up with avoiding me?"

"Come now, would your sister, best friend, and maid-of-honor try to avoid you?"

"Who are you?" Kelani slowly took a seat in the sofa, dropping her purse on the floor beside her. "What have you done with Madison?"

Madison laughed loudly. "I couldn't make it to dinner at Tyler's home yesterday. You know how busy my Saturdays get. I even had to pop by Estrina's. Girl, I was even too tired to make church this morning."

"I hear you."

"Why would you say it like that?"

Kelani smiled at her. "They say, 'The human heart feels things the eyes cannot see, and knows what the mind cannot understand.'"

"Okay, then. You have something to say, Lani?" Madison asked with a hard stare.

"Oh, so now you want to act like you don't know what I'm talking about. Anyway, Tyler's home is gorgeous and his cooking is on point. He'd make a fine chef. He said that he took a cooking class while he was doing his master's degree."

"Good for him." Madison attempted to sound uninterested.

Kelani looked at her knowingly.

"What?" Madison asked, guilty as ever.

"You know what, Madison? I never considered you a chicken, but look at you. You can't even admit that you're in love with Tyler."

"In love? Why would you ever think that?"

"Girl, please. All that hiding that you're doing. I know that's why you didn't come back with us after our engagement party." She lifted a hand as Madison opened her mouth to speak. "Yes, I know you were tired. I've been there and done that. You could at least admit to yourself that you're having feelings for him. That's a start."

Madison relented. "I'm having feelings for him. Feelings I don't want."

"And you're thinking that avoiding him will make those feelings go away?"

"It's a start."

"Good luck with that. Seriously, Madison, you need to let go of that aspect of your life and let God. Good men are hard to find. The least you can do is start praying about your relationship with Tyler. Plus, you need to get to know him. It has been seven years. That's a long time."

"No. Not happening."

"Wasn't that the same advice you gave me when I was sprinting away from Mason?"

Madison mouth swept to the side as she looked at Kelani.

"I am looking out for you," Kelani told her quietly. "Like you look out for me... all the time. It's okay to need someone, Madison. I have never seen you so alive. Not even Carlton brought out that twinkle in your eyes."

"Twinkle?" Madison avoided her gaze.

"You know what I mean." Kelani laughed softly. "Even though I figured you should have at least had a twinkle in your eyes when Carlton walked towards you and got down on one knee. Girrrl, he was strutting like a peacock. Proud and strong, but ooh so wrong!"

Bubbles of laughter escaped Madison. "You are wrong for that."

Kelani's face grew serious. "Promise me you will pray about Tyler," she encouraged. "I'll be praying, too."

Madison was quiet for a moment. "I don't want to, but I will."

"I know." Kelani smiled at her. "Brutally honest, as usual."

Suddenly, Kelani's laughter filled the air. "Girl, you missed Mason's dance class with Tyler. A mess." She shook her head. "How is it that I ended up with a husband-to-be who cannot dance? It's unbelievable."

Madison snorted at Kelani's puzzled expression. "At least you know that, going into the marriage." She snickered. "He was not a sight for sore eyes, huh?"

Kelani grinned back at her. "My poor boo thang. He's trying, though, and that just makes me love him more. I think he'll be at 'C-plus', by our wedding day."

"Awww, how sweeeeet," Madison teased. "I can hear you now—keep going, boo, you're killing it."

She let out a soft chuckle. "I don't care what you say, I love him. He's my bo-bo. Even though he dances like a robot."

Laughter spilled from Madison. "Everything is shaping up nicely for you and your bo-bo's wedding. I saw Mom's group text to us this morning. I need to respond. I was eating when I saw it."

"Yes. Next week, we are going to hunt for my wedding dress."

"I'm so glad Mom is coming with us. At least I will get retail therapy, for I'm sure she will keep bridezilla away."

"I know you didn't say that. I think you'll be a bigger bridezilla than I could ever be."

"You best believe that." Madison laughed. "Have you settled on the style you would like?"

"I was thinking of going with the mermaid look, but I decided on the ballgown style, simply because this is my fairy tale."

"I like that. You will look fabulous—fitted bodice, flair at the waist with a full skirt. It will emphasize your tiny waist. That's ideal for your body type." She grinned at Kelani. "All that eating and you're still skinny."

"All that eating? Don't forget I'm still dancing, so that keeps the weight at bay. And I see you losing the skinny."

Madison laughed. "I know. I gained five pounds. Definitely feeling a bit fuller, but I like it. Always felt as thin as a wafer."

"We're almost the same height—five-seven. You would look great in the ballgown-style wedding dress, too. I suspect Tyler won't be waiting to put a ring on your finger. You better keep all your wedding planning notes. Anyway, I'll be on hand."

"Well, that's that then," Madison responded and then pursed her lips.

Kelani sniggered. "I see you rebuking that spirit. I'm going to let that slide since you made me laugh."

Laughter bubbled from Madison's lips. "No comment."

Kelani settled deeply in the sofa. "I keep forgetting to mention this: when we just started planning for the wedding, the guys met at Tyler's home—to eat, plan, and watch a basketball game. Do you remember?"

Madison knitted her brows. "That was back in February, late February, I'm recalling."

"Exactly! That way back. Over four month ago." Kelani chuckled. "My bad. I kept forgetting to mention this—Laurie-Ann told me that Jayvis told her that while the wedding planning was going on, the guys started to talk about what they wanted more than anything else in the world. Nothing wrong with that. The only thing is—Tyler had nothing to contribute to the conversation. He said that he would talk about it another time." Kelani eyeballed her. "I think you should check that out."

Madison looked into her serious eyes, a smile curving her lips. "You think he wants to join the mob."

"I'm serious, Madison. I understand he may not want to share with the other guys since he doesn't know them well, but I thought you should know," she hastily added, "since you have an interest in each other."

"I don't know about all that, but if anything like that comes up in our conversation, I sure will ask Tyler."

"And that's all I ask."

They were quiet for a moment before Kelani asked, "You're still reading that book?" She asked, pointing towards the center table.

Madison smiled. *"Our Secret Place.* It's really good. It's my third read. You know if I love a book, I'll read it again and again."

"What's it about? I feel like I need to read it. Albeit, I shouldn't be taking book recommendations from you."

"Girl, stop, that was just one book. And, you confessed that you didn't read that genre, anyway."

"It was a mess. I couldn't get past the first page. Yikes." She laughed. "I wish I could unread it."

Madison laughed at Kelani's remorseful expression. "Girl, stop. You will love this one. It's about a young woman who finds herself in a hospital, but the thing is, she has amnesia—she can't remember her name and there is no identification on her. And guess what? She's pregnant."

"Oh, wow!"

"The plot is exciting. There is a couple in the story who is dealing with a miscarriage. From what I have read, the author had multiple pregnancy losses early in her marriage, so she felt led by God to write this story, to help women deal with this grief."

"Look at God. He will use all the situations in our lives for His glory."

"Amen to that. You know what the Word says, '…all things work together for good to them that love God, to them who are the called according to his purpose.'"

Kelani smiled. "It sure does. Living testimony over here."

Madison grinned back at her, nodding her agreement.

Suddenly, Kelani clapped her hands.

"What have you got?" Madison's eyes popped with excitement.

"Girrl, your two handsome uncles decided to pay for our honeeeymoon!" Kelani beamed. "Isn't that amazing? Thank You, Lord."

"Yay! That's awesome!"

Madison couldn't help the smile that lit her face. She loved her uncles Zane and Zadan. Her father had three siblings—forty-five-year-old Alexandria, born after him, followed three years later by his twin brothers, Zane and Zadan.

"Does that mean you'll be able to honeymoon in Jamaica and Europe?"

"Yes. I felt so bad when Mason said okay let's just do Jamaica. He has been to Jamaica a few times, but I have always wanted to visit." Kelani jumped off the sofa and began dancing around. "Go, Jesus! Thank You, Jesus!"

"You go, girl!" Madison said, laughing.

Winded, Kelani plopped down on the sofa.

"I see you," Madison said. "In fact, I'm seeing you back from honeymoon with twins. Don't forget they run in the family."

Kelani flushed.

"Don't pass out on me. I was just kidding."

Kelani regained her composure. "Looking for nieces and nephews, huh?"

"Would be nice. But, by your response, I am sure I'll have to wait a while."

"Yes," Kelani confirmed, not looking at Madison. "We're planning on having children, perhaps, after two years or so." She reached for the book on the coffee table and dropped it in her purse. "Thanks. I'm going to check out this book."

Madison noticed she'd changed the subject.

She let it go.

CHAPTER 18

"Thanks for praying with me, Dad," Tyler said, staring through the windshield of his car in the parking lot of First Missionary Baptist Church.

"You're—" Daniel Bradshaw paused to cough.

Concern filled Tyler as he waited for his father to return to their phone conversation.

"Sorry about that, Son," Daniel said.

"Dad, promise me you will take care of that cough. You have been coughing like that for a while. Actually, since you've had the flu. And, Dad, you've been wheezing more. Something is not right."

"Son, don't worry. I went to the doctor yesterday and he gave me medication for acute bronchitis. I trust God; He's a healer."

"Amen." Tyler smiled. His father's faith had always been strong.

"All the best with your sermon," his father said. "The Holy Spirit will guide you."

"Thanks, Dad. I'm glad you called."

"We're a team, son." He paused and Tyler heard murmurs in the background. "My darling wife, your mother, said that she is praying for you."

Tyler smiled. "Tell Mom thanks. I'll come and see you both after the wedding."

"Great," Daniel responded. "I love you, son. Bye."

"I love you, too, Dad. Bye."

Tyler disconnected the call, silenced his phone, and dropped it into the pocket of his jacket.

He slid from behind the steering wheel of his Jeep.

He felt great.

Bold.

Confident.

Powerful.

"Thank You, Lord, for choosing me," he said quietly, while smoothing the jacket of his signature black Michael Kors suit. He perfected it with a white shirt and orange silk tie with a two-toned basket weave design.

His heart rate kicked up, causing him to glance about the parking lot. A smile whipped across his face when he saw Madison striding purposefully towards the church.

"Madison," he called out, locking his vehicle.

She stopped in her tracks, her eyes floating over the other church-goers to locate him.

He sped to her side, for he had not seen her in forever. "Good evening," he greeted her warmly, taking in the attractiveness of her burgundy lace high-low dress. "Thank you for coming."

She was stoic. "Good evening, Tyler. My appointment was cancelled, so I decided to attend the convention."

"I'm glad you did. I was beginning to think you were avoiding me."

"Please don't think that way. Work has gotten a bit hectic. Thanks for accommodating the wedding planning on the phone."

He smiled widely. "You're welcome, but I would rather see you in person."

She looked away. "I would rather we focus on the tasks that were assigned to us by Mason and Kelani. All the best with your sermon."

"Thank you." He held on to her hand, and she allowed it. "Please keep me in your prayer. I'm trusting that the Holy Spirit will move to bless the people of God."

"I will." Madison made an effort to move forward, but he was still holding her hand. She looked up at him. "I have to go."

"Right. Me, too," he said, smiling and releasing her hand.

She watched him carefully. "And didn't I ask you to stop doing that?"

"Doing what?"

"Acting as if you're trying to melt me with your eyes."

A soft chuckle escaped him. "Sorry, milady, I was not aware I was doing that."

Madison sashayed off without a backward glance.

God, I love that woman. Tyler smiled inwardly. It was as exhilarating as it was terrifying. The opposing emotions tore through his heart. Yet, somehow, they helped to create an amazing picture of their future.

Forty-five minutes later, after a rousing praise and worship session, Reverend Joseph Tanner of First Missionary Baptist Church introduced the person he hoped would be the church's youth minister in the near future—Tyler Bradshaw.

Tyler walked to the podium, set high above the congregation, and placed his Bible on it.

He lifted the cordless microphone to his lips. "Praise the Lord, church!" he said, his eyes circling the congregation before settling on Madison, who was sitting in the third row beside Mason and Kelani.

"Praise the Lord!" the congregation responded.

Tyler piped up, "Thanks for coming out to the second day of our youth conference. It is Friday, so I know you could be anywhere, but you chose to be in the house of the Lord. For that, I am grateful. Please be seated."

Tyler waited for the congregation to settle down.

"I give honor to God who is the head of my life," he declared. "There is no one like Jehovah."

The congregation cheered and Tyler smiled. His eyes drifted to Madison, and he was taken aback as he locked eyes with her father, who was sitting beside his wife, next to Madison. Not that he was afraid of Larry Kanate and his intimidation tactics; he was just amazed that he would go to such lengths, seeing Madison could more than fend for herself.

"Let us pray," Tyler said. Distracted by his mental diatribe, he sounded more forceful than he intended. *Holy Spirit, I need You more than ever,* he silently prayed. *I need more courage, more love, more of You in my heart.*

"Father, You are Lord, and we honor You. Thank You for this opportunity to share Your Word with Your people. Lord, let Your Word fall on the fertile soil of their hearts. In the name of Jesus Christ, I pull down every stronghold and cast down every vain imagination, and every high thing that seeks to come against the knowledge of Jesus Christ.

"Speak through me, Lord, so that Your people will be nourished and blessed by Your Words. I subject my thoughts to Your lordship. As I speak, may Your anointing destroy yokes, shackles, chains, and bondages from the lives of Your people. In the name of Jesus Christ I pray, amen."

Tyler smiled at the congregation. "Before I begin, I want to take this time to thank the pastor and shepherd of this flock—Reverend Joseph Tanner—for the opportunity to stand before you and share the Word of God. I consider it a privilege. Thanks, too, to Elder Sarah Tanner, his beautiful wife and first lady of this church."

The congregation began to clap, and Tyler placed the microphone on the podium and clapped, too.

Retrieving the mic, Tyler continued, "Thanking God for the other leaders of this church, who considered it not robbery to welcome me here and nurture me in the care and admonition of the Lord."

"Praise the Lord!" and "Amen" rang out from the congregation.

Smiling, Tyler said, "I am grateful, too, for the support of my friends – Madison Kanate and Mason Kanate and his fiancée, Kelani Norwood. Glad also to have the anointed Mr. and Mrs. Larry Kanate in the house."

Tyler's eyes warmed as he swept across the bunch and they smiled back at him.

"Let's praise the Lord for all the young people who are here this evening."

The congregation gave up unprompted praise to the Lord as they clapped and shouted.

"Thanks, everyone, for coming out," Tyler said. "Briefly, I want to share with you what God has placed on my heart for a time such as this. If you are here, this Word is for you...and for me." He chuckled. "God is good; He gave me a Word for you and for me. Please turn your Bibles to Psalm 119:11 and stand when you've found it."

He waited before saying, "Let's read together— 'Thy word have I hid in mine heart, that I might not sin against thee.' You may be seated," Tyler instructed.

The congregation sat and looked attentive.

"The Scripture says," Tyler's voice rang out, "'Thy word have I hid in mine heart, that I might not sin against thee.' Oh God, deliver us from sin and the bondages of sin. You see, we must continuously be delivered in our spirits and in our minds, from the bondages of sin. None of us can deliver ourselves from sin. Only God can deliver us from sin."

He smiled as he looked at the congregation. "I am forever grateful to God for sending His son, Jesus Christ, to shed His blood for my sins and your sins."

The congregation knocked their tambourines and clapped while belting aloud praises to God.

After the worship died down, Tyler picked up. "Jesus Christ came to preach deliverance to the captives. The anointing of God on His life enabled Him to preach to the captives—to tell them there is a way out. We cannot be God's people and still be tied or yoked to sinful pleasures. Imprisoned to bad thoughts, ideas, and practices."

Tyler stepped beside the podium, pausing for maximum impact. "There are many people—many people—who are filled with the Holy Spirit, but still in prison in certain areas of their lives. Yes, it is possible."

The congregation was all ears.

"Many people are not free to love because they are held by years of past hurt. They have allowed the hurt they experienced to hold them hostage. But God wants His people to be delivered, to give Him praise and glory. We need to be set free in our minds, body, and spirit to praise God."

"Amen!" rang out like a chorus.

"I am thankful today for the blood of Jesus Christ that delivers. For I know that in the middle of my storm—" he paused to hold it together. "In the middle of my storm, I'm holding on to Jesus. I am praying and depending on the Word of God to instruct me and keep me.

"Psalm 119:105 states, 'Thy word is a lamp unto my feet, and a light unto my path.' Sin will keep you bound, but the Bible tells us where the Spirit of the Lord is, there is freedom."

He moved back to the podium, his eyes scanning the congregation. "I have been set free by the mercy of God. I will not allow the enemy to take me back to where I am coming from. Listen to me—you cannot allow the enemy to take you back to where you are coming from.

"If you have not been delivered and you are tired of living that lifestyle, I have good news for you—there is a pathway to deliverance.

"Here you go—as long as there is a comfortableness with your situation, you will never, ever be delivered. The gateway to being set free is to cry out to the Lord. Cry out to the Lord. The praying person will be delivered."

"Do you have family members who are not saved? Do you have a child who is not living up to his or her potential? Pray for them."

He paused as spur-of-the-moment worship filled the atmosphere.

"When you are God's children," Tyler told them quietly, "there is an expiration date on your problems." He became louder. "I said, when you are God's children, there is an expiration date on your problems! It may be long, but it will not be forever."

That got the congregation excited and spontaneous praise broke out again, and the musicians played loudly as they, too, praised the Lord.

Tyler walked down the short flight of stairs and stood at the altar. "It may have you bound today," Tyler cried out, "but deliverance is ahead for you. Come to the altar and let's pray together. Whatever you need—come. There is room at the altar for you."

Tyler's deep, rich baritone voice rang out as he began to sing "You Deserve It," one of his favorite worship songs by gospel recording artistes, JJ Hairston and Youthful Praise.

He paused and as the band played, he encouraged the congregation, "Come on, everybody, open up your mouths and let's worship the Lord. He's worthy of the glory. He deserves the praise. Come on! Come on, brothers and sisters; open your mouths and worship. Lift your hands and voices and praise God."

High praises along with clapping swept across the congregation.

When Tyler began to sing again, many members of the congregation walked to the altar, and the praise team joined Tyler in song.

Pastor Tanner and Tyler laid hands on those who came forward and prayed for them.

CHAPTER 19

"Will you bring Madison to see us after the wedding?" Paulette Bradshaw's voice rang out through the speakers in Tyler's Jeep. He could hear the smile in his mother's voice. He had just backed out of Mason's driveway when she called.

"Mom, I wish, but as it is, she's bent on only keeping things courteous between us."

"Things will work themselves out, Ty. She is still feeling crushed by your rejection back in the day. Keep praying for her and continue to wow her with your love. Plus, remember your dream."

"Thanks, Mom. It seems I rarely dream these days."

"That's alright, son. We trust the Lord."

"Amen," Tyler agreed, turning on the road leading to Madison's home. "Is Dad still sleeping?"

When no response came, Tyler spoke again. "Mom, are you there?"

"Uh—yes. Yes, I am. Was sipping my coffee."

Tyler chuckled. "I'm not surprised. Your second cup, I'd say."

"You know me too well," she laughed. "Yes, Daniel is asleep. He went back to the doctor yesterday because he didn't think the meds were effective. The new meds are making him drowsy."

"He only took the first set of meds for a week. I suppose I'm so accustomed to him being up and running, it's hard to think he's sleeping, and during the day, too. Strange. Do I need to come home?"

"No." Paulette laughed softly. "He'll be alright. I hate to tell you he's enjoying all the pampering I'm giving him. I don't think he's going to remember how to bathe himself when he's better."

Tyler laughed, too. "Mom, I will buzz you later. I'm at Em's entrance gate. I'm picking her up to do more wedding planning."

"Well, that's a good thing." Her voice was teasing. "Tell her I said hello. And son, keep all the notes."

He chuckled. "I will. And of course, I'll keep the notes. I'll be ready when the Lord gives the green light."

"I like that, son."

He could hear the joy in his mother's voice and that brought out his smile.

"Tyler, Aunt Rachel is grumbling about not hearing from you."

Tyler's smile widened. His mother's older sister, who lived in their neighborhood in Boston, loved talking with him about everything.

"I'll call her soon. I already told her that this wedding has me ripping and running."

"Okay, son. Have fun and I'll talk with you later. I love you. Bye-bye."

"I love you, too, Mom. Bye."

Tyler pressed the button on his steering wheel to disconnect the call.

As he reached for the gate remote, a familiar sense of excitement nipped him and his heart raced. *Lord, help me to keep it together.*

He pressed the button and when the gate opened, he drove through, pressing the button again to close it. After parking before the front patio, he rushed up the steps and rang the doorbell.

He waited…and waited.

He was sure he had heard footsteps and rustling on the other side of the door, but it did not open. He rang the doorbell again.

His insides jittered when the door swung open and Madison stood there, clearly surprised to see him.

"Hello," he attempted a smile while stifling a groan as his eyes landed on the roundness of her breasts under the closely-fitted white t-shirt she wore.

"Hi," she responded drily.

He could see the various expressions in her eyes as she contemplated letting him in.

"I was expecting Mason," she finally said, as she stood back to let him in.

"He said that he would call you to let you know I was on the way."

Tyler entered and closed the door. He could literally feel her rolling her eyes at Mason's trickeries.

"He had to pick up Kelani," Tyler explained, "so he asked me to pick up the things you have for him, since they wouldn't fit in your car."

"Okay." She watched him for a moment. "This way."

She moved through the entryway to the living room.

Tyler valiantly tried to focus on the mission at hand, even as she strolled ahead of him in a pair of yellow shorts. His mission for being at her home was the last thing on his mind, for he couldn't help admiring her toned legs. As his temperature rose a couple notches, he reminded himself to get his thoughts right.

He smiled inwardly. It was as exciting as it was startling, the effect she had on him. He had to admit, he loved the way the conflicting emotions always seemed to run through his mind, painting a stunning picture of the lasting memories he hoped to create with her. Well, if she would only allow it.

She released a soft sigh, and that sound made his stomach flip.

He came back to life and realized he was staring at her. *Whatever.* He wouldn't apologize for staring. Clearly, she was bent on torturing him for his lack of courage seven years ago.

"Nice place," he ventured, his heart thumping hard.

"Thanks." The slight edge in her voice indicated his remark was neither here nor there, as far as she was concerned.

Nice? Her home is amazing. Tyler's eyes scanned the sprawling living room, noting the elaborate detail of the architecture, cutting-edge amenities, and elegance of the styling. With its white, light green, and yellow color scheme, the living room was luxurious, yet livable and functional. Her attention to detail had always been uncompromising.

He smiled inwardly; there was no clutter of any kind. The only things out of place were the three piles of books on the ground, along with her tablet. Despite that, the look and feel of her home whispered perfection.

A huge grin covered his face when his eyes landed on the yellow stone fireplace. Definitely a conversation piece.

"All the stuff for Mason is over there." Madison pointed to a stack of boxes next to the sofa. "You can stack them in your Jeep while I drag on my jeans."

"Sure will," he said, then watched as she walked across the room and began climbing the stairs.

Fifteen minutes later, he had finished packing his Jeep and was sitting on the sofa when he heard Madison descending the stairs. He stood, tucked his hands into the pockets of his jeans, and watched as she walked towards him.

She was comfortably dressed in navy blue jeans and a red long-sleeved shirt that outlined her slender yet curvy frame. A small purse hung on her shoulder.

He smiled at her. "You look nice."

"Thanks." Her voice registered—uninterested.

"Where is your dance bag? Aren't we practicing the wedding dance today?"

"Shucks. Thanks." She ran back across the room and raced up the stairs.

She returned in a jiffy, with a pink and black dance bag dangling from her shoulder.

He took it from her. "That was quick."

"They call me Flash," she joked.

"Okay, Flash." He chuckled softly, encouraged by her sudden spiritedness. His eyes roamed her face and he found himself admiring her lips. He imagined kissing her— slowly, deeply. *A moment of absolute bliss,* he concluded.

"Are you ready?" he heard her ask in a breathy voice.

"Yes." He took her by the hand and led her towards the front door. Her hand felt stiff in his, but he did not let go. He had so much to say to her. He had to find a way to her heart.

He paused at the front door. The blood pounded in his temples as his eyes met hers.

"Em, can we talk?" he asked.

"No, Tyler." Her head tilted as she addressed him. "The time for talking was seven years ago. What we had…whatever it was…that's all in the past."

"I beg to differ."

Fire lit her glorious eyes. "Differ all you want. But since you are clearly having difficulty reading between the lines, let me make it clear. You," she pointed at him, then at herself, "and I, will not be in a relationship."

He was resilient. "With all due respect, it's a little too late for that."

"You can think—"

With a smooth sweep, he snaked a hand around her waist and pulled her flush to him.

"Wha-what?" her dance bag fell with a thud to the floor. She gaped at him as he effortlessly confined her in his arms.

"I am in love with you," he told her, his voice husky. "Let me love you, Em."

Heat and recollections charged the air between them.

Slowly, he lowered his head, hearing her sharp intake of breath as he burned a trail of soft kisses on her neck.

She threw her head back, moaning and clutching his shoulders. "T-Ty…"

His hand grasped the back of her head to keep her in place, his fingers entwined in her hair.

"Ty…Ty…" she chanted his name, sounding intoxicated.

"Hmm." He loved when she referred to him as Ty, It signaled to him he was 'home' again.

She shuddered and he held her close.

"Let me love you," he whispered in her ear while trailing butterfly kisses along her cheek. He lifted his head slightly and inhaled her scent. "You smell wonderful."

A breathless, "Thank you," issued from the back of her throat and she wrapped her arms around his neck to get more of his delightful kisses.

Her body supple, she arched against him, and through the soft material of her clothing, he could feel her breasts pressing against his chest. God, he wanted to touch them so badly.

That thought drove him to her lips. Lips that were made for kissing and more kissing. *Yes, in that order*, he decided. He kissed her deeply, ignoring her murmurs against his mouth, for her hands were at the back of his head, pulling him closer.

155

The delicate pressure of his lips on hers caused her to arch more firmly against him, and their bodies shivered from pleasurable sensations.

She groaned, pulling her lips from his, but he refused to be denied.

One taste and he was hooked.

"A little more," he murmured against her mouth, his voice thick with need.

He didn't have to ask twice.

Her lips hot on his, he backed her up against the door, plying her with tender yet passionate kisses.

Standing on tiptoes, she surrendered, allowing him to explore her mouth.

Their kiss grew deeper, feeding their hunger.

As his lips demanded more, Madison moaned, bucking against him as pleasure ripped through her body.

He felt addicted to her—her soft moans, the way her nails clawed and sometimes gripped his neck.

Her moans struck a primal chord in his body and he knew they had to stop or before long they would be in the Land of No Return.

He tore his lips from hers and held her against his body.

She tensed, then slipped her hands from around his neck and began to punch his shoulders.

"Stop," he said, his voice a hoarse whisper.

But she didn't.

He grabbed her hands, pinning them above her head and pressed her against the door.

She glared at his chest, panting loudly, her chest rising and falling.

"Look at me," he demanded.

"Let me go," she insisted, her breath coming in short gasps.

"I'm not letting you go, Em." *Not now. Not ever*

He felt her tremble, and he released one of her hands.

"Look at me," he repeated quietly, his hand caressing her cheek.

She growled softly, and he groaned at the thought of devouring her mouth again. God, he was aching everywhere.

He stopped stroking her cheek and used his hand to tilt her chin.

She still did not meet his eyes.

"I see I have to find another way to get you to look at me."

He found her mouth again, and he kissed her oh-so-gently.

"Hmm," she murmured, latching on to his lips.

His courage grew, and he lifted his mouth, allowing his lips to hover just above hers. "I'd say you enjoy kissing me as much as I enjoy kissing you."

She pushed at his chest and he pecked her lips.

She pushed at his chest and he pecked her lips again. "We could do this forever," he told her.

She looked at him, her eyes filled with desire and more than a hint of caution. "What now?"

"I have always loved you," he told her.

She shuddered and he summoned his strength and gathered her against him. He wanted her in his arms forever.

CHAPTER 20

Tyler lifted Madison in his arms and laid her on the sofa, then placed a cushion behind her head. She was silent, allowing him to do what he was doing. He sat on the floor beside the sofa, gazing at her swollen lips as she rolled on her side and faced him. She watched him with a hooded gaze.

"I love you, Em," he told her again, reaching for her hand and kissing her palm.

Her eyes warmed, but she did not speak.

"I know I didn't do the honorable thing before I left college," he said, apologetically. "I have come to see the folly of my ways. All I'm asking for, is a chance to love you and for you to see if I am the man that you want to spend the rest of your life with."

She still did not respond.

"We clicked from day one. In every way. There are so many things I love about you." He gazed tenderly at her.

"Didn't I tell you to stop looking at me like that?" she asked, even though the harshness was missing from her tone.

"It's not like I can help it," he told her. "I like looking at you. I couldn't stop, even if I wanted to. I know Mason played us, but I miss our friendship. I miss you."

She rubbed her lips together thoughtfully. "How come you're not dating or married?"

"I wanted to, but I didn't have the courage to reach for what I wanted." His eyes latched onto hers. "That is, until now."

She looked beyond him.

He stroked the back of her hand. "Why didn't you marry Carlton? Of course, I'm glad you didn't."

"Mason at it again." She pulled her hand out of his and clasped both hands under her chin. "The love I felt for Carl was not the kind that would sustain a marriage."

"I believe we have the kind that would sustain a marriage."

"We? There is no we." She frowned. "I'm not sure why you would even be thinking like that."

"I'm not sure why you wouldn't be thinking like that," he countered.

"I have nothing more to say about that," she snapped.

He watched her carefully.

"What?" she asked, knitting her brows.

"I know we have to leave for Mason's, but you may want to delay a bit."

"Why?" she asked, her expression suspicious.

"You looked thoroughly kissed. You might have difficulty explaining...*that* to the rest of the bridal party." He was staring at her mouth.

She gasped, her hands flying to her swollen lips. "Ouch." She cut her eyes at him. "Don't do that again."

"As if you didn't like it."

"That has nothing to do with it."

"It has everything to do with it. I enjoy kissing you and you enjoy kissing me. Do I taste as delicious as you?" he questioned playfully.

"Whatever," she hissed, throwing her legs off the sofa and walking away.

He scrambled to follow her. "Where are you going?" he called out.

"Kitchen."

He hastened down the passageway and found her half-hidden in the refrigerator. He came up behind her and she almost crashed into him when she straightened herself.

159

Her incredulous expression greeted him. "What on earth? Can I have some space?"

"Sure," he said, holding back a chuckle as he took a seat at the long island in her gorgeous kitchen. Creative configuration opened it up to the nook. The kitchen was large enough to feed an army. It was equipped with modern amenities and several white granite countertops with light and dark brown flecks.

Madison tore off a sheet of hand towel and placed ice cubes on it, then wrapped it lightly and held it against her lips.

A soft chortle burst from his lips, and she glared at him. He hastened to fix it. "I'm sorry. I'll be gentler next time."

She quickly moved the make-shift icepack from her mouth. "Next time? You've got to be kidding." She popped down on a chair next to him.

"Em, don't be like that. Give me a chance to love you."

"You fooled me once, Tyler. Once was enough."

"I was not fooling you. I had a lot going on. Things I couldn't even face myself, much less to get you involved."

"I can't believe you said that. We were friends. Friends support each other."

"I did not want to disturb your life." *Perfect life.*

"Why don't you just say, perfect life?" she shot back. "Nobody's life is perfect. Who is to say you won't run off again, when you think my perfect life cannot handle your situation? I still say you had your opportunity."

"I'm in a better place. Thank God. He is still working on me."

She remained unconvinced. "Happy for you."

"Are you denying you have feelings—strong feelings—for me?"

"That's beside the point, Tyler. Plus, look where strong feelings got me. I'm icing my lips."

"It's your fault for tempting me like that."

"Pshhhh! I was doing nothing of the sort."

"It was unspoken. I don't regret it." He flashed her a wicked smile. "We both liked it."

Madison shook her head. "No more of that, okay?"

"I can't promise you that."

"I'm going to pray for you."

"Yes, please."

A soft giggle escaped her at the eagerness in his voice. "That was a great sermon you preached at the convention. Your passion for the Lord was evident. But then, you're passionate about everything."

He smiled at her. "Thank you. God has been good to me."

"You handled that song, too. It was like you were singing at a different level."

"Thanks. Great to hear that coming from you, Miss Soloist."

"Oh, stop," she waved him off, sniggering softly. "I haven't sung in a looong time."

"I can't believe that. You have a great voice."

"Just life. I came off the praise team when I was trying to get my business off the ground then it was one thing after another. Now that business is on the uphill climb, I guess I can talk to our minister of music about rejoining the praise team."

"Sounds great. I like singing, so I did a bit of voice training," he confessed, "but that's not it, I asked the Holy Spirit to sing through me. He has been awesome."

Her lips curved slightly. "I know what you mean. It makes such a difference when the Holy Spirit is in the mix."

"Yes, it does," he agreed, watching her.

She knew he wanted to say something. "What?" she asked with raised brows.

"I was hoping to see you at the end of the church service," he confessed, "but I only found Mason and Kelani. Your mother and father left, too. But your mother texted to say how blessed she was by what I had shared during the service."

"Mom and Dad were leaving, so I just thought I would leave with them."

"You mean run away."

"Really?"

"You know I'm right. You always waited for me back in college. Remember how we would spend hours after, dissecting the sermon?"

He watched her wrestle with how to respond.

"I remember," she finally said.

"Great days, huh?"

When she refused to corroborate, he moved on. "Madison, I know I didn't do right by you, but now I want to make it up to you. I know..." He paused to gather himself.

Madison eyed him cautiously.

"I know that I-I hurt you." His voice broke with emotion. "I'm sorry. It was not intentional. I was trying to save myself. At least, I thought I was, but I only ended up hurting us both."

"Tyler, I hear you, but honestly, I have no intention of going back there with you. The time has passed."

"You don't believe that. You know in your heart we belong together. Why not pray about it?"

"There's no point. I'm not feeling a calling in that direction."

Tyler exhaled deeply. "Okay."

"It has been seven years," she said, justifying her remarks. "You can't just walk back into my life and think you can pick up where you left off. It doesn't work that way."

"I see."

"I somehow doubt that," Madison quipped.

He decided to be honest with her. "I'm adopted," he told her quietly.

Madison's sharp intake of breath echoed in the kitchen.

"I don't know my biological father," Tyler continued, "and I understand my mother died during childbirth."

Madison stared at him for a moment before speaking softly. "Thanks for sharing that. You never mentioned it. Not that it makes a difference in how I see you."

His gaze bounced around the room. "I'd planned to mention it, but the moment never came."

She touched his shoulder to focus his eyes on her. "That's alright."

He held on to her hand and drew forward to place it against his jaw. When he looked at her, he could see a thousand questions running through her mind.

"My life is a series of ups and downs," he told her. "The moment I settle into something permanent, my life gets uprooted. Mom and Dad poured love into my soul, and I love them. I would do anything for them."

"And they love you, too," Madison said smiling. "How old were you when they adopted you?"

"Sixteen." Tyler exhaled, releasing her hand. "At first, it was hard living with them, because I really missed my first dad."

"First dad?" Madison was all ears.

"Before I was adopted, I lived with Pastor David Moore and his wife, Marlene. They were my foster parents, so I refer to them as my first dad and mom or Uncle David and Aunt Marlene." He paused and gathered himself. "They died in a car accident."

"I'm so sorry to hear that, Ty."

"Thanks." He was quiet for a moment and she waited. "I was living in a children's home until I was around six years old, when my foster parents took me into their home."

Madison nodded with understanding. "Oh, okay."

"My first dad was the best," Tyler boasted. "He was determined to be a great father to me, even though I was a bad kid." He chuckled. "He would talk with me about God's love for me, and all the great things that God has in store for me. We went to church every Sunday; Bible Study on Wednesdays, and youth service every other Friday. One Sunday, I gave my heart to the Lord and never looked back."

Madison's eyes sparkled. "Look at God. I love when He brings it together."

"I wished they would adopt me," Tyler confessed. "I thought, any day now, they are going to adopt me; change my last name from Hansen to Moore. I'm not sure why they didn't. I keep thinking Aunt Marlene had something to do with it."

"Why?" It was out before Madison could restrain herself.

"I think she was a bit jealous of our relationship. I would catch her staring at me. Just staring at me…" He rolled his lips together. "I want to say in a bad way, but I wasn't sure. It was puzzling, though. Now, I am wondering if it's because she couldn't have children. Nevertheless, she treated me well, even though we were not particularly close."

He laughed a little, and then divulged. "She would tease me and First Dad that she knew when we were stressed because we would unconsciously run a hand over

164

our heads...." Tyler threatened Madison with his eyes. "Don't laugh. Unconsciously, we run a hand over our heads from back to front."

She zipped her lips playfully with her hands, but her eyes were twinkling with laughter.

"Can I speak now that the threat level is low?" she asked.

They both laughed.

"You used to do that back in the day," Madison reminded him.

"Uh-oh, you said 'back in the day'. Yeah, I like that. I was beginning to think you'd forgotten us."

Madison let out a long-suffering sigh.

He laughed softly, admitting. "I know. I still do it sometimes, if I'm in a stressful situation."

"Well," Madison encouraged, "I'm glad you are in a better place now with two people in Boston who love you."

He smiled. "Yes, they do, and I love them. They had a great relationship with my foster parents, too."

"Oh, wow. Look at that," Madison gushed.

"They would visit us in Seattle, and we used to visit them in Boston."

Madison's eyes widened. "Seattle?"

"Yes. Back then, I lived with my foster parents in Seattle," he told her. "Actually, I was born in Boston. My foster parents lived in Boston for a while, and then we moved to Seattle."

"Well, look at that," Madison said, smiling. "I love Seattle."

"Me, too. Great city and great memories of living there." Tyler's expression grew somber. "Sometimes, I miss my first dad and those days."

"He sounds like a great father, and clearly, he must have loved you, too," Madison pointed out smiling.

"He was. He *did* love me, too," Tyler said, self-consciously.

"Sweet. Awww, somebody is looking all bashful."

"Woman, stop the madness," Tyler said laughing, and then stopped abruptly to tell her, "After he and Aunt Marlene died…"

Madison waited, but Tyler didn't say anything else.

"I understand," she said softly.

"After they died, Mom and Dad adopted me." Tyler's voice shook a bit as he spoke. "Some eyewitnesses said that my foster parents were arguing, since the car was swerving in traffic. However, I found that odd, since I never heard them argue."

"I'm glad you have great memories of them. God knew why He brought you to them. Trust God's heart."

"Thanks." He watched her for a few moments. "Madison, I knew I slipped up, so I was planning to see you after I graduated, but one thing led to another. Even though, I have to admit that I was apprehensive since you hadn't returned any of my calls." He sighed deeply. "I had been working for a little over a month, but one morning I wasn't feeling well so I slept in. I got up, and was heading to the kitchen when I-I heard, well, overheard my mom's sister, Aunt Rachel, and my mom talking in the kitchen."

He looked at Madison. "Aunt Rachel was asking Mom why it was so hard for him to adopt me. I was so hurt. It was bad enough that I didn't know my biological parents. Now, I'm hearing that my dad didn't really want to adopt me."

She squeezed his hands and he sighed and looked at her. "I walked in the kitchen that morning and demanded they both come clean. Dad wasn't home that day; I forget where he was. Aunt Rachel declared that she was joking, but I didn't believe her. Aunt Rachel and I have always had a great relationship, so I knew she wasn't joking. Since

166

they refused to say anything else, I let it go, but I was determined to get my own place. Anyway, I had planned to do that, but that conversation made me do it sooner rather than later."

"Did you ever bring it up with your mom or Aunt Rachel again?"

"No. I didn't ask Dad about it, either, because I didn't want him to feel bad. He is the best dad in the whole world." Tyler smiled. "Mom is great, too. I decided to let it go, but every now and then, I can't help but think about it."

"I understand."

Tyler exhaled loudly. "It was great to let all of that out."

"I'm glad you felt okay to share with me."

He smiled at her. "I would be even better if you tell me you'll pray about a relationship with me."

She regarded him. "I bet you would."

CHAPTER 21

"Man, I can't believe you dragged me away from Grandma Darlene's good food and conversation; plus, the rich ambience of the chateau," Tyler said, staring at Mason's profile as he drove. The men of the bridal party had been staying at Chateau de Kanate for the past three days, while the women stayed at The Kanate. Tyler was taken with the beautiful architectural accents of the chateau.

Mason laughed loudly. "Man, please! Just the thought of seeing Madison had you sprinting out the door. I had a hard time catching up."

"Whatever, man." A smile played at the corners of Tyler's mouth as Madison's image popped into his mind and lingered. "You dragged me away."

"Try not to look so upset," Mason countered, laughter in his tone. "In any case, you've only been at the chateau since Monday. Well," Mason became thoughtful, "that's enough time to get hooked. Grandma Darlene is very engaging."

"I don't know how I'm going to go back to my single life. She's spoiling me."

"By the looks of things, you don't have to worry about the single life for long. I saw you helping Madison with her swing during the golf game yesterday." He laughed out. A deep full-throated laugh. "You're wrong for that in a game that was guys against girls."

"Call me Mr. Helpful." Tyler's lips slid into a wide smile.

"Go big or go home, huh?" Mason laughed even louder. "We saw both of you in dance rehearsal. You two know how to put on a show. Just remember, this is not your wedding."

That brought a chuckle from Tyler. "Don't hate."

"I love seeing you and Madison do your part of the dance." Mason slapped the steering wheel. "Bam! Those tango steps look like the battle of the sexes. You're both enjoying that dance...way too much."

"Like I said, don't hate. You look spiffy in the dance, too. The extra lessons paid off. I give myself a pat on the shoulder for that."

"Thanks, bro. I'm feeling good. Wouldn't want to embarrass my wife."

Tyler was quiet. "I don't think you can do anything to embarrass or disappoint Kelani. She is, as they say, smitten with you."

"And that's the same way Madison feels about you," Mason told him. "She's taking her time, but she'll come around."

"I hope so, but you need to leave her alone," Tyler scolded him. "You told me you're taking your foot off the gas and applying the brakes, yet I still see you gently pushing her. She's a strong woman who knows what she wants. She will reach out when she's ready." Tyler sighed. "I'm trying to be patient because I broke the trust between us."

"Spoken like a man in love," Mason said thoughtfully.

Tyler exhaled softly. "That I am."

Mason pulled up near the front patio of The Kanate. "I'm glad you are," he said, turning off the ignition. He looked at Tyler. "Thanks for loving her, bro. She carries a lot on her plate, because of all the Lord requires of her; however, in all she's doing, I want her to have support. I'm taking on a family and that will be my focus." He sighed. "I want Madison to be with someone who will love her and help her to be all that God wants her to be."

"That I can do," Tyler said quietly. "I have been praying for her."

That brought a smile to Mason's face. "I know you are. Kel and I are praying for both of you."

"Thanks, bro. I need that."

Silence descended in the SUV before they both scrambled to open the doors.

Armela greeted them at the front door before steering them through the entryway and into the formal living room.

"Your parents are in the kitchen and Kelani and Madison are in the sunroom," Armela informed them.

"Thanks, Aunt Armie," Mason said, smiling.

"Let me know if you guys need anything," Armela said before leaving the room.

A few minutes later, Mason and Tyler entered the kitchen and halted.

"Mom. Dad," Mason called out. "Good Lord, make me un-see it."

His mother was puffing out soft giggles as his father was landing soft kisses on her lips; he had her trapped with his hands against the island.

"My good Lord, why are you always blocking me?" his father questioned teasingly. "Don't you see me handling my business? Couldn't you back away?"

His mother playfully slapped his father's shoulder. "Our child needs us."

"Right?" His dad responded. "This had better be urgent."

"My bad," Mason grinned at them, moving further into the kitchen. "If this is retirement, I like it. Something to look forward to."

"I'm loving it," Larry said. "I'm sure you can tell. And I'm going to enjoy it even more after your wedding."

Rozene rescued them. "Is everything okay? I thought Grandma Darlene had you all bound by her great testimonies and gooood food."

"Yes, we're good," Mason piped up. "We're just swinging by to see the girls."

At that, his father's eyes landed on Tyler, who was leaning against the doorframe.

Tyler held his gaze.

"See the girls, huh?" Larry quipped. "I see."

Tyler did not miss the tightening of Larry's mouth, indicating his displeasure at him for wanting to see Madison.

Mom rushed to the rescue once again. "Madison and Kelani are in the sunroom but Laurie-Ann and Rebecca are in their rooms, I believe."

"Isn't this evening the bachelor and bachelorette parties at Abella?" Larry asked.

"Yes," Rozene jumped in, smiling. "That's why they want to see the girls. They won't see them later."

"Smart," Larry huffed out.

Before anyone could respond, squeals of delight sounded as the twins breezed into the kitchen from the opposite entrance.

They hugged Mason's legs, screaming, "Maaason!"

By now, Tyler knew the names of the twins simply by their mannerisms. He watched a smiling Mason happily picking Brianna up and kissing her cheek, and setting her on the floor, then picking Brittany up and doing the same.

Mason held his back. "You two are getting heavy. I need to drink more of my protein shake to lift you up."

The twins giggled and turned their attention to Tyler.

"Good morning, Tyler," Brianna said.

"Good morning, Bri," Tyler responded. "You look very pretty in pink."

Briana looked down at her dress. "Thank you, Tyler."

"Do I look pretty, too?" Brittany asked. "Good morning. Pardon my manners."

"Of course, you look pretty, too, Brittany," Tyler said, smiling down at her.

"Thank you," Brittany beamed.

"Girls, I love your hair," their mother said, admiring their hairstyles. Their fizzy curly hair was tamed, having been neatly braided into a high ponytail.

"Thanks, Mommy!" The twins beamed in unison.

"Hope you said thank you to Kelani," their mother said.

"We did, Mommy," Brittany said, then informed her mother. "Kelani is very creative,"

"Yes, she is," Brianna added, before her eyes settled on Mason. "She helped with my dance routine. I feel soooo much more confident."

"That is true," Brittany said, smiling at Brianna. "You're a great dancer, Bri." She looked at her mother. "Mommy, Kelani reminded us of the Scripture that you had put in our play area when we were little girls."

"You are still little girls." Rozene placed a hand on her heart.

The twins grinned up at their mother.

"Oh, Mommy, you know what I mean," Brittany said, attempting to fix it. "This is the Scripture— Philippians four verse thirteen. Ready, Bri?"

They both recited, "'I can do all things through Christ who gives me the strength.'"

Everyone clapped and girlish giggles rose from their lips.

Their proud papa spoke up. "Would you like us to put that Scripture on the walls in your rooms?"

The twins rushed to his side and hugged his legs.

"Yes, Daddy!" Brianna said, excitedly.

"That would be awesome," Brittany agreed.

"Alright, we will see to it," their doting father said.

They squeezed his legs tightly, murmuring their thanks.

"Okay, let's get you to school. That's still happening, right?" Larry teased, taking both girls by their hands.

"Yes, Daddy," the girls sang in different tones, pulling laughter from everyone.

"I'll be back," Larry said, looking from Mason to Tyler.

"Tyler," Brittany assessed him briefly before asking, "Are you here to see Madison?"

Tyler's heart lurched. *This child. Good Lord.*

The silence was deafening and all eyes were on Tyler.

"Yes, I'm here to see Madison," Tyler responded in what he hoped was a normal voice.

"I'm glad." Brittany smiled widely. "She's in the sunroom with Kelani."

A smile tilted the corners of Tyler's mouth. She was rooting for him. "Thank you, Brittany."

"Okay, girls, let's go," Larry's voice rang out. "Your teachers won't be waiting."

They all walked out of the kitchen and Mason and Tyler bid them goodbye before heading in the opposite direction towards the sunroom.

Mason pushed out a chuckle. "You did well. You always have to be ready for Brittany. She runs the world."

Tyler chuckled, too. "She is something."

CHAPTER 22

Mason and Tyler walked into the sunroom to see Madison and Kelani animatedly chatting on the army-green leather sofas.

Sensing their presence, the women sat up and turned towards the door. They gaped at the men.

"Good morning, ladies," Mason said cheerfully.

"Em, Kelani, morning," Tyler said smiling, although his eyes were on Madison.

Kelani recovered first. "Boo, good morning." She scrambled to her feet and hugged Mason, then Tyler. "Morning, Tyler."

Madison still had not moved, but she acknowledged their greetings.

"This is a pleasant surprise," Kelani said, smiling.

Mason came clean. "I missed you, so I decided to pop by."

"Awww! I love that, boo thang." She hugged Mason, who grinned boyishly. "I really love that. You guys will have to forgive our head wraps," Kelani said, coming out of Mason's arms. "We are preserving our hairstyles for the paaaarty later." She twirled. "It's going to be great."

"If Madison is in it, you know it will be," Mason responded.

Madison seemingly perked up. "We're going to rock her world."

"I can hear you." Kelani grinned happily. "Boo, let's go in the gazebo. I have something to tell you."

"Sure, baby." Mason looked at Tyler, then Madison. "We'll see you guys in a bit. Madison, do you think you can keep Tyler occupied?" he asked in an all-important tone. "Perhaps you can practice your golf swing."

Madison grabbed a cushion from the chair and Mason ran off. "Kelani, you better get your boo thang before I do," Madison threatened.

"This is me about to get him." Laughing, Kelani exited.

"You told him," Tyler teased, taking a seat beside Madison and turning his body towards her.

Madison laughed softly. "I can't wait for him to have children, so he'll leave me alone."

"He cares about you," Tyler remarked, stretching his hand on the back of the sofa so it was behind her head.

By the subtle slant of her lips, he could tell she was irritated.

"And for that I am grateful," she stated. "Nevertheless, he needs to know when to stop. Why did he have to drag you over here?"

Tyler cocked a brow. "I cannot even feign surprise."

She blushed, and by her expression, Tyler was sure she wished she could take the question back.

"He didn't have to drag me, Madison," he said quietly. "I wanted to come here to see you."

She remained quiet, clasping her hands in her lap.

Why? Hung in the air.

It didn't take him a second to catch on. "Because I love you."

Her eyes popped as her head swung towards him.

He had to smile. "I wanted to be in your presence."

Her chin went up defiantly. "I don't want a relationship."

"Look me in the eye and tell me that, Madison."

She bit on her lips and gazed beyond him. When her gaze returned to his face, he wasn't surprised to see uncertainty in her eyes.

His eyes dropped to her mouth and she licked her lips as he leaned in. He felt the heat in his eyes burst into flame as their gazes collided again.

Her eyes widened and her lips twitched as she leaned in.

He held back the urge to kiss the hollow of her collarbone and taste her skin. *She would like that. She would like it a lot.* "Hmm!" came from his lips as he imagined the sweetness he would taste.

He resisted.

He needed her commitment. In any case, this was not the place to steal a kiss.

Suddenly, she sat back and her lips parted, but no words came out.

His eyebrow arched and he pursed his lips briefly. "You were saying?" he asked softly.

"Ty-Tyler," she said, in-between two short breaths, "please stop doing that."

He closed his eyes and prayed in silence. When he opened his eyes, she was staring at him.

"What was that all about?" she asked.

"I was just thanking the Lord for you, for us."

Her eyebrows climbed. "Okay."

"I hope you realize I am a work-in-progress. God has turned my life around, but I am still grappling with some of my not-so-great childhood circumstances. Nevertheless, I am grateful that God is a keeper. He has kept me."

"Amen," Madison said quietly. "What a beautiful thing to say."

"There you have it— a bit more of your chocolate love," he teased playfully.

A tiny hint of laughter bubbled from Madison. "You are too much."

He watched her with bated breath.

What?" she asked softly.

"Every so often, more of you shines through. I love it."

"Whatever," she said, looking away and then back at him. "By the way, didn't Pastor Tanner want you to be the youth minister?"

"Yup," Tyler said, rolling his lips together.

"Yup?" Madison looked at him quizzically.

A grin covered his face. "I'm praying about it."

"I hope it's not the same way you're praying about speaking at Estrina's event?"

It was hard to miss the sarcasm in her voice. "Be nice."

"I just don't get why you won't commit to participating. It's a major event for the children at all the Estrina's locations and other children's homes in the area. We don't have a theme yet, but it will be a power-packed weekend to motivate and empower the children into action. We are going big, hoping that a lot of companies will set up booths. Your life story will motivate the children."

"My plate is full right now. I don't want to drown in work."

"Really, Tyler?" she asked in a sarcastic tone.

"It's a matter of timing. I'll find someone else to help."

"The event is next year. We are thinking some time in February. You have...what—" she counted on her fingers, "—a little over five months to prepare. Well, well. For all your talk about empowering the youth. That's alright, I'll find someone else."

"Don't lose heart. I'm praying about it."

He looked at his hand, which was resting on the sofa between them, and attempted to hook his little finger around hers.

She snatched her hand away. "Stop that!" she all but yelled, her eyes twinkling. "You know I'm ticklish."

"You are?" he asked innocently. "I'll try to remember that." He touched her hand. "Please help me pray about it."

"Sure."

He rested his elbow on the back of the sofa and rested his head in its crook as he looked at her. "What happened to you, Madison?"

She gazed at him thoughtfully. "I'm not sure what you mean by that."

"There is a slight hardness to you that wasn't there before. And you didn't have the invisible cage around you."

She maintained her cool. "You haven't seen me in years, Tyler. I grew up."

Tyler suppressed a pang of guilt. "We all grow up, but you were never like that; you didn't have that edge to you."

She swallowed uneasily. "Life happened."

"What's that supposed to mean?"

"Things are not always as they seem. Things happen in life and you find a way to survive."

"The Em I knew back then would never let anything in life harden her. She would leave it at the foot of the cross and let the Lord handle it."

Madison squirmed, moving her eyes away from him and looking beyond him.

"Unless—" Tyler continued, "—she's upset with the Lord. And no matter how many blessings the Lord pours into her life, that one thing will always take centerstage."

She looked visibly perturbed. "I'm not upset with God. That's ridiculous, and a very dreadful thing to say."

He pushed on. "Maybe deep down you are."

"I'm not. My relationship with the Lord is intact."

"Of course it is, but my spirit tells me you are no longer hungering and thirsting for Him."

She slumped. "What are you—the Holy Spirit?"

"The Madison I knew would allow rivers of living water to flow out of her belly."

"Thanks for the pep talk," she replied flatly. "I'll be sure to take the matter before the Lord."

"I'm not perfect, Em."

"Really?" she said, derision in her voice.

He ignored that. "Of course not, but I am attuned to the Spirit of God; I'm attuned to you. I know you are attuned to me…at least, you used to be."

She did not respond.

He watched her carefully, and in the silence, she looked at him.

He felt his countenance sadden. "I know I hurt you, Em. I am sorry. Understand that I didn't mean to. Please forgive me."

In a long whoosh, she gasped for air, and then blinked several times before tears flooded her eyes.

Tears stung his own eyes, for he knew that somewhere deep inside, he'd hurt her badly. A wave of regret washed over him. He could only hope that she would recover.

He hated the distance between them; it felt wrong.

He moved closer to her, wrapped an arm around her shoulder, and then drew her towards him.

She did not push him away, but settled comfortably against him, her head resting in the crook of his neck.

In silence, he prayed for her…and for himself.

CHAPTER 23

Friday already! A yawn escaped and Madison giggled. She was tired, but it was all good. The time spent at the bachelorette party was everything. A night of endless pampering and lavish indulgences for the bride and her guests.

Delightful.

Memorable.

Altogether wonderful.

The bridal party was exceptional—no words aptly described the comradery among the members. By now, they were all familiar with each other's ins and outs, but that only made matters worse. There was a constant in the group—the echo of spontaneous laughter. Robert provided comic relief. At every opportunity, he recounted childhood stories about him and Mason.

Madison laughed out, recalling Rob's version of what he called "The Onesie Break-up". Mason had refused to let go of his teddy bear onesie up to his early teens, until Rob had "The Talk" with him. The Talk, according to Rob, did not go down well, causing a two-day break in their friendship.

The kicker came when Rob told them that one evening during college, he had visited Mason and he had jumped back in surprise when Mason had opened the door. Mason was not a pretty picture; he had not only shaved off his facial hair, but he'd also shaved his head.

Oy!

During all of their shenanigans, Madison noticed Jayvis' affinity towards Laurie-Ann, especially at the group's golf game. If Laurie-Ann detected it, she looked totally unaffected; however, Madison was sure that she saw a twinkle in Laurie-Ann's eyes when they were all snacking after the golf game and Kelani paired them both to walk the aisle at the wedding.

Of course, since they were the only two left, Robert and Rebecca would walk up the aisle together. While they seemed friendly towards each other, Madison did not detect a burning attraction between them.

Glancing at the clock, Madison reduced the pressure on the gas pedal of her black BMW. There was no need to rush. *Might as well enjoy the fresh morning air.* She punched a button on the steering wheel and the sunroof slid open. She was early for the wedding rehearsal at Chateau de Kanate. She was looking forward to seeing Grandma Darlene. She liked being at the chateau, listening to Grandma Darlene's powerful testimonies about all that God had done and was doing in her life.

A few years ago, Grandma Darlene had shared with Madison that Peter, her husband, had verbally and physically abused her and their sons. He had passed from a heart attack over ten years ago.

Grandma Darlene also told Madison her late husband was "not only abusive, but he was a womanizer of the worst sort." She had shaken her head then told Madison, "Everybody around us knew about his affairs."

Still, Peter Kanate was all about work, according to Grandma Darlene. He had inherited the family business from his father, Etalon, a French-American business tycoon whom the press described as having the Midas Touch. In his father's eyes, Peter did not possess the prowess to help carry out the vision he had for Kanate Management and Realty Corporation, so after Peter inherited the business, he spent many of his waking hours at the office trying to prove just that.

Later in life, since Peter did not get along with Larry, he had taken Zane and Zadan under his wings and schooled them in the running of his empire. Still, he had secretly hoped Larry would come on board, so he had stated in his will that Larry should be the Chief Operating Officer.

As far as Madison knew, her father never took up that position. It was not for lack of trying on Grandma Darlene's part, because her husband had always begged her to convince Larry to run the corporation. Still, Larry was not interested, telling his mother, "Sorry, Mama. Not my calling."

Madison had even questioned her dad about taking up the position in his father's company, but he was adamant that it was 'not his calling'. He also told her that the Lord had delivered him from the hatred he had for his father and that he was at peace with his decision. Madison had always prayed her father would consider being a part of Kanate Management and Realty Corporation; however, with the birth of the twins, Madison was beginning to wonder if her father would ever do so.

Still, it was not all doom and gloom. From the events of her life, Darlene Kanate had decided to make her life a ministry for the Lord. To date, she had set up over sixty Victorious Women's Shelters in several states, in a bid to empower women who had been abused and at the same time give them a second chance at life.

That thought brought a smile to Madison's face as she drove the two-mile stretch of private road to Chateau de Kanate. She enjoyed the soft lights filtering through the cloud of overhanging pink cherry blossom trees.

Her smile widened as she saw the hustle and bustle of the workers on either side of the road, fixing everything in place for the auspicious occasion.

She whipped onto the driveway of the magnificent dwelling that was her grandma's home. Nestled on a gentle sloping peak in the heart of the fifty-acre property, stood the imposing Chateau de Kanate, with its spectacular view of a pristine lake and flourishing vegetation of all colors, shapes, and sizes.

The hustle and bustle went all the way up to the front door. Madison clambered out of the car and waved happily as she made her way through the activities and up the steps. The large oak door flew open and Zalletta welcomed her. Madison gave her a huge smile before hugging her. "Aunt Zal, heeey!"

For Madison, it seemed Zalletta had been with the family since forever. Her dad told her that Zalletta had been there since his elementary years, operating as chief of staff at the chateau. Zalletta had taken over right out of college after her mother died.

"Heeey yourself, lovely lady," Zalletta said, smiling as Madison released her from the hug. "Happy times, right?"

"They sure are," Madison responded. "And I know you enjoy having events."

"I sure do," Zalletta agreed. "I'm looking forward to planning yours. Ooh, I love that tall glass of chocolate milk." She giggled foolishly. "If I was just a bit younger, I would give you a run for him."

Madison laughed out. "Ohhh, please take him away. He's not mine."

"You don't say. You are all he talks about."

Raised eyebrows reached Zalletta. "That's news to me."

Zalletta slapped her playfully on the arm. "Now that you know, do something to make him know you are interested. Go get him."

A chuckle burst from Madison's lips. "Aunt Zal, you're something. Where's everybody?"

"They're all over. I suggest you start with the grand ballroom. That's where your Grandma Elizabeth and

Grandpa Ben are hanging out. We'll all be gathering in an hour or so."

"Okay. Thanks," Madison responded, touching Zalletta's arm before moving away.

"Get it, get it, girrrrl," Zalletta drawled under her breath. "Do not let me slow-oooo you down."

Madison's face creased into a smile as her head swung towards Zalletta. "I'll try," she teased.

Zalletta made a face at her, and she all but hollered as she moved out of the entryway to step further into the spectacular interior of the chateau. Down to the last detail, Chateau de Kanate was one for the history books—grand living rooms, libraries, galleries, terraces, and huge bedrooms with ivory shag carpets and enormous canopy beds draped with sheer white veils. An ivory and gold theme mixed with several shades of blue ran through the general areas of the entire house, but the most unique feature of this magnificent home was the impressive double-helix staircase that gave access to the sleeping quarters.

"Looking for your love?"

Madison's head whipped right to locate the voice of Grandma Liz. She had been thinking about Zalletta's comment and missed seeing Grandma Liz near the entrance of the grand ballroom.

"Yes. N-no. Who?" Madison asked, and then rattled on, "I wasn't looking for anyone in particular." She hugged her grandmother. "You smell nice."

"Thanks, dear."

She saw the twinkle in her grandmother's eyes, most likely put there by the edge in Madison's tone.

Grandma Liz looked around conspiratorially before telling Madison, "Don't be shy about it. Tyler is making his rounds. I had him for a good hour. Now he's with Darlene."

Madison's heart performed an awkward beat. He was reasonable in all things, but he was relentless in his pursuit for her love.

"He'll be good for you, baby," her grandma said. "And you'll be good for him."

Finally, Madison found her voice. "He spent the morning working the family over?"

"No. Nothing like that," Elizabeth said, moving them away from the ballroom toward a nearby passageway. "It was I who engaged him. After all, he has the hots for my granddaughter. And from what I've seen and heard, his heart is not mercurial."

"I can hear you, Grandma," Madison giggled as they walked down the passage.

"I am praying for both of you. Now, I want you to seriously bring this matter before the Lord." She paused at the door leading to the back patio. "He is looking towards the future, but you are running from the past. You've got to let go of what's behind you. It does you no good to hold on to it. Let the good Lord heal your heart so you can be free to love Tyler again."

"Grandma, I would pray about it, but I am not interested in a relationship with Tyler or any man right now. Plus, Tyler is unpredictable and not to mention infuriating."

She watched Madison carefully. "As if you would like it any other way. But, what do we always say? 'Not my will but Thy will be done.' It is hard...hard to find someone who is in sync with you. It is even harder to find a man who genuinely loves God."

Madison considered for a moment. "Thanks, Grandma."

Her grandmother opened the door and gently nudged Madison through it. "I'll see you in a few."

Smiling, Madison walked onto the patio.

She had always admired Grandma Liz, not only for being an exemplary woman of God, but for her determined spirit and the passion she exerted in every task she undertook. Grandma Liz helped to manage the multi-billion-dollar family business, Bennady International Citrus Corporation, with her husband, Benjamin. When she wasn't busy working, she was out and about doing charity work and ministering to women in the various organizations she'd established.

Madison's smile widened and she silently thanked God for her two grandmothers. They were always looking out for her.

CHAPTER 24

The notion of a stroll caused Madison to descend the steps of the back patio. A cheery kind of warm weather welcomed her and invited her to explore. Slowly, she meandered through the beautiful garden to find her Grandma Darlene. Awe-inspired, she paused for a moment, chewing the inside of her cheeks as the elegant purity of the blossoming garden beckoned her.

Eventually, she moved on, taking five minutes to walk deeper into the garden. She arrived at one of her grandma's favorite spots—near a pear tree—and halted. Grandma Darlene and Tyler were sitting across from each other. Suddenly, Tyler broke out singing Ricky Dillard and New G's "Amazing". It was a 'call and response' song, so Grandma Darlene was in high praise.

Gosh, she loved seeing them together like this. Tyler had always been an avid worshipper and not afraid to show it. She had always liked that about him.

She watched as he lifted his hands in worship.

Burning time at the gym was definitely paying off. His lavender button-down shirt clung to his ripped physique.

She rolled her eyes, remembering how Mason and Kelani had found them sleeping arm-in-arm on the sofa in the sunroom. Tyler had sunk deeper into the sofa with his feet on the ground, and she was hugging him with her head buried in the crook of his neck.

While her cheeks throbbed with embarrassment and guilt, Tyler did not even have the gall to look embarrassed when Mason woke them up. He looked like it was business as usual.

Come to think of it, Mason and Kelani looked like what they'd witnessed was an everyday occurrence. By the looks of things, if it was up to Mason, he would amp up the weekend's excitement with a double wedding.

Pshhhh! It was business as usual for everyone...except for her.

Truthfully, it was difficult not to enjoy Tyler, but she had to be careful not to get his hopes up. Not to mention her own.

Madison's eyes focused on her grandmother, who was slowly clapping her hands and nodding while she sang. *Wow.* Grandma Darlene was adorned in a red, form-fitting dress that clung to a surprisingly trim five-foot-six-inch frame. Her wavy salt-and-pepper hair was pulled back in a loose ponytail to show off her beautiful heart-shaped face.

Madison was about to retreat when her grandmother leapt off the chair and called out her name. A guilty smile covered her face as she moved forward.

"My granddaughter!" Grandma Darlene squealed with joy. She had a knack for making her feel like she was her favorite grandchild...actually, her *only* grandchild. Yet Madison knew she loved all of her grandchildren.

"Grandma!" Madison responded, warmth welling up inside.

They hugged, then Grandma Darlene held her at arm's length, her large, light-brown eyes joyful. "You look gorgeous. I'm glad you're here."

"Thanks, Grandma. Me, too. It's a beautiful day to be out."

"Yes, it is." Grandma Darlene smiled at her. "Now greet Tyler and come sit with me. Have you had lunch?"

"Yes," Madison responded, turning self-consciously towards Tyler. "Hi."

She was surprised how quickly Tyler had moved. He was right behind her, and from his expression, she could tell he was hoping for a hug.

She obliged.

188

"Em," his voice caressed her ear as he held her gently. "Glad you're here."

Her entire being quivered at the sound of her name tumbling from his lips. And she could feel him inhaling the strawberry scent in her hair. For a moment, she thought their hug would never end.

You need to release me. She tried sending him the message via telepathy, but since he clearly wasn't getting it, she began making movements to untangle herself.

He released her and Madison walked towards her grandmother. "I didn't mean to crash your praise and worship," she announced, her eyes washing over Tyler before settling on Grandma Darlene.

They both protested.

"Okay, then," Madison said, smiling. "I don't feel so bad."

"You would only add to the worship," Grandma Darlene said. "I haven't heard you sing in a while. What's up with that?"

Madison and Tyler chuckled at her expression.

"You're just not around me enough," Madison teased. "I'm belting out the tunes during praise and worship on Sundays."

"Well, sing loud. Do anything but hide your wonderful voice. And remember your date with the ladies at the center. You know they love your sessions."

"Yes, Grandma, I remember. I only changed the date because of the wedding. We'll be back on regular schedule after that."

"Good," Grandma Darlene said, turning her gaze towards Tyler. "Madison does devotion and exercise classes with the ladies of the local Victorious Women's Shelter. Then, she does an exercise with them that deals with self-esteem." She grinned happily. "I love seeing her in action."

"Thanks, Grandma. You're the best."

Grandma Darlene waved her off. "No. *You're* the best; bringing life-changing messages to those who need it."

Madison blushed. "I do that because I know—there go I, but for the grace of God."

"Amen," Grandma Darlene murmured in agreement. "You two can take off, I need to make a call to tie up some loose ends."

She stood and they hugged her.

"See you shortly," Madison said to her.

"Thanks for the pep talk and the love," Tyler said smiling. "Means a lot."

"You're very welcome, man of God. You know where to find me if you ever need more. I'll be praying for your dad."

"For that, I am grateful," Tyler responded, ushering Madison forward.

"He's able. Remember that," Grandma Darlene called out.

"Yes, He is," Tyler said, flashing her a smile before he and Madison walked away.

"Your father is sick?" Madison asked, glancing at Tyler's profile.

Worried eyes met hers. "Yes. He has bronchitis. To me, it seems like his medication is not working, but he said that he's feeling much better. He still has a nagging cough and his voice sounds hoarse." He sighed. "Mom said that he was coughing up thickened, discolored mucus."

"Hopefully, the ailment with go away. I will be praying for him."

That brought a smile to Tyler's face. "Thank you! Better still, Mom had said to tell you hello, so you can give both of them a call. I'll text Mom's number later."

"Sure. I would love to do that."

190

A baffled expression ran across his face.

"What?" she asked softly.

"Strange, I was just thinking about our trips to Boston when I was younger. My first dad would take me to a coffee shop." He stared intently at Madison before they walked on. "The weird thing is that he never bought any coffee. Usually, he'd sit and watch me eat the treats he bought for me."

"Did you ever ask him about it?"

"No. I never thought it odd back then. It just ran across my mind." He sighed. "How are the plans going for your mission trip?"

Momentarily stunned by the change of subject, Madison gazed at his profile, her expression puzzled.

"They are going well," she said slowly. "The team is excited. We've been to Jamaica a couple of times to visit with one of the children's homes we had set up, but this is our annual trip—the big ta-da, where we do a week of activities for the children. We are scheduled to leave mid-October."

"Great," Tyler said, smiling. His smile widened and he tried to hook his little finger around hers.

Girlish giggles broke from her lips and she moved her hand out of his reach. "Stop that."

When her hand came back to her side, he did the same thing again.

"Stop," she said, her eyes twinkling.

"I'll try to remember that you're ticklish," he said, taking her hand and swinging it back and forth a few times as they moved on.

"You better," she quipped.

He playfully bumped his shoulder against hers. "Be nice," he said, moving them along to a more secluded part of the garden. He brought them to a standstill beside a bunch of yellow roses. In an unexpected gesture, he kneeled, broke off two roses, stripped the prickles from the stem of one, and gave it to her.

She stared up at him through a glaze of moisture, her mouth slightly opened. "Thank you," she managed to say.

It was not her first time receiving flowers, but the fact he remembered that she loved yellow roses blew her mind. She gasped when he shortened the other rose and placed it behind her ear like she used to wear it, back in college.

He smiled at her. "Yes, I remembered. And for the record, I still love how you embrace your natural curls." With mischief in his eyes, he told her, "This you didn't know. I always wanted to pull on them. Still do. They are beautiful and so are you."

His deep voice brought back memories best left behind. She cleared her throat, feeling like a ruffled mess. "Thanks."

He took her hand again and led her towards a long wicker bench, and then encouraged her to sit as he straddled it.

"I want us back," he told her pointedly.

Her knees weakened with interest, but she ignored his fervent gaze, and instead took the time to straighten her long, yellow, fitted-waist dress. "So you keep saying. I've got too much on my plate to focus on a relationship."

"Don't you miss us? I know I do. We are kindred spirits."

She did not comment, so he held on to her hand and used his thumb to caress it. Sensual. His touch sent wild sensations down her arm.

Madison pulled her hand out of his.

"We had something special back in the day, Em," Tyler said, "and I can tell we haven't lost it."

"I don't know about that." She eyed him, putting on her bravest front.

"Really?" He smiled at her, and her heart rate kicked up.

"I told you to stop looking at me like that."

Pearly whites on display, again, he told her, "Just like I told you, I can't help it. I'm drawn to you, and I know you feel the same way. At least, I can tell from the kiss we shared the other day."

She licked her lips.

"And that's exactly how I feel right now. I want to kiss you into oblivion."

Goosebumps cascaded up her arms and she wrapped them around her torso, resisting the urge to rub the goosebumps away.

He brushed his hand across her arms, and the pure pleasure of that feeling was like no other. She felt herself melting towards him. Gosh, she loved his touch.

With a gentleness that surprised her, he slid a hand around her waist and tipped her face upwards towards his. Their eyes met, causing a soft moan to come from her lips, and she edged closer to him as anticipation ran through her.

Kiss me, her heart begged, completely against her will. He had touched her with a need she'd forgotten. Her hand reached up and she circled his strong neck, before using a finger to trace his lips.

He sucked in a breath before pecking her finger.

She whimpered softly, cupping his jaw. She waited…and waited for his kiss. She wished to God he would.

He brushed his lips across her forehead, whispering, but his words were inaudible.

Anxious for his lips, she pressed herself closer, causing a groan to erupt from his throat. Her heart palpitated as his lips hovered above hers, then she froze as

193

she heard and felt the heated breath of his words. "I won't kiss you."

"Wha-what?" she stuttered.

He pulled back slightly. "I won't kiss you. At least, not now, and not until we're in a committed relationship."

Shock made her immobile, her brain refusing to convey anything appropriate to say.

"And this is not a good place for either of us," he said quietly.

Wordlessly, she stared at him, and then realized she was still clutching his shoulders. A sliver of dread rushed up her spine, and she lowered her gaze while releasing him. She attempted to recoil, but his hands around her waist made it impossible. Startled, she stared up at him, her eyes wide with shock.

Before she could make a sound, he placed a finger on her lips.

"I already told you that I am in love with you," he said. "I want to pursue a relationship with you, but I need your commitment."

She inhaled raggedly, her chest rising and falling with deep breaths.

When she made no comment, he slowly released her.

"Is there anything you need to know to help you with that decision?" Tyler asked quietly.

"Ummm...no. I'm good." Then she remembered something. "I wanted to know—what is one thing that you desire more than anything else?"

He watched her for a moment. "I'll tell you that another time, but promise me you'll think and pray about my request. And stop hating yourself for feeling the way you do."

She cut her eyes at him, for she knew he was right.

"We're attracted to each other," he pointed out. "We have a lot in common, and we have history. There is nothing wrong with that. What is wrong is—you're carrying unforgiveness in your heart because of me. I know I did you wrong, Em. I want to make it right because I love you."

Madison swallowed as if forcing down a bitter pill. "I get it. You want a relationship now."

"That's true, but is that what you think is happening here?" His tone was harsh.

She mulled it over. "Okay, fine. I'll think about it."

"And pray about it."

"And pray about it."

"That's all I'm asking," he said, rising. "Now give me a hug."

"I bet you would like that." She rose and stepped away from him.

"Be nice. You can't be beautiful and ugly at the same time."

"Roger that, captain," she said with much sarcasm.

He eyed her. "As if I could kiss you and then take you to the wedding rehearsal. You know how we get with each other. Your father would definitely be giving me the evil eye."

"No comments from this side." She refused to look at him; she remembered the passion that had flared between them at her home.

"Now that's a first," he teased as they moved on.

He was holding her hand by the time they arrived at the back patio.

Mason and Kelani greeted them loudly and with an extra dose of joy. Mason's eyes roamed them, a giant smile forming on his face.

Madison managed to slide her hand out of Tyler's as Kelani clutched her shoulder.

"Ooh, my inner self is freaking out!" Kelani exclaimed, her eyes full of anticipation and excitement. "I can't believe we're getting married tomorrow."

Madison laughed. "Yes, you are. It's going to be awesome."

Soon, the rest of the jovial bridal party joined them.

"Pastor Fotola is here," Grandma Darlene announced from where she stood on the patio steps. She grinned at them as their heads swung. It was obvious no one knew she'd joined them.

"Group text from the wedding planner. It just came through," Grandma Darlene said, holding her phone in the air and moving through the group to get to the door.

Still, Madison noticed her tender smile as she looked from her to Tyler. *Oh my!* Madison drew in a sharp breath, wondering if Grandma Darlene had witnessed their shenanigans. She valiantly tried to rein in her panic.

Mason's joyful foot-stomping caught her attention. He pumped a fist in the air in celebration, singing, and dancing, "I am getting married tomorrow." He pointed at Kelani. "We are getting married tomorrow. Nothing can stop us."

Kelani danced about, chanting, "We are getting married tomorrow. Nothing can stop us." She waved her hand to include everyone. "Nothing can stop us."

The happy gang filed through the patio door singing and dancing. "We are getting married tomorrow. Nothing can stop us. Nothing can stop us."

CHAPTER 25

Madison lowered the windows of her BMW to enjoy the cool morning air as the dark-gray ribbon of road unfolded before her. It was a bleak day; the sky was pewter-colored, but she hoped the sun would break through the clouds and provide a great climate for Mason and Kelani's wedding day.

She was about to make the turn to tackle the two-mile stretch of private road to Chateau de Kanate when she had to stop to allow a small pickup truck to pass. The driver cheerfully waved at her and with a spontaneous grin, she waved back.

Soon, she greeted Grandma Darlene and dashed up the double-helix staircase to access the sleeping quarters. She was halfway up the stairs when her heart rate quickened as Tyler came into view. Her stomach rolled with delight, and she was sure her eyes were twinkling as she took in his black jeans and the long-sleeved, high-collar, red t-shirt that clung to him.

He broke into a light jog as he descended the staircase, equally enthralled to see her.

He looked ridiculously fit and toned. The front of his t-shirt was partially tucked into his jeans to subtly expose his belt.

As they came face-to-face, she lifted her eyes to his and dropped a casual, "Good morning."

She received a flash of pearly whites before he leaned in and gently kissed her cheek. "A good morning, indeed."

The whiff of his aftershave almost made her forget the purpose of her journey. "I'm here to see Mason," she stated quickly, while making movements to proceed. But when he held onto her hand, her eyes found his.

Sweet Lord! Her breath caught at the huge smile that stretched across his face.

"You made my morning, Em," he said with sincerity. "You saved the day."

She watched him and realized he had no intention of letting her go...not ever. "I'm glad to assist," she murmured, her mind all over the place.

"Oh, you were perfect." He laced his fingers with hers and rested them on his chest. "In fact, you were completely and utterly awesome. This was no fingertip save."

She laughed a little. "You are too much."

"Too much for what?"

She slipped her hand from his, and quickly told him, "Just an expression, Tyler. Just an expression," as if he didn't know.

He pushed out a sigh. "You should have told me you were coming. I have other plans. But I forgive you, because you made me happy just by being here."

She stared at him. *Sweet Lord! What on earth?*

"I've made commitments with Rob and Jay," Tyler continued. "We're hitting the streets. Mason has orders to rest."

"Orders?"

"Yup. We told him he needed to stay in and rest. Plus, his barber is about to pay him a visit." He chuckled knowingly. "His life is about to change. We figured he needed to be storming heaven with more prayers, even though we have had several prayer sessions with Grandma Darlene. She has been a tremendous blessing."

That brought a smile to Madison's face. "That's wonderful."

"Rehearsal was great last night, huh?" Tyler said, changing the subject. "Although you ran off without saying goodbye." He wagged a finger at her. "Bad girl."

She giggled softly. "Stop wagging that finger at me, Tyler, or you might lose it."

"Is that a threat or promise? Either way, bring it on," He chuckled softly, dropping his hand out of reach.

She smiled wickedly at him. "You will see."

"Now I'm scared," he said, looking around playfully before landing her a pointed gaze. "Why are you always running away from me?"

"Running? Whatever gave you that idea?"

Shucks! She had to escape last night after Mason and Kelani presented the bridal party with gifts. The wedding rehearsal had left her emotionally traumatized with all the visions of love everywhere. The setting and atmosphere were gorgeous—apple-red and gold decorations dominated the elegant setting. Susan Bowen, the wedding planner from All Things Divine, lived up to her reputation. *Divine, indeed!*

And, ooh that group dance—a mixture of several different genres, starting with the waltz, changing to hip-hop in the middle, and ending with the tango—left her in stitches...way too many girlish giggles. Plus, Tyler was enjoying her too much for her comfort. So much so that Grandma Darlene had remarked, "You two make good music together."

Aaarrrgh!

Neither did it help that with every chance he got, Mason was hinting to the bridal party, that her wedding day was around the corner. "Yup, any day now!" Mason had dared say, at one point, while glancing in Tyler's direction.

As the band and lead singers belted out "Endless Love", while Mason and Kelani danced, Tyler kept following her every move with a love-struck expression. Her temperature soared so many times she thought she was going to explode any minute. And worst of all, he knew it.

By the time the song ended, she had planned her escape route. *Phew! Crisis averted!*

"I thought we had a breakthrough in our friendship last night. You looked like you were enjoying my company."

Tyler's words brought Madison back to the present.

"Was that how you interpreted that? Okay..." Madison responded.

A warm smile blossomed across his face and he gazed longingly at her. "I wish I could stay with you, but I can't. I'm hoping you'll be here when I return."

"I doubt that strongly, because I am heading to the hair salon after this. I'll see you later, though," she heard herself add. *Oh, boy!*

"Great. See you later," he said, continuing to descend the stairs. "By the way, Mom told me you both had a great conversation."

"Yes," Madison agreed joyfully. "It was great to catch up with her."

"Sounds good."

She admired his strong frame, taking in the length and breadth of him.

He paused. "My turn?"

"What?" She proceeded to climb the stairs, muttering, "I don't know what you mean."

He remained silent, but when she added an extra sway to her graceful sashay, she heard him chuckling softly.

A tiny smile curved her lips as she walked across the landing and accessed the area to her father's childhood bedroom, which Mason was occupying.

She rapped a knuckle against the door and waited.

Seconds ticked by.

She pursed her lips to hold back a sigh; she had texted Mason to let him know she was on her way.

Without invitation, she opened the door and strode into the bedroom.

Mason was asleep, but stirred.

"I can't believe you're still sleeping," Madison said.

"Well, good morning to you, too," he grunted, his voice heavy with sleep.

"You sound cheerful. You said you would be up."

"I was. I just dozed off." He hopped out of bed and threw his arms open. "See, I'm out of my night wear."

She took in his army-green shorts and t-shirt with the label, "Love you to the moon...and back." She lifted her eyes to the ceiling. "I can't with you and your boo thang."

He laughed out. "Don't hate. You could be wearing this t-shirt but no, you want to be all uptight."

Madison cut him with her eyes. "Listen, Mason—"

"Alright. Alright." A hand went to his heart. "You can't hurt me on my wedding day."

"It's just like you, starting a fight or stirring up trouble, and then backing out."

Mason's lips curled into a lopsided smile. "You know me well. Come on, bring it in," he said, reaching out to hug her. "I love you."

She hugged him back. "I love you, too. Geesh, your barber needs to run in here. Get rid of some of that bush on your face, please." A soft chuckle escaped her as his eyes widened. "I feel so abused right now," she added, patting her cheeks.

Mason grinned at her, running his hands down his cheeks. "That bad, huh? He'll be here in a few, baby sis." He pointed to the large leather sofa in the seating area. "Let's sit."

He led the way and they sat.

"Your text sounded urgent—life and death urgent," Mason teased. "Or is it that you wanted to see Tyler?"

201

"Man, please." A bored expression covered Madison's face and she dropped her purse on the floor beside her.

He was not convinced. "I feel so used," he told her playfully.

"I hate to burst your bubble, but I am not here to see Tyler. I'm here to see you."

"You could use one stone to kill two birds. Tyler loves you."

"I know. It's because I'm irresistible." *Ugh! I am doing it again, succumbing to his foolishness.*

A frown creased Mason's face. "You should pray about it, Madison. I think you would both be happy together."

"And that's why I'm here. Did you not promise to take your foot off the gas and apply the brakes, where I'm concerned?"

Shock lit Mason's expression. "What do you mean?"

"Yesterday, during rehearsal, you kept dropping not-too-subtle hints about my wedding day, and pulling Tyler into your shenanigans."

Mason did not speak.

"I know you care about me, Mason, but I want you to stop trying to play God in my life. You must remember that God has me in the palms of His hands."

Mason watched her carefully. "You got my behavior concerning you and Tyler totally wrong. You two belong together. I was getting a bit tired of both of you existing instead of living. Come now, what would it take to make a relationship work with him?"

Madison pulled back sharply and exploded, "An act of God!"

Mason looked her in the eye. "Well, so be it."

She hissed her teeth and grabbed her phone from the outer pocket of her purse. "Excuse me while I find my notes app. I need to take notes, for clearly, you're an expert on what should be happening in my life."

Mason pressed his back against the sofa and stared at her.

But Madison was not finished. "Seems like all of my life and in particular for the past couple of years, you kept waiting to see which way I was going to fall so you can snatch me up from the agonies of life. You're worse than Dad," she huffed out with a deadly look.

Mason shot upright on the sofa. "Worse than Dad? We are trying to protect you, Madison."

A jolt of annoyance ripped through her. "Well, if that's protection, I'm sorry for Brianna and Brittany."

"I can't believe you said that." Mason's voice was harsh. "In all my days of knowing you, I never saw you as a quitter. When will you let someone in, Madison? When will you let someone over all those walls you have erected?"

She glared at him. "I see..." Her jaws felt so tight, she could barely get the words out. "I see what you think of me."

"Tyler loves you, but you're allowing whatever had happened between—"

"Whatever, Mason." She jumped off the sofa and rushed to the door. "Don't try to school me. I'm not your child."

Mason raced to the door and blocked her. "I'm sorry," he told her, pulling her hunched frame close and wrapping his arms around her. "I'm sorry, Madison," he choked out.

As she wept on his chest, she felt a few of his teardrops slide down the side of her face.

A few minutes later, they were back on the sofa.

"I didn't mean to upset you. You know I love you," Mason told her quietly. "I'll back away from your personal affairs."

"I don't know where that came from. The tears, I mean."

"Madison…I understand. I know it's overwhelming. I also know I got carried away with the idea of seeing my sister and one of my best friends together. Rest assured that I will leave the matter in the hands of the Lord, but if you need me, all you have to do is call."

"Okay. Thanks for understanding," she said quiet. "Ty-Tyler really hurt me, Mason." She paused to collect herself, swallowing the lump in her throat. "Hurt me in a way I didn't think I could recover." A tiny trickle of tears formed and ran down her cheek.

Mason squeezed her hand. "I'm glad you have the strength to voice that. I believe that is the beginning of good things. Let not your heart be troubled."

"Thank you." She spoke softly, collecting herself.

Mason smiled at her. "All things are working together for your good. I believe so."

"Amen!"

He lightened the tough moment. "If you ever need my help, you can always do the wink-wink signal."

She chuckled softly. "I'll remember that."

"Come on, bring it in." He reached out and hugged her, and she hugged him back.

"You have got to cut your beard. Yikes!" Madison shrieked, pulling away.

Chuckling, he released her. "That's my bad."

She came clean. "I'm sorry for comparing you to Dad. I know you're both trying to help."

"That's alright. I know." Mason breathed a sigh of relief then looked her in the eye. "Now that we're friends again, will you admit you knew I would have liked Kelani?"

Madison laughed aloud. "You're still at that?"

"Yes, I am. She said you talked about me a lot, and I found it odd, because you barely mentioned her to me. I think it was deliberate." He watched her. "Now, I've waited forever to get the truth out of you, so tell me."

Her eyes twinkled.

"Aha! I knew it," Mason shouted, slapping the back of the sofa.

Madison laughed. "But I haven't said anything yet."

"You don't have to. I know you."

"O-kay. The more I got to know her, the more I liked her. I may have spoken about you a bit more as the time came for you to come home from your trip. But that's because, knowing her story, I realized she wouldn't trust easily. I also know...you don't like to be told what to do, so I prayed and left it to the Lord."

She watched Mason as he wrestled with what she had said. She smiled at him. "Honestly, there is nothing like seeing two people who I love...in love with each other. It brings a double portion of joy to my heart."

He smiled at her. "Then, it's settled. Are you going to make it for 4:00 pm?"

She laughed softly, brimming with new hope. "I say 3:59, and not a minute earlier."

CHAPTER 26

Madison's eyes widened with shock as she gazed across the ballroom at Tyler. She must not have heard him right. But, when someone pushed a microphone in her hand, she knew she had indeed heard right. *Oh. My. Lord.* Her knees felt weak. This will be going down in history with a bold headline, one she had not yet come up with.

Jesus, fix it. The sequence of events leading up to this was etched in her mind.

An usher had quietly nudged Tyler from his seat at the bridal party table and then Madison saw him talking in what seemed like hushed tones to Susan, who was pointing at the wedding program. Next, she observed Tyler making his way around the room to the band.

Interesting. Her eyebrows lifted when a cordless microphone was handed to him, and he walked back to take up a spot across the room. *Ooookay, he must be filling in for the male lead singer.*

A few minutes later, the moderator called for the bride and groom to take centerstage to do their first dance. Mason and Kelani looked phenomenal on their big day. She smiled because of the dazzlingly glamorous picture Kelani made in her strapless white Alexander McQueen ballgown that showed off her figure. The scooped neckline hinted at her cleavage and perfectly accentuated her stunning features. She had ditched her braids for a sleek, twirled chignon that was beautiful from every angle and created a polished look that was fit for a princess.

Mason looked divinely dashing—stylish in a Calvin Klein black slim-fit tuxedo. Debonair. Handsome. Confident. Happy. The world was at his feet. He moved with ease and infinite grace, flashing a boyish, charming smile at every opportunity.

As Mason and Kelani walked to take up their positions, Tyler called for Madison to help him with what he said was one of her favorite songs—"Endless Love".

Screams of delight came from Kelani, followed by shrieks of "Yes!" from the rest of the bridal party. The delightful roars and deafening applause from the guests exploded in the room.

A shiver snaked its way down Madison's spine as she made her way across the floor. She could only hope she would remember the words of the song. She glanced across the room at Tyler, who smiled encouragingly at her. She resisted the urge to threaten him with her eyes and instead smiled at Mason and Kelani. Yup, by their huge smiles, they were rooting for her. That bolstered her confidence somewhat.

A tilt of her head told Tyler she was ready, and she saw him signal to the band to start the introduction to the song.

The ballroom grew silent and although it could be her imagination, it seemed that the audience looked rather thrilled to see her and Tyler together. She intended to focus on Mason and Kelani, but when Tyler crooned out the first line of the song, he pulled her in.

Soulful and deep. Deeeeep. That brought out a warm smile, and then the shock held her immobile for the next line of the song—"My first love..."—was hers. Tyler was her first love. *Focus. Focus*, she commanded her thoughts. *This is for Mason and Lani.*

By the time she got it together, Tyler was repeating the opening lines and smiling encouragingly at her.

She glanced out at the sea of faces before her.

Watching.

Waiting.

Heart pounding, Madison closed her eyes and launched off with the next lines of the song. She looked at

Tyler and a smile popped on her face as he stretched his hands towards her and continued to sing.

They poured their love into the song as they serenaded Mason and Kelani...and each other. When Tyler began walking slowly towards her while singing, Madison couldn't breach protocol, so she walked towards him, too.

The guests were spellbound, seemingly holding their breaths...right alongside her. She had to remind herself to breathe, or she would never be able to sing.

Eventually, she and Tyler met and held hands, delivering an emotional yet powerful finale. By then, they were serenading each other with passion that could set the city ablaze.

"My love." Tyler sang like a sweet caress.

"My love," Madison echoed, "my love."

Poignant, heartfelt, and stirring, they sang the last line together—"My endless love."

The ballroom was soundless as they embraced each other and Tyler tenderly kissed her cheek. Suddenly aware that they were not alone, they broke apart and started to clap for the bride and groom.

Their guests, who were all hushed, broke out in thunderous applause. Tyler and Madison bowed then rushed centerstage to hug Mason and Kelani.

Madison could feel all eyes not on the couple but on her and Tyler. It didn't help that Tyler was smiling tenderly at her as he steered her back to the table and made sure she was seated before taking his seat.

It was beginning to feel like planning her escape route was becoming a habit when she and Tyler were in the same space.

Forty minutes later, she quietly slipped from the ballroom and made her way to the balcony. She held on to the billowing fabric of her fashionable apple-red chiffon gown so that she wouldn't trip. By the time her hand grasped the wooden rails of the balcony, the folds of the chiffon were teasing her toned legs. She closed her eyes and then opened them to enjoy the beautiful stars twinkling in the sky and beckoning to her.

By all accounts, the wedding was a celebration. A quintessential fairy tale, the setting was magnificent—unique yet intimate. Picture perfect. No stone was left unturned to transform the grand ballroom into a magical apple-red and gold palace to make beautiful memories. The glamorous event showcased the gold-detailed ceiling and jaw-dropping architecture of the ballroom.

Yay! The gourmet food and specialty beverage selections—served by white-gloved attendants as befitting the setting of grandeur—were the bomb. As expected, the bridal party dance was a hit with the delighted guests.

Madison's smile widened as she recalled singing with Tyler. Her heart lurched. *I really enjoyed that.* She sensed a sliver of heat rushing through her body, tripping over itself to reach her heart.

Truth be told, she had enjoyed, too, the way he'd looked at her earlier that evening, when she had arrived at the chateau and joined the rest of the bridal party in a room adjoining the ballroom.

She was adjusting the folds of her gown when she glanced across the room and saw him enter. Her pulse kicked up several notches—as it did these days—and the room suddenly felt warmer. As he began to move towards her, she felt herself glowing with all kinds of emotions.

Joy.

Pleasure.

Desire.

By the time he arrived at her side, they were smiling foolishly at each other.

His eyes swept over her—hair, face, neck, dress, shoes, and tremulous smile—before returning to gaze at her. "You look beautiful, Em," he said tenderly.

Pleasurable sensations ignited and glowed in her heart at the untainted passion in his eyes. "Thank you," she managed to say, glancing around him and noticing the rest of the bridal party was pretending to be engrossed elsewhere.

That brought on a smile. And just like that, she was jerked out of her recollections as arms crowded her.

She did not have to ask who was invading her personal space. After all, this was where they had escaped to the last time.

"Em, I missed you," he whispered passionately. "Why are you always running away from me?"

His voice suave and full of need, Madison's body quivered at the sound of her name rolling off his tongue. "Ty, I'm not—" She moaned as his lips danced along her shoulder towards the crook of her neck. *Dear God! Help!*

In the small space, she turned to face him.

He pulled her against his body and she planted her hands on his chest, feeling the ripples of his muscles.

"Don't do that," he warned teasingly. "I'm a minute away from getting seriously freaky."

Happy sparks sizzled in her chest at his statement. *Dear God, what am I going to do with this man?* She slid her hands around his neck. Well, she had to. Her knees were buckling.

He eyeballed her like she was his prized possession. "For singing like that, I give you five smoking-hot stars."

"And I'm giving you the same," she replied. "We did well."

"We were great together." Smiling, he rolled his eyes to the sky. "Everybody knew it."

She giggled softly, then paused as his eyes dropped to her lips.

As he made eye contact again, she realized she was staring at him...just like he was staring at her. Oh, she wanted him.

"Ty." Every single hair on her body stood on end. "I-I..." She stuttered, pausing as they both heard the vibrating of his cell phone.

******

Tyler took his cell phone from his inner jacket pocket, while still hugging Madison's waist.

He breathed a sigh of relief. "It's Mom, I told her I'd call after the wedding, to tell her how it all went down."

He decided not to take the call but instead began to text her. *Mom, still at the wedding.* ☺ *Call you soon.*

But before he could press the send button, his phone began to vibrate again.

"Mom," he answered joyfully, "I was just texting..."

He listened, then asked, "When did that happen?" as he pulled away from Madison.

Listening intently, he unconsciously ran a hand over his head, from back to front. "Okay, I'm catching the first flight out." Agonizing, he listened before saying, "Bye, Mom. I'll see you soon."

Tyler disconnected the call and stared across the balcony rails at the impending vortex swirling before him.

Petrified.

That was putting it mildly.

As a string of terrifying thoughts curled in his gut, he felt rigid, as if rigor mortis had just set in. He'd hoped he wouldn't have to go down this road again. At least, not for a while.

He heard Madison calling his name, but he couldn't answer. All he heard was the tremor in his mother's voice as she told him his father was in the hospital and that chances are, he wouldn't make it.

As horrifying thoughts passed, his throat dried up and he squeezed his eyes shut, trying—and failing—to process what he'd just heard. Suddenly, he felt light-headed, as if his body was being lifted off the ground. Darkness blanketed his vision, and he gripped the rail just as his body started tipping forward.

CHAPTER 27

Everything hurts, Tyler moaned mentally, while staring at the ceiling in what used to be his room at his parents' home.

His body craved to be free of the torment. If only he had the energy...the courage. He had felt like he was barely alive since his father died a week and a half ago. Even with all the praying he'd been doing, he felt no reprieve.

He swung his feet over the side of the bed and felt like he was rising from the darkness of his father's passing and swimming towards the surface after a deep dive. He turned on the bedside lamp and was surprised that is was after 1:00 p.m. He surmised his mother must be tired of trying to get him out of his room. He sighed, realizing she must be hurting but was playing strong for him. That thought made him walk over and pull on the strings to open the long ceiling-to-floor drapes.

Sunlight flooded his room like a beacon of hope, accentuating the medium tone wood floor and the ribbon fireplace with natural wood incorporated into its design. Suddenly, he felt hopeful. He decided there and then, he was going to be strong for his mother. He pulled the drapes in to reduce the sunlight then wandered over to the two-seater leather sofa.

He lounged there with his hands behind his head, taking pleasure in the rustic decor of his incredibly inviting bedroom. Woven textiles softened the décor and ambiance in the room, a direct contrast to his contemporary style homes in Boston and Orlando. Albeit, he had not yet gone to his own home in Boston. He just needed to be close to his mother right now.

Daniel Bradshaw had been not only a beloved husband, father, and pastor, but also a renowned community leader. He could only imagine the crowd size at the funeral on Saturday. Several of his parents' family members were already in town, but only Aunt Rachel was staying with them.

Lord, help me, Tyler pleaded silently. *I have to believe that all things are working together for my good. Some good must come from this.*

Strangely, Larry Kanate had become a tower of strength for him. *Downright weird.* That was not a relationship he thought would ever have developed to such depth...especially so rapidly. However, when he had almost fainted after the wedding, Madison had called her father and he had jumped into action. He had led Tyler back to his room at the chateau, and then called the family doctor. While they were waiting, he had gathered a few family members including Madison, and had led them in prayer concerning Tyler's health and the situation he was facing.

After Tyler was cleared by the doctor, Larry had insisted that he spend the night at the chateau. Madison found an early bird flight for him, and in the morning, Larry drove him to the airport. Since then, he'd been calling daily to check on Tyler, and they often ended their conversation with prayer.

Since leaving for Boston, he had spoken with Madison twice. Okay, he had been avoiding her. He didn't have much to say or much to offer. He was aware that she had been praying for him and had reached out to his mother several times.

Knock.

Knock. Knock.

"Ty," his mother called out, her voice quiet and gentle.

"Come in, Mom," he said.

She entered, smiling at him. "Good morning, son. You're up. That's wonderful,"

"Good morning, Mom." He forced a smile he did not even come close to feeling. "Yes, I decided to drag myself out of the doom and gloom."

She moved confidently into the room and stood before Tyler, her hands akimbo on her supple hips. Paulette Bradshaw was tall and elegant, and always in First Lady mode.

A tiny smile curved Tyler's lips as he took in her pretty red sweater and ankle-length black skirt, showing off her coffee complexion. His eyebrows shot upwards, taking in the dramatic bun on top of her head. "Mom, you're looking lovely. Are you and Aunt Rachel heading out?"

"No." She smiled at him. "I'm just putting my best foot forward. People are popping by every second." She sat beside him. "I know I can stop them, but I don't want to. They are grieving, too, and they want to express their love for Daniel."

"Mom, you are a great human being." He reached over and hugged her. "I love you. I could not have asked for a better mother."

She squeezed him tightly before releasing him. "And I could not have asked for a better son." She smiled lovingly at him. "You were right on time."

"Even after all the issues I put you and Dad through."

"Pshhhh! That was nothing compared to the joy of having you, our one and only son. You know how grateful we are that God gave you to us."

He smiled. Perhaps his first genuine smile since he'd heard the terrible news. "The feeling is mutual."

They were silent for a moment, each reflective.

"You're taking Dad's passing rather...well, for lack of a better word," Tyler mentioned.

"I have my moments, and it gets worse at night when I climb in bed without him." She paused to gather herself and Tyler squeezed her hand, which was resting on the sofa between them.

"But you know what," she told him, "we were always determined to live each day as if it was our last. Life is fleeting, Ty. Things happen, but I trust God. I trust Him."

She watched Tyler before carefully telling him, "You have loved Madison forever. I would never get tired of you telling me all the things that you and Madison were doing in college. You are a good match for each other, Ty. Please don't let your father's death crush you into thinking that life is hopeless." She paused to make sure he was listening. "I want you to reach for the life that God has for you. It's about time for that dream to be fulfilled. You can't run away from it anymore."

"Thanks, Mom. I know, but it's so hard. I am relying on God to see me and you through this...this difficult season. I keep seeing Dad, healthy and active, running around to do all he could for the people of God. I...I'm going to miss him."

"I know, Son, I know. I-I am trusting God. He will help us."

"I love you, Mom." He hugged her. "You are the best."

"I love you, too." She hugged him tightly before releasing him, and questioned, "Does that mean you're going to make a move on Madison?"

He chuckled softly, thinking how she would not let up. "I need to get past Dad's funeral."

"That I understand, but I want you to move on with your life. I want to be alive when my grandbabies are born."

Tyler laughed aloud. "I'll handle it."

"Come on, bring it in," she said, reaching out and hugging him. "I will see you for lunch then, since you

216

missed breakfast? I'm sure Rachel needs your company, too. You know how she likes to chat with you."

"Yes. I'll be there in a few," Tyler said, watching his mother making her way to the door. "Even though I don't know if I'm good company right now."

A hand on the doorknob, his mother paused. "She'll be happy with whatever you offer. And while you're at it, please call Madison. She is very concerned about you."

He sighed. "Mom, I don't have much to say right now."

"Tell her that. Do anything but shut her out." Her tone was serious. "You do not want her to go back into hibernation."

His eyes popped. "Okay, I will," he said quietly.

"Good, son," his mother encouraged before leaving the room.

Tyler got up and retrieved his cell phone from the nightstand. Dropping on to his bed, he dialed Madison's number.

"Good afternoon," she answered quietly.

"Good afternoon," he responded. "Sorry about missing your calls."

"It's okay," she said in a monotone voice.

"Em, please don't sound like that. I—"

"Like what, Tyler?"

"You know what I mean," he offered. "I'm just having a hard time."

"Of course, you're having a hard time. Your father died. That is understandable. What I don't understand is why you're refusing to take my calls. You keep doing this running away thing when you think the world has done you harm."

He sighed loud. *This is the last thing I need.* "Don't give up on me. I am looking forward to seeing you all on Saturday, despite the circumstance."

She softened. "I'm not your enemy, Ty. Just stop doing the runaway thing, okay?"

"I'll try, but it's not easy," he confessed.

"Just know that there are people who care about you and your happiness."

"I know. Thanks."

"I'll call you when we arrive on Thursday. We decided to come in two days early, so we could settle in."

"Do you need me to pick you all up from the airport?"

"No. Since it's so many of us, Dad rented a vehicle and we'll head straight to the hotel."

"Mason and—"

"Yes, they are cutting their honeymoon short because they wanted to support you. Plus, Rob, Jay, Laurie-Ann, and Rebecca will also be attending the funeral."

Suddenly, Tyler felt grateful. Grateful for all the people whom God had placed in His life to love him. There was a certain bliss in being alone, but the term 'circle of love' now took on a new meaning for him.

CHAPTER 28

That's a perfect spot, Madison thought as she gazed from the balcony outside her bedroom. The pretty blue sky seemed to majestically fuse with the mountains over yonder. Awe-inspiring. Beautiful. Peaceful.

Lord, this is the day that you have made; I will rejoice and be glad in it. A tiny smile curved her lips as her gaze shifted to where the sun was trying to peep from the clouds in a bid to illuminate the sky. Still, it could not destroy the preferred union of the sky and mountains.

She slid deeper into the huge, padded wicker chair, thinking how she had opened herself to Tyler once again, and once again, he was playing the fool. She closed her eyes, feeling a dull ache in her heart. Just then, her doorbell sounded, and she made her way down the stairs to the front door.

"Dad. Mom. Why didn't you use your key?"

She was surprised when her parents had called to say they were out and about and wanted to stop by.

"Good morning," they greeted her with hugs.

"Great to see both of you." Madison watched as her father closed the door. "The question is what brought you to my neck of the woods? On a Wednesday morning?" she asked curiously.

"That is not the welcome I expected from my first daughter," her father teased as they made their way to the living room.

Her mother playfully swatted Madison's shoulder. "Is it against the law for us to stop by?" she questioned, taking a seat beside Madison on the sofa, while her father sat across from them.

Madison shook her head, her expressive eyes wide. "Of course, you're both welcome to visit. Anytime. Would you like something to eat or drink?"

"No, thank you for asking," her father replied, while her mom shook her head.

"Are you ready to roll tomorrow?" her mom asked.

"Ready enough. I'm not packed though, but I'll do that later. Thank you both for planning to attend the funeral. I appreciate it and I know Tyler does."

"It's the right thing to do," her father responded.

"Yes," her mother agreed, and then she eyed Madison. "Do you plan to release yourself from what happened between you and Tyler?" her mother asked bluntly.

Madison's defenses climbed. "Why would you ask me that, Mom?"

"It is obvious that you and Tyler have a thing for each other." She smiled gently. "We can all see that, but you will have to lose that...haughty spirit."

"Haughty? Mom, what on earth—" Madison stopped, too stunned to finish her statement. Clearly, her parents were on a shock and awe campaign, but she also remembered Mason mentioning that 'haughty spirit' to her.

"My thing is—what's your end game?" Her mother's eyes held a bit of reproof. "You may be enjoying the ride, but will it get you to where you need to be?"

"Mom, I'm not doing anything of the sort."

"Baby, you are quick," her mother filled in. "You get things done, always. That's your nature. You move and you make it happen...so now you've come upon a situation that floored you and in order to survive, you've built up many walls, to protect yourself."

"Mom, we have had this conversation."

"And the fact that we're having it again means the situation has not been resolved. I am trying to help, Madison, because, I see that you're not allowing the Lord to resolve the situation. Instead, you're leaning on your own understanding."

220

Jesus, fix it. What on earth! For the first time in her life, Madison wanted to tell her mother a few choice words; however, her upbringing would not allow it. "Okay, Mother," she managed to say.

"I've been talking with Tyler quite frequently." Her father spoke up. Clearly trying to diffuse the situation.

"Dad, you've been talking with Tyler? Frequently?" Madison's eyebrows crammed together. *This day could not get any stranger. Dad and Tyler chatting? Frequently?* She had to squeeze back the hollow laughter that was dying to pop out.

"Yes," her father responded.

Madison's eyes wavered between her parents before settling on her father. "I hate to ask, but, about what? I thought you didn't like Tyler."

"I like Tyler, alright." Her father smiled. "I was just uncertain of his intention towards you. I wanted him to know that I was watching." A thoughtful expression crossed his face. "The more I saw you both, the more I realized you love each other. Confirmed when you both sang at the wedding."

"You both looked like love." Her mother laughed softly, "I believe it was obvious to everyone in the room."

"Really, Mom!" Madison exclaimed, but she did not look at her mother.

"Yes, really," her mother replied. "Madison, sometimes God has a way of taking us full circle. He will show the prize but not the journey to the prize." She touched Madison's hand. "You recall the story of Joseph. If you are trying to walk in your destiny, there will be roadblocks."

"Yes, I remember that story," Madison responded in monotone. "And I see what you are saying, Mom."

Her mother was not put off. "Baby, loving someone is great, but sometimes love is complex and hard and tiring.

You may not have known all that Tyler went through in his life that caused him to behave the way he did back then. He's older now, and I see the way he has been looking at you. He's certainly not hiding it. I think you should pray about the matter and see how the Lord leads you."

"I thought about a relationship with him and all I can see is him running off again, like he's doing now. Once was enough," Madison huffed out. "Why can't I love a simple man? No, that would be too much to ask. I have to go for someone who constantly rips my heart out and stomps all over it."

Her statement rang out in her head as she faced her new reality. *Did I just confess that I love Tyler?* She pulled herself together.

"Mom and Dad, you know how much I admire your relationship. I thought I could have something close to that with Tyler." She choked, and her mother grasped her hand and squeezed it. "It took me a loooong time to get over Tyler and I cannot put myself in that position again."

"Oh, Madison, all things, not just some things, *all things* are working together for your good," her mother encouraged. "That season has passed, and this is a new season and you are both older and wiser."

"Madison," her father called for her attention. "Don't think by any means that your mother and I have a perfect relationship." He chuckled loudly. "Do you remember when I secretly bought you that playful pup?"

Madison beamed. "Yeeeesss, Dad. I loved Bubbles...up to his dying day. I didn't want to replace him."

"Well, your mother has a no pet in the house rule. Soooo, you, me, and that dog almost had to sleep outside."

Rozene waved him away, laughing softly. "Stop. I'm denying all of that."

Larry smiled at his wife. "I see the guilt all over you. Anyway, Madison, I wish some of our issues were that simple." He looked tenderly at Rozene. "You may recall when you and Mason came home at the end of your first year of college—how you both were saying that we were behaving differently towards each other."

Madison eyes widened as she recollected.

"I see you remember," her father said. "During that time, your mother and I were having a soul-crushing takedown of each other."

"It was not a pretty situation," Rozene added, "but we survived it, and I believe that made our love for each other stronger."

Larry nodded in agreement. "We have had terrible seasons when we didn't think we would make it." His gaze softened as he looked at his wife. "Some days, neither of us wanted our marriage. Only our relationship with the Lord and counselling helped. Today, I can confidently say we're glad we've weathered the storms of life."

"We are nurturing each other," her mother filled in. "And we are making sure that our marriage remains Christ-centered. Of course, we are holding each other accountable."

"Amen," her father said.

"Thanks for sharing that," Madison said.

"As your mother encouraged, put the matter before the Lord. Let Him work it out." He smiled at Madison. "Remember, you have to go out on the limb; that's where the fruit is. They say love needs both roots and wings. You have your roots, I think you need the courage to fly."

Madison looked away from them.

"Did you know Tyler was adopted?" her father quizzed.

Madison looked puzzled. "I see you both have really been talking."

"I'm going to take that as a yes," her father said.

Aghast, Madison's gaze bounced around her living room before settling on her father. "I'm surprised he mentioned it to you."

"And perhaps that would help you to understand his behavior towards you in the past...and the present," her mother added.

Madison could not quite recover from the shock of the news. *Dad? Tyler?* It would be a relief if she ever saw any kind of relationship developing between the two.

"He didn't go into details," her father said. "And I did not press him."

"Thanks for letting me know, Dad."

"Are you going to be okay?" her mother asked.

Madison's mind was reeling. "Yes. I'm just a bit surprised he shared that with you considering..."

"Considering how I treated him?" Her father's gaze became solemn. "I'm sorry. That was wrong of me, and I apologized to him. You are both grown, and he did not exhibit any action that suggested he was dangerous or that you were in danger because if him." He sighed. "The truth is, the more we talked the more I found out we have more in common than not."

"Okay," Madison said slowly, not sure she understood.

Her mother looked at her tenderly. "God has an opportune time to bring us into our destiny."

Suddenly Madison's eyes grew wide, and before she could hold it together, her eyes filled with tears. Her body quivered as tears rolled down her cheeks. For she remembered how the Lord had led her to Estrina's and her growing passion to advance the lives of those who were less fortunate.

Indeed, the Lord was in the mix, making sure that she understood what these children had been through, so that she could have a greater understanding of her own future.

Her mother comforted her as she sobbed, and she heard her father praying. "Oh God! Oh God of all grace and mercy. We thank You, oh God, that Your name is a strong tower. Lord, this morning we can run into it and we know we are safe. We place our daughter before You..."

CHAPTER 29

Sympathetic expressions flashed across the attendees' faces before they tried for polite, encouraging smiles as they expressed condolences. Still, Tyler was grateful for their support at his father's funeral. The gathering was huge—family members, church members, city leaders, pastors, deacons, and elders from many churches, as well as other well-wishers; however, Tyler would be lying if he said he remembered much of the greetings or words of comfort they offered during the solemn occasion.

He was grateful, too, for the support of Madison and her family. She'd offered to visit when they'd arrived, but he'd backed away at breakneck speed. He couldn't deal with company.

When they had arrived at the church earlier, she and her family had greeted and hugged him and his mother. He'd hugged her, but he was sure she could feel the distance. It didn't help that he could hardly look her in the eyes.

Now at the graveside, he clutched his mother's shoulders as she wept. He did not cry at the funeral. He'd already shed all his tears since the news of his father's passing. Plus, the last thing he wanted to do was dump all his fears and hurts…and baggage in front of everyone. In any case, he had to remain strong for his mother.

Strong? Oh God! He could feel the vacuum in the vast wilderness in his soul. He needed peace from this raging unrest. He was fighting feelings that made him think he'd been abandoned again, this time on the precipice of life. God, he was tired and needed to hold up the white flag and surrender.

A lump formed in his throat and he quietly coughed until his throat was clear. He beckoned to one of the ushers for a chair so his mother could sit. The usher brought two chairs and he helped her to sit and then sat beside her with his arms around her. He couldn't wait for this part of the funeral service to pass.

He heard the pastor's voice droning on. He realized he'd missed most of what the pastor had said at the church. He closed his eyes as they covered his father's grave. He'd lost the two fathers he'd come to know.

A sharp pang of guilt hit him. Maybe he should have come home when he'd heard his father cough or that he was making a second trip to the doctor. But from what the doctors told him, the bronchitis quickly turned into pneumonia and it was downhill from there. His father still trying to run around certainly did not help his case.

Soon it was time to head back home where there was food galore for the attendees to partake of, if they wished to do so. The engine's roar filled Tyler's ears. Mason had offered to drive, and he had agreed because he felt winded. He'd driven his mother's white BMW, so he sat with his mother and Aunt Rachel while Kelani took the seat next to Mason. It was a quiet half an hour ride home, except with Aunt Rachel belting out directions for short cuts.

When Mason guided the vehicle near to the front door, Tyler assisted his mother as she got out. Once his mother was seated in the living room, Tyler beckoned to Aunt Rachel.

Her bloodshot eyes met his.

Tyler touched her shoulder. "Please make sure no one stresses Mom out. I'm going to get her a bottle of water or something to drink."

When Tyler returned, several family members were keeping guard around his mother. He uncapped a bottled water and gave it to his mother.

She took it, offering a tiny smile. "Thank you."

"You okay, Mom?" Tyler asked.

"Yes, son. I'm trying to hold it together. You can mill around. I'll be here."

"Okay, Mom." He watched her carefully before moving away.

"Hey, bro," Mason greeted him. "Praying for you, man."

"Thanks. I need it." Tyler blinked quickly to push away the tears that were threatening. "I'll be back. I just need to step outside for a few. I feel like I can't breathe in here." *Actually, I feel like a bomb is strapped to my chest.*

"No problem, bro."

With that, Tyler moved away, nodding and escaping apologetic smiles and those who wanted conversation. He made his way across the huge living room, through the side door, and gained access to the passageway that led to the back patio.

As he opened the door, the scent of fresh-cut grass hit him, but not enough to stop him. He descended the patio steps like he was being chased and walked the beaten path away from the garden towards a covered building his parent used as a workroom.

He opened the door, closed it behind him, and walked over to the black leather sofa. He did a split-second mental debate on whether to sit or stretch out, then decided lying down made more sense.

Finally alone, he exhaled loudly. *Ah, silence!* "Lord, I pray for strength and courage."

Some fifteen minutes later, he was staring at the ceiling when he heard a gentle knock on the door. He remained quiet.

The door opened and he raised his head only to look into the intense and slightly unsure eyes of Madison. His stomach lurched. Funny, how he'd felt the same way the first time he saw her.

He didn't even pretend to be strong. Throwing his feet on the ground, he reached for her.

Pulling the door closed, she rushed to his side, sank on the sofa, and he rested his head on her lap.

"Ty," she murmured his name, rubbing his head. Her voice was smooth as silk to his ears.

Tears coursed down his cheeks, and he allowed his tears to flow. He heard her whispering encouraging words and threw his legs on the sofa so he could comfort himself in her arms.

She hovered over him, hugging him as best as she could, while he wept.

Shortly thereafter, his tears ceased, but his body began to convulse intermittently. She tenderly kissed the top of his head as if he was a child and he hugged her tighter, for that was exactly what he needed.

When he quieted, he saw her wiping her tears. And, in the midst of his grief, joy rose in his heart.

She gently rubbed his head and he moaned softly in contentment. "Ty, it's going to be alright," she said softly. "I know it doesn't seem or feel like it, but all is well. God is good. And in times like this, when you can't trace His Hands, trust His heart."

Her words were sound and beautiful. They made his heart smile. *God, I love this woman.* "Thank you," he mumbled.

She prayed for him.

"Almighty God, help us to shift from what we feel, to what You have said in Your Word. Oh God, the struggle is painfully real. Lord, I place Tyler into Your capable hands. I pray You will continue to keep him, to lead him and to direct his steps during this very agonizing season.

"Help him to be strong in You, Lord, and in the power of Your might. Give him the faith to rise above all that is happening. Comfort him, Lord, through the power of

Your Holy Spirit. Allow him to use this season to cling to You.

"I pray for a fresh anointing for him. Give him a vision of his future, Lord, so he will not despair but instead be fruitful, increasing in knowledge and understanding daily. Remind him that Your plans for him are for good and not evil.

"Father, I pray for a hedge of protection around him and over his mind. Shield him from the strategies and lies of the enemy. When the enemy comes in like a flood, Lord, I ask that You lift up a standard against him. I declare that the angels of the Lord encamp around Tyler.

"In the name of Jesus Christ, I destroy every spirit of discouragement and hardness of heart. I decree and declare that no weapon that is formed against him shall prosper, because the Spirit of the Lord rests upon him. He is anointed. He is blessed. He is empowered. Thank You, Lord. You are our strength and our redeemer. In the name of Jesus Christ, I pray, amen."

"Amen," he mumbled, still holding her close. "Thank you." *Ah, peace. Just what I need. Thank You, Lord.*

He was grateful, too, that they had always been attuned to each other.

CHAPTER 30

How much more can I take? Tyler paced the floor of his living room feeling as if he wanted to kick something. His head was beginning to pound, so he squeezed his eyes shut and massaged his forehead.

Obstacles.

Rocky paths.

Hurdles.

The host of hell must hate me.

It had been over three weeks since the death of his father. He was holding it together, even helping John Leeds, the family lawyer, to sort out his mother's financial affairs. Now this strange, new occurrence had him on the edge of darkness pondering what had become of his life.

Larry Kanate watched him with compassion. "Tyler, don't run yourself to a wreck. There is a lot of good in this news."

"Good news, Mr. Kanate? Pardon me for not seeing the light." He plopped down on the other end of the sofa that Larry was sitting on.

"Let me get you something to drink," Larry said, encouragingly. "I promise, it's going to be alright."

Tyler watched him head towards the kitchen, and gratitude filled his heart. He had been surprised a few days after the funeral when Madison's father had called and informed him that he and his wife were hanging around in Boston as the Holy Spirit led. They were familiar with all the city's attractions, since Mason and Madison had attended MIT; however, Tyler took them to lunch on the weekend.

Tyler wished he could stay longer in Boston but he had to head back to work. Still, he was mainly in Boston for his mother's sake. Since the death of his father, he felt it was his responsibility to make sure his mother was coping.

Yesterday, when he had visited her, he had concluded that she was doing well, under the circumstances. He then decided to head back to Orlando by the weekend. He was on his way to his apartment when Mr. Leeds called to find out exactly when he would be leaving for Orlando. During that conversation, Mr. Leeds told him that it was important he and his mother stop by his office the following day. So they had, almost two hours ago.

Mr. Leeds gave them two letters—one addressed to him, the other addressed to his mother—handwritten by his father. Mr. Leeds had indicated that he did not know what was in the letters, but he was given specific instructions to hand them over after his father's will was read.

Tyler recalled himself and his mother staring at each other as they sat on the sofa in Mr. Leeds' office. "Let's do this on the count of three," he had teased.

His mother had smiled cautiously at him. "No need, I'm in," she had said, ripping open her envelope.

He had watched as she read her letter, smiling all the way. That had encouraged him to open his own letter, and he began to read.

Phew! Soon, he had found himself smiling, too. Shouts of joy whipped back and forth in his mind as he read. He was still reading when he heard his mother's gasp. He was in deep, so he glanced her way but didn't give her his full attention.

Then, he had heard himself gulp. His mental shouts of joy had died instantaneously, as his heart cried out. Unable to bear the pain, he had jumped off the sofa, his head whipping towards his mother.

Her tear-filled, wounded eyes met his. She had been visibly shaken.

His chest had tightened with fear and he had fallen to his knees sobbing.

In a flash, his mother was by his side. Hugging him. Comforting him. Whispering words of encouragement, through her tears.

Eventually, she had prayed for him.

Soon, silence had covered him like a wet blanket, submerging his soul in utter despair. He could hear his own heartbeat, and his mouth had filled with bile. He glanced at the letter in his hand, tears still running down his face. He would never be the same.

Tyler's tortured mind began to re-read the letter that had changed everything.

"Dear Son,

Writing that brought on a smile. I love you. Your mother and I love you very much. We feel privileged that God has chosen us to be your parents. We could not have asked for a better child. We are very proud of the man you have become. Above all, you have nurtured your relationship with the Lord and we love seeing all that God is doing in and through you.

Now, if you are reading this letter, do not despair. Remember, the Lord giveth and He taketh away. Moreover, everything God does is well done. Therefore, let not your heart be troubled. The aim of this letter is to ensure you are equipped for the successful future God has planned for you.

Please take care of Mom for me, as I know you will. I know you love her, and I see her loving you right back. When I see you both in action, I can only say—look at God. He is an on-time God.

Thanks for being a shining beacon of hope to so many, especially our young people. We see how the Lord has prospered you in the field of architecture, showing you favor with man. I know you believe that the Lord called you into ministry and you are waiting for the right timing. Fear not! You will know when the time is right, for the wind will be blowing in that direction. Allow God to lead you into that season.

Now son, I have a delicate matter to talk with you about. One that will have a profound effect on you, but I know and pray you will weather this storm. Remember— God is watching over you.

I was hoping to tell you in person but I shied away from it, for no good reason. And of course, there was never a good time to break the news. So, here it is—your first dad who loved you very much and whom you love, was your biological father. Yes, Pastor David Moore was your biological father.

I know you are in shock to hear this news, but as you can well imagine, the situation was complicated. Your mother's name is Katrine Hansen. We knew her simply as Suzette. You look just like her. Before you leave Mr. Leeds' office, he will give you another envelope. It has a picture of your mother. Your father was touched she gave you his middle name. Please forgive your father for not being truthful about his middle name. His middle name is Aiden and not Adam.

I met your mother once at the Zim's coffee shop, the same one that David would take you to. As you know, I am not a coffee drinker. I met Katrine when I had to pick up David from Zim's one evening. I did not know of your father's and Katrine's relationship until she "disappeared" from the coffee shop. Meaning, she left and your father could not find her. That was when I was brought into the picture.

For years, David lamented about Katrine. I believed he cared deeply for her. From what he had told me, she helped him overcome the death of his own son. Yes, he and Aunt Marlene had a son who died shortly after he was born. His name was Nathan.

A few years later, your current mom (Paulette) asked me to stop by Zim's and pick up an order. I did. The owner, Ned Zimmer, came out front to greet me because Paulette had become a frequent customer. I started talking with him and I asked about Suzette. He looked puzzled, and then told me that no one by that name had worked there. I refused to give up, so I visited Ned the following day, and showed him a picture of Suzette, which David had left with me. That *was when I found out that your mother's name was Katrine Hansen. Ned also told me that she had left because she was pregnant and on top of that she was an undocumented immigrant.*

Using my contacts around the city, I found you but was told that your mother had died during childbirth.

David was sick for days when he heard she had died. Then, he wondered if you were his son. Whether or not you were, he wanted you to be a part of his life. The wonderful thing is that DNA testing confirmed that you were his. He was sad that your mother had passed but he was ecstatic to gain a son. I am sure you realized how much he loved you.

As you can tell, your arrival at home was a bit unnerving for Aunt Marlene, since Katrine and David's relationship occurred during his marriage. It did not help either, that David loved you more than life itself. David loved you so much that he asked that if anything should happen to him, Paulette and I were to adopt you. He wanted to make sure that your humble beginnings did not affect your life. Of course, we adopted you. He did not have to ask twice, we loved you then, and we love you now.

Son, at this point, I know you are hearing and feeling many things. Please know David

236

*and I love you. You have been nothing but a
good son to us. We are thankful to God for
you. As David always reminded you—God
is watching over you. So soar like an eagle.*

*On another note, don't forget the dream.
Don't give up on the dream. Sometimes,
God has a way of taking us full circle. He
will show the prize but not the journey to
achieve the prize. Walk in alignment with
God and He will bring it to pass.*

*Do not give up. Do not run. Stay. I love you,
son.*

Your Dad."

By the looks of things, his mother had had no idea.
Shocked, his lips trembled of their own accord.

The silence in the vehicle was beyond deafening as
they headed home. He and his mother were too stunned to
communicate.

Even so, on another level it was now making
sense—being summoned by his first father's legal firm
after he had graduated with his bachelor's degree and the
good financial position in which he had found himself after
he'd left the lawyers' office. It was at that time, he had
learned that his first father was a hedge fund professional
before he took on his passion—architecture. In his later
years, he was called to pastoral ministry. It made sense
then, that his first father had invested heavily in real estate
and owned rental properties in Boston and Seattle.

After dropping his mother home, he made sure she
got in safely. He knew she wanted to talk, but he quickly

kissed her cheek, telling her he would see her later. He had to get away.

When he drove to his home, he was surprised to find Madison's father in his driveway. He'd forgotten that Mr. Kanate was dropping by.

Larry's return from the kitchen brought Tyler out of his reverie and he took the bottled water Larry extended. He uncorked it and drank some before covering it and placing it on the coffee table. He stared out in front of him.

"Tyler, God has your back." Larry took a seat near him. "Don't forget that."

"I'm sure He does." Tyler said, but his expression looked like someone who had been held hostage. "I'm just tired of getting the wrong end of the stick."

"I understand," Larry encouraged. "Sometimes, the situation will cause you to think that God has taken a vacation from you. But remember the Scripture—'Yea, though I walk through the valley of the shadow of death, I will fear no evil: for thou art with me; thy rod and thy staff they comfort me.'"

Tyler's firm lips curved. "Why are people so evil? I have known these two men for most of my life, and they did not have the courage to tell me. How is that love?"

"There is no excuse," Larry stated.

Tyler stood then plopped down again. "I suppose my first dad didn't want anyone knowing he had a child with another woman who was not his wife. That would have ruined his precious reputation," Tyler huffed out. "No wonder Aunt Marlene would look at me like that."

Larry's eyes searched Tyler's. "Good will come from this. I promise."

"I know, Mr. Kanate, but it hurts," Tyler's eyes filled with tears. "I feel like I'll never get close to anyone, again, so I'll never get hurt."

"That's your pain talking, Tyler, and I understand. You will need time to heal. God is going to work it out. You have to trust the Lord to move you to a new place of understanding. Resist becoming wrapped up in what you feel. Focus, instead, on what you *know*. Your future is secured in the hands of the Lord."

Tyler looked beyond Larry, trying to contain his emotions.

"I told you the story of how my father abused me and my other siblings...not to mention my mother. He was a horrible father. I hated him. Seriously, I hated him. Talk about a life of misery—that was our daily lives." He looked at Tyler as if to make sure he was listening. "He was a good provider for his family, but that was it." Larry shook his head. "But you know what, when he died, I was hurt.

"He died from a heart attack," Larry filled in. "I realized that I never had a chance at a relationship with him. I had to go to counselling because I was carrying too much, which was not only destructive for my health, but bad for my family."

"You went to counselling?" Tyler's eyebrows shot up.

"I sure did. I wanted to be better for myself and my family. It was a bit scary at first, so Rozene went with me. The thing is, I knew I needed help. My family means everything to me. I have not been perfect, far from it, but I trust that God will help me to be the son, husband, and father, He has called me to be."

He smiled at Tyler. "And on that note, I apologize again for my attitude towards you concerning Madison. I know you love her. I had to make sure."

"That's alright, Mr. Kanate. I know the drill. You're right—" he smiled for the first time since he'd heard the not-so-good news, "—I love her. I always have."

"That's good." Larry's smile widened. "But you need to work this situation out. Get counselling if you need to, in order to overcome this challenge in your life. God has a calling on your life and I can tell that the hand of the Lord is on you."

"Thanks, Mr. Kanate." Tyler released a deep sigh. "Guess I now know why my biological father kept visiting that coffee shop."

"Despite the way you entered this world, you were born out of love. Pray about it and see how the Lord leads you. I'll be praying, too. If you decide to find out more about your mother and her family, I know a good private investigator that I can recommend." He smiled at Tyler. "You have some of your mother's features."

Tyler remained stoic. He had no thoughts on the matter. In any case, he could hardly tell, since the photo was black and white and his mother was peeking out from behind a tree.

"As you go through," Larry added, "I want you to explore God as your Father. He will not disappoint you. He's a keeper."

Tyler sank against the sofa as tears welled up. "I'm not sure my body can withstand any more of these shocking events. All I want is a future I can endure."

"Tyler, this will take some time for you to process. You will make choices, but remember, anyone can make an easy choice. Please make your choices prayerfully."

Larry prayed for him. "Lord," he began. "You are a father to the fatherless. You…"

CHAPTER 31

The scent of freshly mowed grass filled Madison's nostrils as she waited for Kelani to emerge from Mason's car. She came out of the car then twirled, girlish giggles erupting.

"Mrs. Kanate!" Madison exclaimed from her front patio.

"Yeah! Good to see you, my lovely sister-in-law," Kelani said, whipping out a brilliant smile.

They hugged, squeezing each other tightly then turned and waved at Mason.

Madison pulled Kelani through the front door. "Ooh, you're looking fine, too," Madison said, eyeing Kelani's royal-blue jumpsuit.

"I try." Kelani closed the door then grinned at Madison.

"Mission accomplished," Madison said, hugging her shoulders as they moved towards the living room. "Married life is looking great on you, sister. Albeit, I don't seem to be able to see you."

Kelani grinned at her. "I can't be running like I'm single."

"Well, excuse me, Married Lady. Do what you do. I'm not going to be a hater."

They both collapsed on the sofa, laughing.

"I don't see you for almost two weeks, and you've gone gangster," Kelani teased Madison.

"I'm just getting warmed up. Watch out."

Kelani grinned at her. "So glad you're back. I can tell the mission trip was a success by the pics and the joy in your voice when we spoke."

"Oh, it was everything…seeing the look on those children's faces when we were delivering their toys, books, and all kinds of treats. I wouldn't miss that for the world. I feel privileged to have shared in that experience."

"Awesome! And those kids love you." She squeezed Madison's hand. "Anyway, I was hoping you didn't have to do the weird airplane shuffle to get past the other passengers to get in your seat or the bathroom." Madison had mentioned that she had given up her aisle seat to a passenger who needed quick access to the bathroom.

A burst of laughter erupted from Madison. "You've got to stop this madness."

"Let me show you." Kelani began to demonstrate—pretending to clutch the back of the seat before her and then wagging her buttocks from side to side as she attempted to slide out of the make-believe row of seats.

Madison laughed even louder, and soon Kelani collapsed on the sofa laughing loudly, too.

Ah, the sound of laughter. I miss that so much, Madison thought.

All she was doing these days was sitting on the recliner in her bedroom with a cup of cocoa, reading nightly until sleep came. Simply because she was annoyed at herself for being in the same untenable situation with Tyler.

After the funeral, she had been on top of the world, since a certain level of understanding was developing between them; however, her heart that had once quickened at the mere sound of Tyler's voice, now felt like a boulder in her chest. Something had gone horribly wrong between them and she couldn't put her finger on it. Of course, he was not forthcoming with any information.

All she knew was, a little over three weeks after the death of his father, Tyler had stopped calling her. During that time, he was still in Boston, so she had reached out to him several times, but it was obvious that he was bent on putting distance between them.

Before she had left for her mission trip, she had called him again, but their conversation had been nothing short of emotionless. Even so, she had been anticipating his return to Orlando.

Madison rested her elbows on her thighs and leaned forward, her forehead on the heel of her hand. She wondered if she could live like this.

For an instant, she thought she had heard someone calling her name. *Oh, goodness!* She stared at Kelani, who was looking at her with great curiosity.

"Kelani, sorry about that," she responded. "My mind traveled for a moment there."

Kelani watched her carefully. "For a moment? You were gone for a looong time."

Madison shifted uneasily on the sofa.

"You have it bad for him, don't you?"

An involuntary laugh left Madison. "I am not going there with you."

"Okay, Ms. Lady, a bit feisty this evening."

"No such thing."

Kelani changed the subject. "I heard that you've rejoined the praise team. That's good news."

"Oh, yes." Madison smiled. "I didn't realize I had missed worshiping with the team, although I only sang with them one Sunday before rushing off for the mission trip."

"Well, I'm glad you did, because I wanted to ask if you could lead praise and worship before the production starts."

"Lani—"

"Pretty please. Nothing long. Just ten minutes or as the Holy Spirit leads. I really want the atmosphere set before the ensemble begins to minister. Oh, oh, Rob said that he would be able to moderate."

"Great. He's good at that."

"We have about a month and a half to the production and it's full steam ahead. Rebecca took the lead while I was off on my hooooneymoon."

Madison grinned at her. "I hear you, Mrs. Kanate. I can tell you had a great time. You're still glowing."

"Guilty," Kelani said, throwing her hands in the air.

Madison laughed aloud.

"Anyway," Kelani said. "With your permission, I would like to promote Rebecca to be my second-in-command."

"Sure. With the relevant pay increase, I take it."

"Yes. I will see to it when I return next week."

Madison nodded absent-mindedly.

Kelani's quiet tone cut into her thoughts. "Do you want to talk about it?"

Madison sighed loudly. *There is nothing to talk about.*

Tyler was not interested in a relationship, but she didn't have the courage to tell Kelani. She couldn't believe it herself.

"Not sure there's anything to talk about," Madison said. "Oh wait, there is—why am I so unlucky in love? Why can't I learn my lesson?"

"Madison, don't put it like that. Tyler loves you. Listen—" Kelani took on a confidential tone, "—it seems like something else happened after we left Boston. I overheard Mason talking with him on at least two occasions about it. It sounds serious, too. I tried to pry it out of Mason, but he was tight-lipped. He just asked me to pray for Tyler and his mom."

Madison knitted her brows. "What could have happened?"

"I don't know. I wondered if they found out something that his father did. But like I said, it sounded serious, so you should be praying for him."

Madison rubbed her lips together. "Okaaaay."

"He's back in town as you know, so I'm sure he'll be making his way to see you."

"Not so sure about that. But, whatever."

Kelani touched her shoulder. "I'm praying for both of you. Everything will work out."

"Okay."

"Soooo, we have good news."

"We," Madison looked at Kelani.

"Yes, me and boo. I hear him coming through the front door. When you and Tyler get married, you need to take that key from him."

Madison laughed aloud. "You mean fight him and snatch it from him."

Laughter burst from Kelani.

Mason entered the living room and walked towards them. He looked from one to the other. "Everybody is happy. I like that."

Kelani stood up and embraced him, and he pecked her lips.

Mason looked at Madison. "What happened? No hug?"

She shook her head, and then rose and hugged him.

"That's more like it," he said, releasing her and taking a seat between both of them.

"I hear that I need to take my key from you," Madison told him.

"I know that did not come from my wife." He gazed suspiciously at Kelani before looking at Madison. "And no, you cannot have it back. I am your back-up key man."

"Okay, big brother," Madison said, grinning at him.

"I like that," Mason said, giving her shoulder a gentle shove.

Madison pulled forward to get a better look at both of them. "So, what's the good news?"

Mason and Kelani smiled at each other, and then Mason pulled Kelani under his arm. "I'm going to be a daddy."

245

"I'm going to be a mommy," Kelani said, snuggling closer to Mason.

"I'm going to be an aunt!" Madison leapt off the sofa hollering and dancing around. "Yay! Thank You, Lord." She stared at them then started to dance around again. "This is great news. Congratulations!" she said, group-hugging them.

Mason and Kelani laughed softly.

Madison returned to her seat on the sofa. "Wow! Me—an aunt. Go, me! Does Mom and Dad know that they will be grandparents?"

"Yes," Mason said.

"They are ecstatic," Kelani added.

"Yes, they would be." Madison shook her head knowingly.

"I'm just about to hit seven weeks, so no bump yet," Kelani said, rubbing her belly.

Madison grinned at her. "Seven weeks pregnant after only eight weeks of marriage? You two weren't wasting any time!"

Kelani laughed aloud. "You are sooo wrong for going there."

"Yes, very wrong," Mason agreed, chuckling loudly.

"At least you brought good news." Madison grinned at them. "I am happy I'll be an aunt."

"Yes, Aunt Madison, and I can see you spoiling this child."

"Just a little."

"Right?" Kelani pursed her lip.

"Girl, behave." Madison waved her away. "Next week, when I'm at the academy, let's begin to make plans to accommodate this exciting news. Anyway, you should be taking it easy. All the dances for the production are completed, right? So you don't have to stress yourself."

"I'm pregnant, not an invalid," Kelani said in a playful tone.

"I know, but you should still take it easy and follow the doctor's orders," Madison stated.

"See, now I have both you *and* Mason to contend with," Kelani retorted.

Mason smiled at her. "Baby, I'm just trying to protect our little girl or boy."

"Oh Lord, the doting daddy," Kelani teased.

Mason chuckled softly. "That I'll be."

"Yes, big brother. We're going to take care of Mommy and baby," Madison added, high-fiving Mason.

Kelani rolled her eyes to the ceiling. "Lord, help me."

CHAPTER 32

Tyler pressed his back against the mattress and pulled his knees to his chest. He held that position for a moment before yawning and stretching lazily under the bedcovers. *There's a certain bliss in being alone,* he thought.

He rolled on his side and his hand bumped his Bible and the notes he had been writing. He gently eased away from them and was making himself comfortable when he glanced at the clock on the nightstand. *Almost eleven already. Where did the evening go?*

It had been over a week since he had returned to Orlando, and he could hardly believe how slightly nippy the weather had gotten in mid-November. Summer had been hot and humid, but today, the tropical weather had been pushed away. *Unexpected but definitely not an inconvenience,* he concluded. He liked the cooler weather.

His mind flitted over all his situations before running a comparison between the two men whom he'd come to know as father. He had no doubt that they had loved him. And he had loved them, too. He remembered their words of encouragement, their love for the Word of God, and their passion for community and outreach missions.

"What could I have done differently?" Tyler asked loudly, still attempting to fathom the events following his father's death.

His eyebrows pinched together.

Everything had been a blur, until he found a solution to take away the sting in his chest. Work. Work—the one word that had defined his life since he had returned home. Work was the fuel that drove him so he would not have to think about the two men who had lied to him.

Tears stung his eyes as his heart stuttered and careened to a stop.

His imagination had been running wild, conjuring up all kind of scenarios about them. Now, thanks to them, he was having trust issues.

When he was not at work, he was at church, or at home spending time in the presence of the Lord. He had not been praying much but he had been spending time researching different topics in the Bible.

Alone…and lonely, with seemingly no break from the tempest that was raging in his heart, he made a decision.

A decision he hoped would set him on a path to freedom.

He jerked in surprise as his cell phone rang. Reaching for it on the nightstand, he watched it ring for a moment before deciding to take the call. "Hello, Em."

"Ty, how's it going?"

"It's going alright. How's it going with you?"

"It's going alright. Just wanted to touch base with you since it has been a while."

"I'm good," he said drily, then tried for a softer approach. "Just going to work and church."

"Same here. Work and church, and more work and church. Oh, the academy and Estrina's, too."

Silence stretched between them, and sorrow tugged at his heart. He tried harder to be engaged in their conversation. "I thought you would be asleep by now."

"I was just about to hit the sack when you ran across my mind," she told him.

"Thanks for checking on me. I heard you're going to be an aunt."

She laughed softly. "Yes. I was pleasantly surprised."

Her joyfulness made him smile. "Yes, good surprise. I see babysitting in your future."

"Mine and yours," she quipped in true Madison style.

"That is so."

"Aunt Madison. Sounds good to me."

He could hear the smile in her voice.

"You'll be hearing a lot of that," he told her.

"And I will not get tired of hearing it." She snickered, then stopped and asked, "What's up with you not visiting me? You've been back for a while."

"Em…" he began, then paused to find the right words.

"Ty, what's really going on with you?"

But he knew the question was—what's really going on with us?

He hesitated, blood pumping unsteadily in his ears.

"Are you there?" she asked.

"Yes." He swallowed hard. "I have been meaning to visit you, to talk with you about a few situations that have occurred since my father passed. But now, it doesn't really matter. I am thinking of pursuing the path of singleness."

He overlooked her loud intake of breath and pressed on. "I have been researching and praying about it, and I think that's where I'm heading."

Tension crackled through the phone line, and the vacuum between them grew wider than ever. His heart was beating too fast. Strong and uneven. *Say something,* he encouraged his unhelpful vocal cords. But he couldn't think of anything worthwhile to say.

Eventually, Madison spoke, her voice faint and filled with pain. "Singleness? Why would you select that path?"

"It's best for me at this point in my life. It's my way of honoring God. As the Apostle Paul indicated in the Word, singleness is a way of life that would allow me to give undivided devotion to God."

"Oh, okay," seemed to squeeze from her throat.

He knew dread had filled her.

"Em, singleness is not a death sentence. You know being single is a privilege, a gift from God."

"I know, Ty; you don't have to tell me."

"I'm glad you understand, because there is an underlying assumption that singleness is not healthy or it's an indication that something is wrong. I know that singleness is not for everyone, and I am not saying I would never get married. But, right now, being single is what I need."

Madison made no effort to respond and he, too, was at a loss for words.

The ticking of the clock seemed louder in the awkward silence. He pushed away sadness and guilt. He didn't want her entertaining any illusions of a relationship between them...at least, not now.

"Okay," Madison finally said in a frosty voice. "Good night."

"Thanks. You—" he paused.

She had already disconnected the call.

Pure shock stiffened his body and engulfed his expression as he stared at the screen until it faded to black. Blinking in rapid succession, he released the phone and watched it fall on the bed beside him.

He had told her what was on his heart, but why was he feeling like he needed to rush to her side and comfort her? His instinct screamed at him to do it. Still, he couldn't, and that saddened him.

Being single was his way out of this chaotic life. His situation had stretched him far beyond his comfort zone, and the key to survival had to be a life of singleness so he could focus on God.

A spark of panic ignited in his belly and he pulled the bedcovers up to his neck. Closing his eyes, he willed the fog in his life to lift and display the new road ahead. It had to be a new road. A new road to the freedom he had imagined.

CHAPTER 33

Madison resisted a pent-up shriek of despair as she opened the electronic gate to what used to be her home—The Kanate. She pulled up on the circular driveway, near the front patio, and switched off the ignition.

A feeling of nostalgia washed over her and she began to blink rapidly as tears welled up. That feeling was back again. Fear permeated her being as it had more than seven years ago, but this time it was strangely intense. Her heart screeched in agony at the dawning of her new reality. She had to fix it; she couldn't will it away.

As she had prayed earlier, the Holy Spirit had urged her to go back to The Kanate. By now, she'd learned when the Holy Spirit placed something on her heart, it was best to say, "I surrender."

She leaned back in the seat and closed her eyes. Her mind screaming, alarmed at the place where she now resided—a kind of shadowy half-existence.

It was all too familiar. Unreciprocated love—thrown back in her face, and again, she was unprepared to take the catch. Just when she had decided to say goodbye to past hurts…just when she had decided to move forward towards the future…just when she had figured out what she wanted out of life…for the rest of her life…that was the precise moment that the man she wanted had decided to move in the opposite direction. Tyler did not want her. He wanted her friendship, but not her love.

Her heart lurched as she heard a sharp knock on her car window. *Oooh God! Dad! I really don't want to talk.*

She tried for a smile, making movements to indicate she was about to exit her car.

He stepped back.

Grabbing her purse, she exited the vehicle, locked it, and looked at her father.

The joy on his face was in great contrast to the expression on hers, and she flew into his arms and began to weep.

"It's going to be alright, baby girl," her father told her comfortingly as she wept. "It's going to be alright."

Her head on his chest, she wiped her eyes, telling him, "I don't know what came over me, Daddy."

"It's okay. You can cry on Daddy's shoulder anytime."

"Thanks, Dad." She hugged his waist as they moved up the patio steps and into the living room.

"Would you like something to drink?" her father asked as she took a seat on the sofa.

"No, Dad. I'm just glad to be here." She rubbed her hands over her cheeks, trying to erase the evidence of her tears.

Her father sat next to her. "Everything will work out fine. Trust God."

Madison's slightly swollen eyes hit the floor. "I don't know, Dad. This burden is too much," she trailed off lamely.

"Of course, it's too much. You shouldn't be carrying it."

Her head swung. "Dad, I was doing fine until Tyler decided to rise from the ashes and upset my life. Again." Her outburst startled her, but she had to clear her chest.

"Dad," her voice trembled and a stream of tears rolled down her cheek. "I can't feel my heart. It's hard and unyielding. I feel like I am in a time warp with no end in sight."

Her father pulled her closer and wrapped his arm around her. "Don't you worry; broken hearts can be mended. I am praying for you."

She hugged him back and relaxed against his chest as he rubbed her back.

A few minutes later, her father released her and handed her a wad of tissues from the box on the coffee table.

Madison dried her eyes and looked at her father, who had again taken a seat next to her.

He was looking at her with what she knew would be tough love.

"First daughter, there are some things that even a father can't do for a daughter." He smiled gently at her. "Even though a father wishes he could. I hate seeing you like this. You are now carrying your pain in your eyes. You have to admit to yourself that you are in love with Tyler. The horse has already bolted…a long time ago, I might add. I know you have closed that door for some time now, but even the best intentions can be up for reconsideration."

She exhaled loudly.

He touched her shoulder. "You need to go up to your room and lay this situation before the Lord. Do not leave until you are confident that you have laid it all at the foot of the cross."

Madison nodded, her curls bouncing slightly.

"You have to believe that God knows what is best for you, Madison. That He only gives good gifts to His children. And remember, even though I try to be an awesome father, He is the best father you could ever have."

"Awww, Dad, thank you. You're a great father." Madison gave him a wide smile. "But I understand what you are saying."

"Thank you," her father responded, returning her smile. "This is just another season. This too shall pass. Stand on the Word of God. Stand on Jesus Christ, the solid rock, and let Him strengthen you."

Madison perked up, gazing admiringly at her father. Something in his voice gave her hope.

"Let the Word of God anchor you in this situation. A divine release from God has the capacity to turn your night into day. Let that fear you feel draw you closer to God." He touched her hand where it rested on the sofa. "That fear is telling you that your redemption draws near. So begin to see your deliverance. Don't forget who you are in Christ. And remember, you have a double portion of your mother's anointing. Use it."

Fifteen minutes later, Madison was still at The Kanate, but this time lying on her bed. Her Bible laid open, but she was unconsciously gazing at the changing rays of light floating over the foot of her bed to the wall, as beams came through her window. All was quiet save the tick-tock of the clock on the nightstand, which read 10:18 a.m.

She moaned, turned on her side, and pulled the bedcovers up to her neck. She no longer wanted to hide. Well, that hadn't helped, anyway. But her soul was tired and she couldn't continue at the rate she was going.

A relationship between her and Tyler was definitely not happening. And her hope was dashed during their telephone conversation last night, when Tyler had declared that singleness was the path he may be pursuing.

That bombshell had left her staring into space. Speechless.

She had tried to scream for help, but no sound, no words escaped her lips. The agony permeating her soul was severe, robbing her of rational thoughts.

Singleness? She wanted him to repeat, because she couldn't believe it. But, he had said it. Plain as day. No apology. Nothing. Well, excepting all the reasons being single would be advantageous for him.

After she had disconnected the call, the world had stop turning. No surprise there.

She swung her legs off the bed and rushed to her walk-in closet. She opened the door, turned on the light, and walked to the back. After moving two suitcases, she saw it—a large blue plastic container that stored some of the things she'd kept when she'd moved back home after college.

On her knees, she opened the container and began to remove several books, posters, and girly stuff. "I need to clean up this closet," she muttered, knitting her brows. *I am surprised Mom hasn't called me to get my things.* She reached in and took out more of her stuff before she was finally gazing at the gift bag in which she'd stashed all the pictures of her and Tyler.

She grabbed it and sat on the floor.

Catching a breath, she emptied the photos onto her lap, then proceeded to look at them one by one before dropping them back into the bag.

They looked so young and happy…smiling in all the photos. All excepting the ones when she sneaked up on him with her camera. She chuckled. He didn't mind taking photos, but only when he was ready.

She gazed at a photo of them, taken at their first Christmas production. He was smiling and hugging her shoulder, while she was clutching the bunch of yellow roses he'd given her.

She stared at him—the man with whom she'd been in love since she was only nineteen years old. He had grown even better looking, more suave, more appealing to the eye, more confident…more of everything.

She read the small card that came with the flowers.

Congratulations! You are one in a million. Love you, Ty.

"I love him."

Her declaration caused her to fall flat on her back. It was only now that she was realizing how deep her feelings for Tyler ran. Her brother had been right all along—Tyler had ruined her for any other man. She was completely and utterly his, and had always been.

Moisture filled her eyes as her stomach trembled. "I am in love with, Tyler Aiden Bradshaw."

Her pronouncement fresh in her mind, she raced out of the closet and climbed into bed. There was a quietness in her soul even though her lungs felt like they were on fire.

Run!

Take flight!

Sprint...

Those words seemed to bounce off the wall in front of her.

Then everything stopped as her father's parting words rang loudest.

That fear is telling you that your redemption draws near. Don't forget who you are in Christ. And remember, you have a double portion of your mother's anointing. Use it.

If she was going for all-out honesty, she had to admit, she had never stopped dreaming about Tyler; she had never stopped loving him. He had always been in her heart.

Her heart galloped. More than seven years later, he still made her heart thud...

She picked up her Bible and read aloud what used to be her favorite Scripture verses—First Corinthians 13:4-7: "Love suffers long and is kind; love does not envy; love does not parade itself, is not puffed up; does not behave rudely, does not seek its own, is not provoked, thinks no evil; does not rejoice in iniquity, but rejoices in the truth; bears all things, believes all things, hopes all things, endures all things."

She sighed loudly. She'd spent so much time locking everyone out, that she'd forgotten how to love and allow herself to be loved. She had become an effective bystander in her own love life.

"Lord, help me to believe," she pushed out. "Help me to be attuned to You. I know You are a way-maker, and today, I want to move forward, in Jesus' name."

She paused, then flipped to Psalm ninety-one and read aloud. "'He who dwells in the secret place of the most High shall abide under the shadow of the Almighty. I will say of the Lord, 'He is my refuge and my fortress; My God, in Him I will trust…''"

A sigh of relief left her as she completed her reading and placed the Bible beside her. She felt comforted. Safe. The safest she had felt in a long time.

A tiny smile crept up her face. This was her safety net—abiding in the presence of the Lord. When her heart had been crushed by Tyler's rejection years earlier, she'd stopped believing in a loving God.

So, the all-is-well charade had begun. Seven years in the making, it was baked to perfection. But, she hadn't planned on Tyler showing up and invading her space.

Tears rolled down her cheeks, soaking the pillow beneath her head. She couldn't remember ever feeling so utterly exposed.

"Lord, please forgive me," she whispered tearfully. "Deep on the inside, many things broke. My heart. My spirit. My hopes. My dreams. My outlook on life—along with my love for You. It has been ha-hard, Lord. Seven years of mental torture—questioning myself as to how I got it so wrong. Feeling stupid and inadequate for letting my emotions lead me down the wrong path. Unable to love anyone else because my emotions were tied up elsewhere."

She allowed the tears to fall.

"Now Tyler is back, Lord, stronger than ever. But, I also have strong reasons to run in the opposite direction. I was the one who carried my broken heart, day and night.

Despite that fact, Lord, I don't want to run. The pull towards him is great because I am in love with him."

Tears rolled down her cheeks.

"Well, now he's talking about pursuing singleness. Oh God, at best, my options are discouraging. It seems like I have found myself in the same situation again." She let out a longsuffering sigh. "But I prefer to think that we have been momentarily derailed…for the umpteenth time. So, I present him to You, Lord. And, I am leaving him right there, at the foot of the cross."

A sigh of relief escaped her.

"Lord, I admit I felt overwhelmed coming here. There is now peace in my soul. To that end, Lord, I say, do whatever is well pleasing in Your eyes concerning my relationship with Tyler.

"Father, I ask that You restore My love for You. I love You, Lord, because of who You are. Despite my foolishness, You refused to let me go. I am eternally grateful that You didn't. Put a longing in my heart to spend more time with You, to read Your Word, and to hear from You. Increase my faith and give me the ability to believe You, Lord—Your love. Your Word. Your promises. Your power. Help me to acknowledge You in all that I do.

"Lord, Your Word states, 'the just shall live by faith.' Help me not to despair but live a fruitful, faith-filled life of gratitude in service to You. And, Lord, I am waiting on You. I am waiting because I know that You hold my destiny. You know the way that I take, and when You have tested me, I will come forth as gold. You will find me faithful. I trust You, Lord. In the name of Jesus Christ, I pray, amen."

An hour later, Madison walked across the circular landing and accessed the passageway leading to her father's study. She knew it was his favorite place in the house. She listened and heard the sound of typing, so she knocked on the door.

"Dad, I'm leaving now."

"Come in," her father responded. She heard the love in his voice and knew he had been praying for her.

She opened the door to find him spread out in the chair behind the large desk. He gave himself a stretch, and then waved her over to the sofa as he closed his laptop.

He took off his glasses and placed them on the desk. "How is first daughter doing?" he asked, rocking back in his chair. "Ah, don't answer that," he said, smiling as he lifted himself to full height. "Your breakthrough is all over you." He clapped loudly. "Watch out, world!"

"Dad!" Madison chuckled loudly. "You've always been my greatest cheerleader." She shook her head playfully. "I've gathered a few over the years, but you're still my number one."

"You better know it," he added half-seriously. "It's good to see you up and running again." He wiped his forehead. "Phew! She's not doing a wall slide. She's not giving up on life." He threw his hands in the air. "Yes! She scores! She wins! Yes, Lord! She's baaaack!"

Madison laughed. "Was it that bad?"

"Never mind that. I'm glad all is well."

"Thanks, Dad."

He watched her proudly, and she smiled at him.

"Dad, did I disturb you? You sounded like you were typing."

He chuckled. "You're still listening at my study door."

"Yes, nothing has changed. I had planned to camp out there, too, if you didn't let me in."

They both laughed, recalling how she would camp out at the door of his study when she was a little girl. Yes, she had always been close to her mother, but only her father could fix certain issues.

"I have decided to play a more active role in my father's company," he told her.

"Dad, am I hearing right? Of course, I'm excited, but you were always against doing that."

"Well, the season has changed, and I believe that the Lord would have me do it."

She smiled at him. "Well, alleluia! I know Uncle Zadan and Uncle Zane must be happy, and Grandma Darlene must be ecstatic. A dream come true."

"Yes, they are all thrilled." Her father returned her smile. "The twins are getting older, and since I am retired, I now have more time on my hands. Anyway, I'm taking it slowly. Mostly reading company information. I started around two weeks ago. Right now, I go to the office when I need to."

"I'm proud of you, Dad." She stood up. "I love you. Thanks for everything."

He stood and hugged her. "I love you, too, first daughter." He released her, telling her, "I am extremely proud of the woman you've become."

"Thanks, Dad." Smiling, Madison clutched her purse. "I'm sure my staff is wondering where I am. I'm about to hit the home stretch then head to work."

"Sounds good."

They both headed towards the door.

"Is Mom on board with your new job situation?"

"You bet she is." He smiled widely. "She's glad, too, that I don't have to race through the door, like back in the day. She called an hour ago and I told her you were here. Of course, I quickly told her you were alright."

He laughed loudly, and his voice echoed as they walked down the passageway. "Yes, I had to stop her in her tracks. I could see her running out the glass doors of

Rozene Kanate Ministry, with just a wave to Sienna at the front desk."

Madison laughed, too. "Yes, Dad, you did well. Mom will move mountains for her kids. I hope I will be as great a mother as she is."

"I am positive you will be," her father reassured her.

Madison smiled happily.

"It was great to see you on the praise team," her father mentioned.

"Yes, it's great to be back. Didn't realize I had missed worshipping with the group."

"Well, something else to give God thanks for," her father said.

Madison hugged his waist as they descended the stairs, and he hugged her shoulders.

Her heart warmed. And for the first time in ages, she felt hopeful, even joyful. She was back in alignment with God.

Chapter twenty-eight of her life would definitely be different...in a great way.

CHAPTER 34

"Great job, everyone," Madison complimented the dancers on the stage at Rozene Bennady Performing Arts Academy as they completed their final rehearsal. "God has been good, so let's make Him known. We are praying for you. Be ready to go live in another hour."

"Thanks, Ms. Kanate," the group of dancers said in unison.

Brianna tugged on Madison's arm. "I feel more confident and prayerful in my dances. Did that come across?"

The look on Brianna's face caused Madison to focus on her sister. Having danced since her youthful years, she could identify with the feeling. She looked at Brianna from the top of her dramatic bun to her white ballet shoes and flipped her two thumbs-up. "Yes, Bri, you will not leave a dry eye in the audience." She patted her shoulder. "Yes, you ministered in dance during rehearsal."

"Thanks, Madison!" Brianna smiled proudly before running off the stage with a few of the other dancers.

Smiling, Madison gazed around the grand auditorium, decorated in Christmas colors.

Magnificent.

Even so, Madison's mind was on Tyler. With the event coming up, she hadn't had a moment to think about him and whether or not he would even attend the production. She didn't want to get Mason's hopes up by asking about his friend, so she threw her energy into making the production a success.

"Lord, be glorified," Madison said quietly, attempting to focus. She was about to return to her office when she saw Kelani walking slowly towards her.

Concern lit Madison's features at how tired Kelani looked. "Are you okay?"

"Ah, morning sickness turned into all-day sickness. Nothing is staying down."

Madison eyed her suspiciously. "Are you feeling okay now?"

"It usually wears off, but today was a long day." She touched Madison's shoulder. "Stop giving me that look, and stop worrying."

"Why didn't you tell me?"

"No need. Mason is playing nurse and doctor. That's why he called to see if you could observe the final rehearsal. I was resting." Kelani rubbed her belly. "Don't worry, I won't be doing a lot. Everything is in place and we have many happy helpers."

"I am watching you. You still have pain in your eyes."

"Yes, my belly is cramping every now and then." She put up a hand. "Don't worry, I already have Mason doing that. He insisted on staying backstage."

"Well, that's a relief."

Kelani chuckled. "Oh, stop."

"I am sure glad your husband knows you well."

Kelani sighed. "Rob is here, in the sitting area outside your office. He is waiting for any further instructions concerning moderating. Then in another half an hour, we are gathering as usual, for prayer before the production begins. I would be grateful if you would pray with us."

"Sure, and please find a comfortable seat, near to the stage entrance…so we can all see you."

Kelani chuckled. "You mean keep an eye on me."

"Guilty," Madison said, before leaving to find Rob.

Forty-five minutes later, Rob welcomed the enthusiastic audience and called for Madison to lead them in praise and worship.

Madison's gaze swept over Kelani, who was sitting close to the entrance of the stage. Kelani smiled happily at her, giving her a thumbs-up.

Madison returned her joyful smile before stepping into the limelight. The band was already playing softly.

"Praise the Lord!" Madison said amiably.

Mingled shouts of "Praise the Lord!" and cheers greeted her.

"I am Madison Kanate, and this evening, I am here as a vessel of the Lord, to lead you in praise and worship. Amen?"

Pockets of "Amen!" filled the atmosphere and the musicians raised the volume of their music.

"Alleluia!" Madison shouted. "Let's take this time to tell the Lord how grateful we are to be in His presence. Come on, lift your hands and voices and tell God how grateful you are."

Hands in the air, the audience worshipped.

"Father, we are grateful to be in Your presence." Madison's voice rang out. "We could be anywhere, oh God, but you saw it fit for us to be here, so God, we are here to praise You, to lift up Your holy name. Oh God, we love You," Madison professed loudly, "we were created for no other reason but to glorify You. Alleluia!"

"Alleluia!" came from a lone voice in the audience, as Madison's voice broke and pockets of sniffles were heard as the audience continued to worship.

The music reached a beautiful, dreamlike crescendo.

"Alleluia!" Madison cried out. "Father, Your Word says that You inhabit the praises of Your People. We praise You, Lord, so we ask that You shower us with Your blessings.

"Blessings of God—fall on us.

"Healing of God—fall on us.

"Favor of God—fall on us.

"Anointing of God—fall on us.

"Glory of God—fall on us.

"Jesus! Jesus! Jeeeesus!" Madison uttered, before belting out the song, "What a Beautiful Name" by gospel recording group, Hillsong Worship. Her gorgeous soprano filled the auditorium, bringing glorious worship to what was already a sacred moment.

As the song came to a close, Madison hollered "Alleluia!" from deep within her soul.

The audience followed suit, and when they had quieted, Madison spoke. "You see, brothers and sisters, when you are planted on the solid rock—Jesus Christ—the storms of life come. They come, not simply to threaten us; they come to make us stronger. Don't be fearful. The Scripture says, 'Therefore, my beloved brethren, be steadfast, immovable, always abounding in the work of the Lord...' Be planted in the Lord! Be immoveable in the name of Jesus Christ. For He who promised is faithful. Amen!"

"Amen!" several members of the audience cried out.

Madison left the stage.

Soon, she heard Rob addressing the audience. "We thank God for His presence in this place. Amen!" He paused as the audience cheered. "This evening, it is my honor and pleasure to present to you, our dance and drama production—'In His Presence'. I have no doubt that you will be blessed by it. I will be back at the end of the production to introduce you to the cast and other key players. Don't forget that some of the proceeds from this year's event will go to Estrina's Children Home. Enjoy."

The audience cheered then silence fell in the auditorium as the lights dimmed.

"Ladies and gentlemen," came a booming voice from the speaker, "Rozene Bennady Performing Arts Academy, presents 'In His Presence,' a theatrical production surrounding the birth of Jesus Christ, God's greatest gift to humanity. This exhilarating production incorporates dance, drama, and music to celebrate God's total and unconditional love for us. Sit back, relax, and enjoy."

Almost two hours later, Rob called Madison to the stage after he had introduced the cast of the production, which by all accounts had been successful.

The cast stood on the stage as Madison introduced her mother and father to the audience, and then her mother spoke briefly about inheriting the academy from her parents, whom she called to the stage.

"Ladies and gentlemen," Madison said, "it gives me great pleasure to welcome to the stage, the COO and chief choreographer of the Rozene Bennady Performing Arts Academy—the awesome, fearless, Aunty K, Aunty Kel, Aunty Lani, the one, the only, Mrs. Kelani Kanate!"

The audience rose, shouting and clapping alongside the cast of the production.

When Kelani did not appear, Madison teased, "She is now Mrs. Kanate, so you can understand that things have changed with our lovely, courageous leader."

However, when Rob rushed to the stage and whispered that Kelani would not be coming out, Madison's professional training took over, even though her heart rate kicked up.

"Unfortunately, our lovely COO is taking care of another matter, so on behalf of all of us here at the academy, I want to thank you again for coming out. We thank God for His presence in this place. And we know you were thoroughly blessed." Madison glanced behind her. "Extra special thanks to the leaders, teachers, the cast of the production, all who helped to make this event successful. We love and appreciate you. God bless you all. Have a good night, everyone."

The music picked up, and Madison tried not to rush off the stage. But as soon as the curtains closed, she ran across the stage. She was looking around for her mother when Rob and her father rushed up to her.

"Madison," her father said in hushed tones. "Mason and your mother took Kelani to the hospital."

"Hospital?" Madison questioned, her tone a bit jagged because it suddenly felt like she couldn't breathe.

"Yes. She is spotting," her father told her quietly.

Madison tried to restrain her emotions as the dancers waved at them. "Is she going to be alright?"

"They are still running tests," her father said. "That was the last update. Travel with Rob and we will get your car later. Brit is helping Bri to pack her stuff and I'll drop them home. Armela is waiting for them. I will make my way to the hospital after that. Rebecca and the team will make sure everything shuts down here and the cast gets fed and presented with their gifts and trophies."

"Mr. Kanate," Rob butted in, "if you'd like, I could take Brit and Bri—"

"Thanks, Rob, but I'll take my daughters home."

"Yes, sir."

"Thanks, Dad." Madison hugged him. "We'll see you soon."

"Okay. See you soon," her father said, hugging her. He turned to Rob and shook his hand. "Take care of my daughter. Drive safely."

"Yes, sir." Rob glanced at Madison. "Ready?"

"Yes."

With that, they left.

Almost three hours later, Madison discreetly glanced around the waiting area of Kelani's private hospital

269

room. Bloodshot eyes met hers—her grandparents, Rob, and Mr. and Mrs. Clarkson. Kelani had lost the baby.

Oh God! Madison's eyes welled with tears and she looked away. Mason had been inconsolable until their father arrived. He had taken Mason away from the scene and when they had returned, Mason was at least not wailing as much, but a range of emotions continued to ripple across his face.

The group had not ceased praying while they waited, but when Dr. Trevor Jude finally appeared, he told them Kelani seemed to have had a spontaneous miscarriage and he was running several tests to make a more definitive diagnosis.

When the group finally got to see Kelani, she went berserk, screaming at the top of her lungs, and then wailing with a death grip around Mason's neck. The doctor asked them all to leave the room except for Mason and his parents.

The whole scene broke Madison's heart, for she remembered the joy on Mason and Kelani's faces when they'd announced that they would be parents. Since the announcement, she'd made sure that Kelani was not doing too much at the academy.

Lord, help them, Madison silently prayed, desperation lacing her thoughts. She couldn't think of anything else to pray.

The doctor came out of Kelani's room, an apologetic expression covering his face.

"Kelani is still a bit groggy, but you can see her. I'm suggesting small groups, with Mason always present. He's still in the room. So, after his parents leave, visit in pairs. Mr. and Mrs. Kanate will be out in a moment."

"Thanks, Dr. Jude," Grandma Darlene said.

The doctor quietly told them. "I don't have to tell you Mason and Kelani have a long road to recovery ahead of them. I am thankful that they will have your love, support, and prayers."

CHAPTER 35

After a final wave, Tyler drove away from the newlyweds' home. It had been a rough three weeks since Kelani had left the hospital, but he was extremely grateful for the signs of progress. On his visit today, she was out of bed.

She did not stay in the living room with him and Mason, but he was glad she at least made polite conversation before mentioning that she was getting back to her reading in the sunroom. He knew Mason was holding them both together, but he could tell that Kelani's miscarriage had deeply affected their marriage.

Ah, this life that we live. You never know what it will throw at you, Tyler mused. *Lord, I pray you will continue to strengthen them and in the fullness of time give them children who will be a blessing to them.*

He could hardly believe that Christmas had passed in a haze, and January was almost ending. Albeit, he had spent two days with his mother during the Christmas season. Dealing with all the emotions surrounding Kelani's miscarriage and the loss of his own father made it hard to be jolly in the festive season. He was on high alert—praying, calling, and visiting Mason and Kelani to give his support. Of course, he made sure Madison was not on hand when he visited. They were all following the doctor's orders so as not to overwhelm Kelani. Plus, Kelani needed a drama-free zone.

Em. Tyler smiled inwardly. She was his next mission, because he needed to fix whatever was going on between them.

Shortly thereafter, he pulled up near Madison's front patio and cut the engine of his Jeep. He reclined the seat since he didn't know how long he would have to wait. Communication between him and Madison had been pretty much nonexistent. He wanted to kick himself, for he was mostly to be blamed for that.

The secrets that were revealed about his birth had sent him into a tailspin—to a place he had long forgotten, and thought he had conquered. As he navigated the dark corridors of his mind, he could hear the echoes of the past—*abandoned. Unlikeable. No one wants you. No one loves you. No one. No one. No one.*

Yes, the shadows of time long past had reappeared. He could feel their pull to stay in a place of unforgiveness.

How could his mother not have known?

Was she lying to him, too?

Yet, he had to believe her. She didn't know...no idea.

Even in his sorrow, he could see the regret in her eyes. Her dearly departed husband did not trust her enough to tell her his one big secret.

Well, at least, Aunt Rachel had come clean about the conversation he'd overheard between her and his mother in the kitchen, back in the day. That conversation was about his first dad. She had witnessed his love for Tyler but couldn't figure out why he wouldn't adopt him.

Tyler pushed out a heavy sigh. All the fight had been squeezed out of him and he felt powerless. Nevertheless, he'd valiantly decided that something good had to come from this madness, for after all, he was alive, and even that had to count for something. He had been caged for so long, he just wanted to fly, to breathe, to be himself. So, he forged ahead, refusing to glance back at the darkness. Instead, he looked to the light of God's Word to give his heart a new narrative.

Pressing.

Hoping.

Praying.

Pushing forward into the light.

A breakthrough from his mental struggles came when he'd attended the Christmas production and seen Madison in full-blown worship. Her cries of "Alleluia!" had somehow unshackled the chains that had held him bound. He'd left the production early to spend time in the presence of God.

His total surrender came early morning, two days ago, after a night of tossing and turning. He rolled out of bed wailing for God to rescue him.

When he had quieted, he prayed.

"Father, my heart was ripped open. Help me believe that this is not how my story will end. God, it would be easy for me to give up. But I know too much to turn back now. So I lay every dream and desire that I have at Your feet. Take them Lord, and let Your will be done in my life on earth as it is established in heaven.

"Your Word says to all who have received You, to those who have believed in Your name, to them You gave the right to become children of God. I am…Your child, and You…You are my father."

His voice broke, and he wiped his tears. "Lord, my heart is torn, but help me to trust You. Help me to press forward. Help me believe, again…that You are watching over me. In the name of Jesus Christ I pray, amen."

He didn't feel any different when he rose, but he knew he had done the right thing. A calm came over him, and he felt at peace as the Scripture—"For God hath not given us the spirit of fear; but of power, and of love, and of a sound mind"—reverberated in his mind. And as the Word of God ignited in his heart, the shame that had been laid upon him was lifted.

Tyler came out of his recollection as the lights from Madison's car indicated her arrival. He observed, too, that the courtyard was brightly lit by fluorescent lights.

When Madison opened her garage and pulled in, he exited his vehicle and locked the doors. He waited outside, thankful she had not closed the garage door.

Madison exited her car, her purse in hand, and locked it. "Hi there," she called out, hanging her purse on her shoulder. "Come on in."

Come on in. Tyler almost looked behind him. His mind swirled in several directions as he marched forward. "Hello."

Madison smiled at him as she closed the garage door.

His stomach flipped. *What is going on? A confound him mission?*

She waited for the garage door noise to die down. "I didn't know you were waiting. I didn't get the memo." She held up her phone in jest, stared at the blank screen, and then eyed him teasingly. "Oh, I'm just getting the memo now."

He pushed back the sides of his jacket and slid his hands into the front pockets of his pants, watching her cautiously.

She spoke before he did.

"It's pretty nippy out here. Come on in and I'll make us cocoa." She moved forward and opened the door, but he was still rooted in place.

"Em, are you okay? What's going on here?" A muscle twitched at the line of his jaw.

She turned to look at him. He couldn't miss her overarched brows even if he tried. "You mean if I have turned into some kind of psycho killer?" She offered a casual shrug as if that could not possibly to be true. "Come in, Ty."

Amusement covered the glint of guilt in his eyes, and he moved forward.

They arrived in the living room, and immediately started taking off their jackets. That caused brief chuckles from them. It was just like old times...though neither of them was brave enough to say it.

Sweet, Tyler thought as he gazed at Madison's traditional, professional attire—black pencil skirt, tailored jacket, and green inner...*Good Lord!* Enthralled, he watched as Madison peeled off her jacket to expose her green, sleeveless blouse.

Their eyes locked, and Tyler ignored the siren that went off in his head as his gaze slid down her body, then zipped back to her face. His body tingled, crying out yes all the way, as if it had reported for duty. *Focus. Focus*, he warned himself.

Madison's eyes warmed, but she did not encourage his overture. Instead, she toed off her stilettos then walked to the bottom of the stairs, where she slipped on a pair of waiting flip-flops.

Stomach tight, Tyler's gaze swept around the room. He swallowed hard. Lying on the coffee table was a photo of him and Madison. He was smiling and hugging her shoulder, while she was clutching the bunch of yellow roses he had given her. He inhaled then exhaled a lungful of air, moving away from the table. He did not want her to know he had seen it.

"Sorry to visit unannounced," he said, as she walked towards him.

Madison waved off his concerns. "No problem. I figured if you had to," she air-quoted, "break in, with Mason's help, what you have to say must be important."

"I tried to reach out to you, yesterday and today, but you were not forthcoming." When she didn't say anything he pressed on, earnestness in his voice. "I called and texted you several times, but you didn't respond."

Planting her hands on her hips, she tilted her head to the side. "Do you blame me?"

Pressure built in Tyler's head. "I'm trying, Em."

Her eyes softened. "Let's head to the kitchen. I hear a cup of cocoa calling."

Tyler nodded, followed her into the kitchen, and took a seat at the island. He watched as she filled the kettle with water, set it on the stove, and turned on the burner.

"Can I help?" he asked, as Madison reached for packets of cocoa in the cupboard.

"Nothing to do," she said, turning to glance at him before resting the packets on the counter.

"Okay," he murmured.

Madison moved and took two huge cups from the cupboard, and seemingly stared off into the blue.

"Am I going get that cup of cocoa or what?" Tyler askcd.

"You would have gotten it sooner if I knew you were coming," she retorted.

"Not true," he stated.

Her head whipped right. "This I've got to hear."

"You came home late. You, my dear, Em, were gallivanting on the streets of Orlando." He pointed to the island. "That's why I am not sitting there and sipping my cocoa."

She laughed softly, shaking her head. "I have one Mason in my life. Seriously, I don't need two."

"Oh, you don't have to remind me."

She didn't respond, but simply picked up one of the packets of cocoa, tore off the edge, and deposited the contents into one of the cups.

Tyler automatically followed suit.

"Not that it's any concern of yours," Madison said, "but Kelani asked me to stop by Estrina's to drop off a few things for Malachi."

"Thanks for letting me know."

"You're welcome, Mason the second."

"Stop being ugly, Em." Tyler said, moving towards the refrigerator.

Madison watched him. "I'm not being ugly. It's the truth."

"You're being ugly," Tyler grumbled.

He returned to her side, whipped cream in hand, and watched as she poured hot water into both cups, and then added a dash of cinnamon from a small bottle that was resting among several in a tray on the counter.

Madison took a spoon from the drawer below and stirred. "And you are just like Mason, always trying to slice and dice your way out of your wrong-doings."

"Me? Now, you are wrong for saying that."

She took the whipped cream from him and topped off the cocoa with it. "You know I'm right." She slid him the cup.

Amusement danced in his eyes. "Maybe a little-little bit." He accepted it and took a sip. He watched Madison and was sure she was holding her breath. "It's perfect...as always." His voice had taken on an intimate edge.

She cut her eyes at him, but not before he saw the hint of a smile. "Okay, if you like, we can sit at the island, unless you prefer to sit in the living room."

"The island will do."

She grabbed two napkins and looked at him. "Where are you sitting?"

He grinned at her. "Wherever you are sitting."

She rolled her eyes to the sky, walked to the island, and placed her cup of cocoa on it.

He was right behind her, pulling out the stool.

For a moment, she stared at his cup before taking a seat.

He smiled inwardly, for he knew she was wondering when he'd set it down.

He took a seat, swiveling so he was directly facing her.

She took a few sips, then turned to face him. "Now—"

"Wait," he urged, resting his cup on the island.

Her eyes widened as she waited.

He leaned towards her, cupped her chin, and gently dabbed her mouth with her napkin, and she patiently endured it.

"All clean," he said, looking satisfied before releasing her and turning to pick up his cup. He turned back to her and realized she was looking at him.

"What were you asking?"

She visibly pulled herself together. "Wha-what could be so urgent to have you camping out in my yard?"

His Adam's apple bobbed on a swallow as his nerves assaulted him. He sipped more cocoa. "This is really good," he said appreciatively. "I wanted to catch up with you."

She popped an elbow onto the counter and gave him a look. "You know I shouldn't be talking to you right now?"

"I'm sorry for the limited communication between us."

"Are you?" A frown tightened her features.

"Yes, Em, I am," he said gazing at her.

"There you go with that look again."

"Isn't that the way I've always looked at you?" His mouth set in a hard line and eyes blazing, he snapped, "Honest to God, Em, I like looking at you, because you make me forget my horrible beginnings."

It was out before he could stop himself.

A heavy silence followed. The admission disconcerted them.

Aghast, Tyler all but dropped his cup on the island before leaping off the stool and rushing out of the kitchen.

CHAPTER 36

"Don't leave here like this, Ty!" Madison called out, trailing on his heels and then grabbing his arm.

That brought him to a sudden halt, and he almost tripped over his own feet before righting his posture.

He did not look at her.

"Please," she encouraged.

A few seconds passed, followed by several more. His well-defined lips relaxed, softening their stiffness. He gave her a terse half-hearted nod, and she held his hand as they walked back to the island.

They drank without speaking, awkwardness creeping between them.

"What have you been up to?" Madison asked, breaking the silence.

Tyler set down his cup with a sigh, abandoning all pretense of calm. Unconsciously, he ran a hand over his head, back to front, and was about to do the reverse when Madison grabbed his hand.

He froze.

In one step, she closed the space between them.

Standing between his legs, she placed his hands around her waist, then cradled him to her chest, rubbing his head.

He hugged her closely and breathed in her essence. *God, I love this woman, who knows how to disarm me with her love.* He knew she was silently praying for him, and relief flooded his body.

When she saw he was relaxed, she released him and took her seat. The whole situation had brought out a strength in her and a weakness in him that she had only seen in the distance.

"Talk to me, Ty. Make me understand what is happening with you. What is causing this stop-and-go in your behavior towards me? One minute, you are chasing me down, and the next minute you have me chasing you down. Seriously…I have been there and done that, and trust me, it was no fun."

"I know, Em." His gaze grew soft and she heard the slight tremor in his voice. "I never ever thought I would be that guy who would say to you of all people—this time it will be different. I wanted you to remember me as someone who cherished you. This was not what I dreamed of for us…but, here I am. I have to believe some things are worth doing twice…that the second time around would be better."

His gazed latched onto hers. "I fell for you so fast, I got scared." He looked away. "I never felt like I was good enough for you, and I couldn't offer you any of the comforts that I know you were accustomed to, so…I ran."

"I'm sorry you felt that way. I hope I didn't give you—"

"No." He looked at her. "No, you didn't. Anyway, it's not like I can ever provide for you like that, but at least now I can provide a decent home for you."

"Ty, I'm not sure why you would even be thinking that way. You should have given me the choice. You cannot imagine the vacuum you left in my life." Her eyes welled up, and she looked away, blinking rapidly, and then dabbing her eyes with her fingertips.

He pulled forward and touched her shoulder, wincing when she shrugged him off.

"No one knew," she admitted, "I cried, night after night, asking myself why."

"Em, I'm sorry. I should never have done that to you. I promise I'll make it up to you."

"I don't know about that, Tyler. You seemed to have a new hobby—disappearing and reappearing at your leisure. I thought we were doing well the other day, until you pulled the same," she air-quoted, "disappearing-lack-of-communication act. And I thought you had run off in a blaze of glory to live a life of singleness. Now that's what I call dropping a bombshell."

"Em, I'm sorry. My emotions were all over the place after Dad died. Abandonment is my latent struggle, and it seems to show up every time it gets a chance. So of course, I had a desire to be alone. And I wanted to forget you, but I couldn't. I was tired of being hurt by the people I love, not to mention the fact that the people I love seem to die, leaving me alone."

Madison rubbed his hand. "I am really sorry to hear that. You know life is a series of ups and downs. I know that God has given you all that you need to take you through this season."

"It's still rough mentally, but I believe He has." He watched her carefully. "Anyway, you would be confused and want to disappear too if your adoptive father wrote you after he died...to say that your foster father was actually your biological father."

Madison's brows slammed together. "What did you say?" Dread filled her tone, and she clutched her hands to her chest.

"You heard me. The good Pastor David Moore, the man I have been calling my first father, is actually my biological father. I'm sure Aunt Marlene knew, which would explain the looks she would send my way. He apparently met my mother at a coffee shop in Boston—"

"The one he would take you to when you visited Boston as a child?"

"Yes." He shook his head. "Now I am resting in the Lord, because I've had it up to here." He lifted his hand above his head, before pulling the letter from his pocket and handing it to her.

"Ty, you don't have to—"

"I want you to read it."

She took the envelope from his hand, pulled the letter from it, and began to read. Her finger tugged on her lower lip as she read.

Tyler watched her ever-changing expression—joy to more joy, joy to shock, shock and more shock, shock unending—before she slowly folded the letter and put it back into the envelope. She mopped her tears with the napkin under her cup before handing it back to Tyler.

"I'm really sorry that you found out that way, Ty."

He pushed out a short sigh. "Me, too. Thank God for your father. I needed to lay out on somebody's couch, and his couch was perfect and timely. I could not have asked for a better counselor-friend-advisor-prayer partner wrapped in one." He chuckled. "Even though we started off on the wrong foot."

"That's my papa."

"You should hug him tighter," Tyler advised. Pain filled his gaze, and he stood and held on to the back of the stool. "You have no idea what it is like to not know your parents—the struggles with the feelings of abandonment."

His gaze pierced her.

"I crept into the production the other day, and it was your alleluia that unshackled the yoke on my life. I tell you, after that praise and worship session, I was done. I went home and spent the night before the Lord. I needed answers. So, thank you."

She touched his hand. "You're welcome."

He leaned against the island. "So this is me. My life is far from perfect and so am I. I love you and I'm asking you into a relationship, but I want you to think about it. Plus, I have decided that I'm going to accept the position of youth minister at church, after I wrap up this project. My VP is not happy, but I promised that we would work something out if he'd allow me to work in Orlando. He already said yes."

Tyler looked directly into her eyes. "I enjoy my job and Lord knows I am good at it, but I feel the Lord calling me into ministry. Plus, you know what? I am grateful to have God as a father. The other day I was wondering what I could do to show the Lord that I love Him. I came to myself when I realized that I wanted to give back to the Lord that which He has given me—my life. I want to make my life a ministry for Him."

"That is just beautiful," Madison gushed.

"Thanks." Tyler sighed, looking away from her. "Em, please think and pray about being in a committed relationship with me. I'll be fine with whatever decision you make."

"Okay," she said, walking to stand before him. "Thanks for sharing everything. I will be praying for you…and about us."

"Thanks. I'll be heading off, then."

"Ty, I'm really sorry, you had to find out about your biological father in that way."

He was silent for a few moments, before responding, "Me too."

They walked in silence to the living room and he pulled on his jacket before they moved to the door.

"You had asked—what is one thing that I desired more than anything else?" He watched her carefully. "The answer is family. I want to have a family."

Her eyes grew soft. "A family."

"Yes. More than anything in the world," he said, reaching for the doorknob. "I'll talk with you later."

"Ty."

He turned to look at her and she embraced him, wrapping her arms around his waist.

He held her close, ignoring the way his heart rate sped to what seemed like a million miles per minute and thrashed about in his chest.

They held each other for a moment, as if each knew that the other needed it.

Fighting off all his emotional needs, Tyler gazed down at her. "Have a great night."

"Thanks, I will. You, too."

"And remember, sometimes doing the right thing is not always the easiest."

She reached up and kissed his cheek, whispering, "I'll remember that."

Momentarily stunned, he heard himself say, "See you soon."

With that he bolted—happy and extremely hopeful—through the door.

CHAPTER 37

"Shameful," Kelani jostled Madison with her elbow.

Madison jumped. All because she was caught up with the magnitude of the man—Tyler Aiden Bradshaw. "What?" she feigned innocence, her back pressing against the wall in the hall at Estrina's.

"I'm going to leave that alone." Kelani zipped her lips.

Her expression caused a quiet, girlish giggle to erupt and Madison covered her mouth to prevent further laughter. "You need to stop."

"I need to stop?" Kelani eyebrows climbed in amusement. "You need to stop ogling that man."

"What?" Madison feigned innocence again, as unexpected pleasure filled her.

Kelani shook her head slowly, and for a second time, pretended to zip her lips. "Your secret is safe with me, and everyone in this family."

Before Madison could respond, Kelani gave her two thumbs-up, causing a soft chuckle to escape her. "You need to behave," Madison told her, unable to help her happy grin. "You're making folks look in our direction."

"Right?" Kelani shook her head. "I'll see you in a bit. Off to check on Malachi."

"Okie dokie, I will check on him before I leave," Madison said thoughtfully, watching as Kelani made her way towards the back door.

Before long, her gaze was back on Tyler, who was making his way to the podium. Of course, she was happy to see him. Not only was he a welcome sight, but the fog had lifted from his life and it was obvious that he was on a new path...a new road to freedom. He'd again escaped from the snare that had been set for him and his eyes were fixed on Jesus Christ.

She watched Tyler with pride while attempting to settle the butterflies thrashing around in her stomach. She had given him a special spot—Motivational Speaker—on Estrina's Building Bridges community weekend program. She knew many of the children would be blessed by what he had to share and that he, too, needed to release himself from the baggage he had been carrying.

She smiled inwardly, thinking how confidently he had walked towards her in the foyer forty minutes ago. Suave and altogether wonderful, he was dressed in a fitted navy Calvin Klein suit, white shirt, and red tie. His bowlegs and disarming smile had her reaching for him by the time he arrived in front of her.

He had hugged her gently and kissed her cheek, whispering, "Good morning. Someone is happy to see me."

"Happy Saturday!" she greeted him before quietly diverting his attention to her father, who had just entered the foyer and was looking at Tyler like a second son. Soon, her parents, grandparents, Thomas and Edna Clarkson, Mason, and Kelani joined them. She could see the joy on Tyler's face when he saw Kelani. She still had not bounced back. In fact, no bouncing was happening. Kelani was still carrying her wounded heart in her gaze. Understandable. Nonetheless, it was great to see her out and about.

Madison apologized for leaving them, but she had to make her rounds in her role as a member of the planning committee. Before she could move away, Tyler subtly hooked his little finger around hers and while she quelled a shriek, she couldn't help the smile that blossomed on her face.

Everyone pretended not to notice their shenanigans, but the gleam in Mason's eyes told her that he had seen the play.

She had quickly fled the foyer, her heart skipping beats. Despite everything, her body constantly quivered in anticipation of Tyler's touch.

He had called, but had not visited or offered to take her out since the evening of their frank conversation over three weeks ago. She assumed he was giving her space to think and come to a decision concerning their relationship.

In one of their nightly calls, she asked if he would be getting in touch with his father's and mother's families. He'd told her that he didn't know, however, he was not closing those doors. She had also asked about the dream that his father had mentioned in the letter. It could be her imagination, but he sounded as if he was smiling when he had told her that she'd know about the dream in the fullness of time. She couldn't wait. It sounded special.

Madison's countenance brightened. For the past three Mondays, Tyler had sent her yellow roses at the office. She had placed the small cards that came with the flowers on her nightstand, where she could read them again before retiring for the night.

Loving you is easy because you are beautiful, inside and out. I thank God for you. Thinking about you, as always. Have a wonderful day. I love you, Ty.

I love your smile and everything about you. My heart skips beats when I think about you. Have a victorious day. I love you, Ty.

You soothe my soul. You're always in my heart so I know we belong together. Have a blessed day. I love you, Ty.

They had come a long way. She was enjoying the ride, the connection, the friendship, and—she dared to think—the courtship.

She let out a breathy sigh as Tyler's voice snapped her out of her musing. She decided that a closer view would be in order, so she walked along the wall and sat at the end of the front row.

"Good morning, everyone!" Tyler's voice rang out as he stood at the podium. He waited for a response.

Low murmurs of "Good morning, Mr. Bradshaw," sounded around the room.

He looked out at the late-teens and young adults and flashed a winning smile. "Okay, let me try this again. Good morning, everyone!"

"Good morning, Mr. Bradshaw!" rang out in the hall, followed by pockets of snickering.

"Much better," Tyler encouraged. "Now, I feel like you are alert, and I need you to be alert, even after your sumptuous snack. I heard that it was really good."

A chorus of "Yes!" erupted in the room.

"Awesome!" Tyler touched the screen of his tablet. "I want to thank the management and staff of Estrina's for giving me this opportunity to speak with you. Thank you, also, to Mrs. Reid, our gracious moderator, for that wonderful introduction." Smiling, he looked behind him and saw that she had taken a seat. "And thank you," he stretched out his hand towards the audience, and then returned the microphone to his mouth, "thank you, in advance, for being a great audience."

The room buzzed with excitement.

He smiled at his captive audience. "Again, I am Tyler Aiden Bradshaw, and I am adopted."

Suddenly, the room grew quiet.

Tyler smiled at the children. "It felt great to say that—I am adopted. Like many of you, I lived in a home just like this, for the first six years of my life. When I was almost six years old, a wonderful foster family took me into their home. It was hard at first, but I grew to love them." He smiled peacefully. "I loved them very much. They taught me about Jesus Christ, and I gave my heart to the Lord."

Tyler left the podium, cordless microphone in hand, and walked down the short flight of stairs. "Around ten years later, my foster father and mother died in a car crash."

Audible gasps resounded.

Tyler waited then spoke, "Yes, I was devastated. I finally had a mother and a father, and then I was back to square one." He walked and stopped near the middle of the front row.

"I wanted to hate. I cried. Again, I wanted to know why I couldn't be like some of my friends who had a mother and a father. I wanted to know why I was not worthy of affection. Yes, I fussed at God. But I remembered that my foster parents always taught me that God is watching over me. Come on, let me hear you say, God is watching over me."

"God is watching over me!" the children shouted.

"Yes, He is," Tyler said. "Now, I am telling you my story so that you know that God is watching over you, too. So, after the death of my foster parents, I was adopted by my father's friend and his wife. They are whom I now refer to as my dad and mom. I love them and I am grateful that God gave them to me."

Spontaneous applause broke out in the room.

"Thank you." Tyler smiled widely. "Thank God. But the saga continues. About six months ago, we buried my father."

Pockets of gasps echoed around the room.

Tyler remained stoic. "That was a rather painful experience. Of course, I cried. Again, I wanted to hate, to become hardened by my experience. I wanted to be bitter because of some things I had learned after my father passed. But again, I remembered…"

"God is watching over me!" the audience yelled.

"And, that is what I want you to remember going forward—God is watching over you. No matter what is taking place in your lives, remember…"

"God is watching over me!" the group shouted, and applause broke out.

Tyler quickly walked back to the podium.

"Yes, God is watching over you and me. So that's a little about me; however, God has placed something else on my heart to talk with you about. I call it—The Struggle Within."

Tyler touched the screen of his tablet and it sprung to life.

"The Struggle Within," he repeated. "The deepest struggle you will have—will start within your spirit. It is a struggle in your innermost being, as you ask yourself the question, who am I? And this struggle gets worse when you don't know who your parents are."

He paused to let that sink in.

"But this is a struggle that you must resolve. You must resolve this struggle, or you will do a lot of damage to yourself and others."

His eyes landed on Madison and he smiled before continuing. "Because, you see, that struggle…that pain in your heart, if left unresolved will be like a volcanic eruption in your life—destroying everything that it touches."

His eyes wandered around the room. "So today, I want you to give that struggle to Jesus Christ, and allow

Him to take care of you. Every struggle that you give to Him, He will take, and He will help you."

A round of applause broke out, so Tyler paused until it died down.

"Now, you have got to be big enough to learn to lean on someone—because sometimes, your hands are not big enough…your feet are not strong enough…to carry your struggle.

"Sometimes, the struggle is too great, and you will need to talk with someone about it—a counsellor, your foster parents, your pastor. Someone who can help to quell the struggle within you. Someone who will pray with you and help to steady your hands and feet when you feel like you are falling apart or when you feel like giving up."

He stared towards the back of the room. "Yes, you will have to learn to lean on others to help you get through the struggle within, or you risk destroying the blessings of God on your life."

He paused to let that sink in. "You have to genuinely look at yourself. Ask God to help you. Say to the Almighty God, 'God, You are the father of the fatherless. Here I am—Your child. Work on me, Lord. Help me to be right. Help me to do right. Lead me, Lord, and I will follow.'"

Tyler paused. "God will give you the strength and courage that you need. So, if you are going to have victory over your struggle you must arise. Arise—say that word."

"Arise!" the children shouted.

"Yes, arise," Tyler encouraged. "Philippians 4:13 states, 'I can do all things through Christ who strengthens me.' And Psalm 18:29-30 tells us, 'For by You, I can run against a troop, by my God I can leap over a wall. As for God, His way is perfect; the word of the Lord is proven; He is a shield to all who trust in Him.'"

Tyler glanced around the hall. "So, the talk is over, it is time to work to resolve this struggle within. With every step that you take toward resolving the struggle within you, you will find that God is helping you, and He is moving you towards your healing. God has called me—and you—to use the many talents that He has given us to make a difference in this world, so we will not let the struggle to find out who we are hinder us. We must be the light that drives darkness away from the lives of others. Be someone else's daybreak.

"God has called you and empowered you. Each of you has an assignment to touch the lives of certain individuals, and your work will bring glory and honor to God. I have a question for you—what are you doing with what God has blessed you with?"

Tyler paused for effect.

"What God has given me won't allow me to sit still. I am motivated. It's not about me; it's about the investment that God has made in my life. I must do the will of God. God loves fruitfulness. I am going to show up and use my talents to inspire someone.

"Today, I want you to lean on God and the people that God has placed in your lives to love you and help you. We are going to pray and ask God to help us. For we know that when God speaks everything changes, because He has infinite authority."

He stood beside the podium. "If you are counsellors and leaders to these children, please come forward," he said.

As the individuals Tyler called stood below the stage, he spoke to the children. "When God speaks, the universe responds. He is the author and finisher of my faith and your faith. And I can tell you that God does amazing things. Everyone has his or her own particular brand of struggle and only the intervention of God can break your

294

brand of struggle. Given the choice, most people step backwards from the light, simply because they enjoy their sins and struggles more than they love the opportunity for resolution and salvation. But today, I want you to come forward so we can talk with you and pray with you."

He smiled at the children. "I'm going to sing one of my favorite songs and meet you at the front of the stage." He then walked forward, singing "Turning Around for Me" by gospel recording artiste, VaShawn Mitchell, as the children—some running, some walking—came towards him.

CHAPTER 38

Later that day, Tyler almost let out a wolf-whistle of appreciation. His eyes flared with unmistakable desire as Madison walked across the landing to descend the stairs. He admired her seamless, red satin dress and strappy evening slippers. Her small red purse hung on her shoulder. *Simply beautiful, as always.* His gaze riveted, he cocked his head to get a better view of her as a medley of pleasant emotions washed over him.

Her eyes met his, and a wide smile graced her lips.

After the epic prayer session at Estrina's, he was exhausted and rest was in order. But he could not forget the tenderness in her gaze as he spoke, so that had given him the extra boost he needed to invite her out.

He wasn't too surprised when she bashfully told him yes, hugging him briefly. He knew he had held on to her a little bit longer than was appropriate, but he'd needed the warmth of her love. True, too, she did not seem to mind, even with her parents standing not too far off. In fact, he wanted to high-five her for showing her independence.

He had gone home hoping to rest, but he was all nerves, staring at the ceiling and watching the clock, even though he had set his alarm.

He had decided to suit up—his signature black Calvin Klein suit—and looking at her, he was glad he had. Albeit, in his excitement, he had arrived twenty minutes early, in his newly-purchased gray Lexus ES350.

Madison stopped on the last step, her hypnotic hazel-colored eyes telling him, *I love you to the moon and back.*

He could not help but return her tender gaze with a dazzling smile. She was the one person who had the ability to astound and overwhelm him at the same time, and in such an exquisitely enchanting way.

They didn't speak for a while, but simply looked at each other. Well, he was star-struck.

Radiant and beautiful, she straightened his tie, and then her fingertips tap-danced on his shoulders.

He waited...well, froze.

"I knew I would fall in love one day," Madison declared softly. "I knew, too, that the man I fell in love with would be special, in many ways." She smiled at him, and he shot her a toothy grin, his entire body buzzing.

"I imagined many things about the man I would fall in love with," she continued, running a hand over his head.

He heard himself purr. One of those long purrs that said, *Heaven. I'm in heaven.*

Smiling, she placed her hands on his shoulders. "But, above all, I imagined a man so engrossed in his relationship with Jesus Christ, that the only reason he glanced right was because he had found the one."

She leaned forward and whispered in his ear. "That was the look I saw in your eyes in the hall when I was nineteen years old, and I knew there and then, I had found where my heart belonged."

Her warm breath coupled with her perfume—distinct and soft with a hint of strawberry—almost sent him into a tailspin. She almost had him sniffing her.

He grasped her by the waist to steady himself. "I—" he began.

She cupped his chin and ran a finger over his lips to silence him.

Good Lord, I am about to become unglued, he mentally deliberated as the hairs on his body awakened under her caress.

She flashed him a wide smile. "My mother told me that love needs roots and wings. She also said that I have the roots, but I needed to have the courage to fly. I am feeling all courageous. I have discovered my wings and I want to fly." Smiling, she stepped slightly away from him, and softly said, "Can you ask me again?"

His lips curved in a toothy grin, deepening the single dimple in his lean cheek. "Em, I love you. Will you be in an exclusive relationship with me?"

A smile blossomed on her face. "Yes. I love you, too, Ty."

"Oh God!" His eyes popped as his body tingled. Joy bells were ringing. The sounds came from everywhere. *I am delirious with joy.* "Could you say that again?"

"I love you, Tyler," she said softly. "I never stopped loving you." And just because she felt he needed to hear more, she continued, "I choose you. I choose us. No hesitation. No holding back. I am home."

"Woot! Woot!" he shouted with glee.

In his excitement, he lifted Madison by the waist and held her up, turning and turning with her. She clutched his shoulders, squealing with delight.

He lowered her to the floor and held her closely, kissing the top of her head, and murmuring, "I love you. I love you," his voice resonating with boundless emotions. He felt alive.

An hour later, Tyler sat holding Madison's hand across the table at Perfect Touch Restaurant. They had barely eaten, but their hearts were content.

Madison peered at him. "You look happy."

"That's easy, I'm with you. I'm..." His words trailed off, as a bout of joy hit him. He smiled widely while playing with her fingers. "I'm always happy when I'm with you. There is a certain joy in knowing that my light is back."

Her eyes grew overly bright. "Your light?"

"Yes. The light of my life. During college, I looked forward to seeing you every day. You reminded me of the sunrise, bringing me hope as you lit my way." He smiled, his fingers caressing her palm. "There's no covering or hiding the sun. One way or another, it will rise."

She gasped softly, and he delighted in the sweetness of it.

"That...is beautiful," she said tenderly, and then she tensed. "I'm going to need my hand back," she told him.

His eyes pinned her, before releasing her hand. "You know being attracted to me is okay," he teased.

"Of course." She smiled sheepishly at him, resting her hands at the edge of the table near her chest.

"Can I tell you a secret?" he whispered.

"Sure." Her ears perked up as she stared at him wide-eyed.

"I am very attracted to you."

Her eyes dropped to the table and she fiddled with her napkin.

He cocked his head. "I have rendered you speechless. Now that's a first."

She lifted her eyes to his then rolled them skyward, but the twinkle he saw in them was a dead giveaway.

"We'll talk about it when you are ready. I can't believe you're that bashful," he told her, smiling at her discomfort. "Can I tell you a secret?" he asked in hushed tones.

"Another secret?"

He chuckled softly at her apprehension. "Yes, I've got more, of a different sort."

She smiled. "Shoot."

"Remember back in the day, I had told you that I rarely dreamed."

Madison's curls bounced as she nodded, anxious to hear the rest of his story.

"The dream I am about to recount is the one that Dad mentioned in his letter."

"Oh. My. Lord." She smiled widely at him. "Are you saying, the fullness of time has come?"

He chuckled softly, taken by her jubilant expression. "Yes. It has."

"I am all ears."

"Shortly after my foster parents died," he began, "I dreamt about my wife. I watched her from the back patio as she stood in our beautiful backyard, admiring the amazing landscape—the array of green trees, well-manicured lawn, and beautiful gardens. Apparently satisfied, she moved towards the gazebo that was nearby, and then she stopped to gaze at a patch of roses…yellow roses."

A gasp burst from Madison's lips, and he watched as she tried to contain her excitement. "Go on," she encouraged.

A smile curved his lips. "I was mesmerized by what I saw—her curly, honey-brown hair was aglow because of the soft morning sunlight." He stopped talking for a moment, watching her wide-eyed expression. "So in my dream, I step out on the patio and call out to her. She hears my voice and her head swings, and she smiles at me. A smile that tells me she loves me and has been waiting forever for me to come home. My heart rate kicks up several notches because I love when she smiles at me, with those warm hazel-colored eyes. Then we begin to walk towards each other, and immediately my eyes widen…"

"Why?" Madison asked breathlessly, her expression incredulous.

A second passed.

Tyler flashed her a brilliant smile. "Because she is…" Tyler mouthed the rest of the answer.

Madison gulped, then girlish giggles burst from her lips. "Wow."

Tyler looked at her tenderly. "I had this same dream on and off until I was around eighteen, when I decided my mind was playing tricks on me. I rationalized it—it was a way to protect myself, since my foster parents had just passed. I did not know my biological parents, so I was projecting the image of the perfect family that I would have. Plus, where would I get money to purchase such a home?"

"Unbelievable," Madison said, smiling.

"I never told anyone about the dream. Maybe I never believed it myself, but nearing my twentieth birthday, we had a family life conference—Friday to Sunday—at church in Boston. I will never forget that Saturday evening service." He marveled. "It was youth service and the preacher called for all the young people who believed that they were called to be in ministry. Of course, I went to the altar. It was always a given that I would preach." He paused to gauge her reaction.

She was with him. "Go on."

"When it was my turn, the pastor prayed for me, and confirmed what God had already laid on my heart concerning pastoral ministry. Then, suddenly, he stopped and stared at me."

Tyler gave a short laugh. "I thought, *What on earth?* He was staring at me and not staring at me. Then, he lowered his microphone and asked me to step forward, away from the others. I did and while I was moving, he'd apparently called my father."

Tyler shook his head slowly, as if the memory was still unbelievable.

"Would you believe that pastor recounted my dream?" Tyler's eyes popped. "Em, I could not believe it. And he told me, that is your wife. You will know her when you see her."

Tyler smiled at Madison. "That explains my odd reaction when I first met you. I knew it was you. I loved you then, and I still love you now."

The object of his desire stared at him tenderly from across the table. Smiling, she squeezed his hand. "I love you, too," she told him. "That was an amazing dream and an equally amazing prophecy. Thank You, Lord."

Her simple touch quieted the fluttering of his heart. He closed his eyes briefly before telling her, "When God sends a prophet to talk with you about something He has told you, it's because you have ignored your own conscience. I pray that God will keep my heart and mind sensitive to Him so that I will not only remember, but do whatever He requires of me."

"Amen to that."

"The best course of action to take when God speaks is to follow through."

She smiled at him. "I see you are bent on pursuing that particular dream."

His eyes roamed her face. "I am done chasing that particular dream. I'm waiting on the Lord for my next move."

It was her turn to flash him a toothy grin.

He signaled for the check and when it was all squared away, he asked, "Are you ready?"

She nodded and when they rose, Tyler extended his hand to her. She slid her fingers into his, and they walked towards the entrance of the restaurant.

Soon, they were on their way. They were both quiet, each wrapped up in thoughts.

The courtyard was brightly lit when they arrived at Madison's home.

"Here we are." Tyler said, as he brought his car to a standstill near the front door.

"I still prefer the Jeep," Madison said, picking up on a conversation they had had earlier, while on their way to dinner.

Tyler smiled at her. "So I gathered; however, a car is more fitting for certain occasions. Remember, I still—"

"Have the Jeep," she interjected.

He gazed at her in silence before reaching for the hand that was toying with the cup holder. He caressed her hand, and then paid her a special level of homage—softly touching her knuckles with his lips.

He felt her shiver, and gently released her hand.

"I'll come in briefly to make sure everything is okay," he said.

"Okay," she said softly.

Tyler switched off the ignition and raced around the front of the car to open Madison's door. She swung her legs out of the car and then stood before him. He hugged her waist as he reached around her to close the door.

As they moved towards the front patio, Tyler locked the vehicle. The light February breeze did nothing to cool his amorous thoughts. He took the key from Madison's hand and opened the door. They walked in and while he closed the door, she flicked on the light and disarmed the alarm.

They stared at each other until nervous laughter filled the air. They both wanted to. They both knew they couldn't.

"I'm going to back away while I have the strength," he told her quietly.

She flashed him a tense smile but said nothing.

He moved towards her, then circled her waist with his arms and hugged her closely. "I love you."

Her arms wound around his neck. "I love you, too." Her voice was muffled because her head was buried in his neck.

God, he wanted to kiss her so badly. He took a deep breath, kissed her cheek, and made a lame attempt to pull out of their embrace.

She held on to him, pulling him closer.

For the love of God, don't do that. "No. Not a good idea," he said softly, kissing the top of her head. "You need to let go."

"I don't want to," she pleaded softly.

"I don't want to, either, but it's best. I wouldn't be able to stop myself."

"Okay." She released him and spoke to his chest. "Have a good night."

"I will," he managed to say. "See you tomorrow."

He opened the door and stepped through. A cool gust of wind jarred him from his passionate thoughts. "I'll call you when I get home. No, I'll call you from the car."

She perked up, clutching the doorjamb. "Okay."

Swept away by the joy in her eyes, he brushed his lips across hers and caught her gasp in his mouth.

"Lock yourself in," he told her, smiling.

She gave him an ear-to-ear grin before slowly closing the door.

At the click of the lock, he raced to his car.

CHAPTER 39

Madison moved the stepladder from the corner of Tyler's kitchen and placed it near the cupboard. She climbed on it, and at that height, she could observe the length and breadth of the kitchen.

By the time Tyler dashed around the island and arrived by her side, she had reached for two huge cups on the top shelf.

"I could have gotten those for you," he said.

"Huh?" Startled, she turned, and he clutched her waist to steady her.

"Are you trying to kill me?" she puffed out. "Don't be sneaking up on me like that."

"No. Not trying to kill you." He ran a hand over his mouth to hide his grin.

She peered down at him. "Don't think for a minute I didn't see the laughter in your eyes."

He gave her a lopsided grin. "Guilty."

"And he admits it." She paused. "Errr…."

It was then that Tyler realized he was still holding her by the waist. He lifted her and began turning.

Laughter bubbled from her. "Put me down," she begged.

He chuckled, too, loving her laughter.

"Ty, put me down," she begged, girlish giggles erupting. "I'm about to lose these cups."

He slid her down his chest and placed her on the ground.

She stared up at him, her arms around his shoulders with the two cups dangling.

Kissing her was his only thought, but he resisted, releasing her. "Are we having cocoa now? Thought you wanted to finish first."

"We're finished. We just need to do a final check." She placed the cups on the counter. "Okay, let's check out our handiwork."

They moved to the dining room.

"We have done well," Tyler said, watching Madison rearrange the dishes of food on the table.

She glanced at him and smile. "We make a great team. High-five."

He came towards her, but she was still fixing the dishes.

He waited.

"I would high-five you, but that would be difficult without your hand," he teased.

"Oh! Oh!" She turned and grinned at him. "High-five."

"No," he scowled playfully, walking away.

Madison laughed. "Come here."

He did. Wearing a wounded expression.

"You are something," she said hugging his neck.

He lowered his voice. "Good something?"

"Yes." She rubbed his head. "Good something."

He purred, nuzzling her nose with his.

She giggled, burying her head in his neck. "I love you," she said breathing him in.

"I love you more," he responded, kissing the top of her head.

She lifted her head and smiled at him. "Every time you kiss the top of my head, I feel so loved."

"You are loved." He grinned at her. "Don't you see my heart on the floor every time you look at me?"

She smiled at him. "Of course. Do you know why?"

"Tell me."

"Because, that's where mine is when I see you."

His mouth felt slack and he closed his eyes, attempting to rein himself in.

She gently nipped his lower lip before covering it with her own.

He should have tried sidestepping, but he couldn't fight it.

He was aching everywhere. It had been three weeks of playing the cat-and-mouse game between them. Three weeks of exhibiting tormenting control over his body. God, it had been tiring. Tiring for him, for sure, but he could almost see her at times commanding her body to stand down.

Still, it amazed him how his libido had just flared up and could explode with just a touch of her hand. Keeping his passion at bay was turning into a full-time job. No one ever told him that when he'd found the one, the urge to be one with her would have him constantly on his knees.

God, I love her. He growled low in his throat as he kissed her, pressing her into his frame.

She shivered, and satisfaction ran through him.

He released her lips, and took his sweet time dragging his mouth against the soft skin of her neck.

Unprepared for the heat of his lips, she moaned loudly, gripping his back. She went limp against him and he lifted her into his arms and walked to the living room. He laid her on the sofa and sat beside her.

He watched her eyes slowly adjust from the lull she seemed to be in.

She smiled vaguely at him.

He wiped her lips gently with his thumb. "Are you going to fall out every time I kiss you?" He laughed softly. "And must everyone know you've been kissed?"

Immediately, her hand flew to her mouth. Eyes wide, she asked, "Are my lips swollen?"

"No. But what a time to be concerned."

She harrumphed, pulling herself to a sitting position, her back against the side of the sofa. "You're wrong for that."

"You are wrong for that. All that temptation. I am a mere mortal."

Her eyes twinkled. "I know we are waiting, but—" she held on to his hand, "—I like being near you and I really like kissing you."

He smiled at her. He liked that she was beginning to express how she felt. She had been bashful about the physical aspect of their relationship.

"You are not alone. I like kissing you, too, but honestly, I can't wait to make love to you."

Her cheeks flushed and she looked away.

He squeezed her hand. "As if you don't want to do good things to my body."

She laughed out.

"That is not a good laugh," he teased, poking her side. "I'm afraid of you."

"Stop!" she yelled, cracking up.

"You weren't saying that a while ago when you took advantage of me. I feel so used."

"I bet you do."

He poked her side several times and she doubled over, laughing.

"Help! Someone help me!" she hollered, trying to avoid his fingers.

Her obvious joy made his spirit soar. He stopped poking her, pushed his back against the sofa, and watched her. "That's what you'll get when you misbehave."

She grinned at him. "I better be a good girl, then."

"I somehow doubt that."

"You better be glad I love you."

They eyed each other and then started to lean in.

Madison sucked in a breath as her phone rang. "It must be Mason or Kelani," she said, glancing at her purse on the small sofa across from them.

She moved towards it, pulled out her phone, and looked at the screen. It stopped ringing and she dropped the phone back in her purse. "Looks like a wrong number," she said, turning and almost colliding with Tyler.

Contact with him caused mindless chatter to slip from her lips. "I wonder what's keeping Mason and Kelani. I hope they're okay. Would you like your cocoa now?"

He wrapped an arm around her waist, and then breathed in the strawberry scent in her hair. "No, I don't want cocoa. I want you."

He felt her body jolt and an involuntary gush of air escaped her lips. "Ty..." she paused, spreading trembling fingers over his chest as her knees weakened with interest.

Her nervous movements drew his attention. "You're nervous. Don't be." He lifted her chin, forcing her to meet his eyes.

"Ty, you..." She touched his jaw, her gaze searching.

His name on her tongue brought chill bumps to the surface of his skin. He waited not a moment longer to kiss her.

When their mouths met, their kiss felt like something flammable.

Something electric.

Something ablaze.

He kissed her longer than he probably should, his heart in his throat, beating way above the regular rate.

They groaned with desire, clutching each other. He attempted to lift his mouth from her, but her breathless murmuring held him in place. All his instinctive responses—let go, back away, flee—were quickly leaving him.

Oh God. He didn't want to stop, but he had to, for they had long passed the proverbial red line. He skillfully withdrew his lips from hers, and she buried her head in his chest.

"I know. I know," he said, gathering her close and raining light kisses on the top of her head. "Soon, babes, soon."

She softened in his arms.

He prayed for the strength they both lacked.

Before long, their world righted itself again.

Tyler held her hand and they walked back to the sofa and sat. He pulled her into his side and placed his arm around her shoulder.

"Thanks for my flowers. I enjoy receiving them. I'm keeping all the cards."

"You're welcome. It's my pleasure."

He angled his jaw to receive a kiss, and she pecked him tenderly.

He chuckled good-naturedly. "I took your suggestion to start with flowers."

"Good job." She chuckled softly, recalling she'd cheekily told him that in the parking lot at Zilano Italian Restaurant, when he'd mentioned she had to stop taking ugly pills.

"What's the story behind you liking yellow roses?" he asked. "Back in the day, I looked it up and yellow roses represent joy and friendship."

"No one ever asked." She stared ahead. "It started off as my secret shame, and then it became something exceptional."

"Tell me."

Madison rolled her lips together. "During my first semester in college, I worked with Dr. Mary Green, aka Dr. G., on a business communication project for the senior staff of a technology company. She taught the Business

Relationship class. As the semester progressed, we developed a great relationship and I learned a lot from her. Of course, the project was successful, and was accepted by the company." She grinned. "We made money from it."

Her smile slowly disappeared.

"At the end of the semester, during my oral evaluation, she told me that I was excellent in all that I did, but several times she noticed I had a tendency to lean too much on others—" Madison tapped a finger against her jaw, then finally spoke, "—giving the impression that I lacked self-confidence. She told me that it was not an attractive quality and that when I am in business, others may use it against me."

She sighed. "She was right. I need to stand up for what I believe in, and do so with conviction." She smiled at her recollection. "Dr. Green always had yellow roses in her office. She said that they reminded her of the joy of teaching and the friendship she shared with her students."

Madison shifted slightly to look directly into Tyler's eyes. "The yellow roses remind me God has gifted me abundantly with wisdom, knowledge, and understanding to do whatever He has called me to do. That I am equipped, strong, and well able."

Her answer surprised him. "Wow. Life-changing action. I love it."

"Indeed."

He smiled at her. "What else?"

She met his teasing grin. "How do you know there's more?"

"Babes, I know you, and I see you holding back."

She came clean. "When you gave me the yellow roses after my first production…Since you had taken the time to ask about my favorite flowers, for me…that was a sign that you cared, that…"

"I loved you," he filled in.

"Yes," she answered quietly. "And, I couldn't have enough yellow roses because back then, they represented your love for me."

Without saying a word, he wrapped her in his arms, breathing in her essence. He wanted to kick himself for the pain he'd caused her.

"Ty, I'm okay," she mumbled in his chest. "We've already crossed that bridge."

He kissed the top of her head. "I know, but I'm still sorry."

"Wait a minute!" She pulled out of his arms and eyeballed him. "What were you talking to Mom and Dad about after church?"

He toyed with her finger, but did not respond.

"Ummm? I saw Mom looking at me," Madison said. "Were you all talking about me?"

"Yes."

She perked up. "What about? Are you all planning my birthday party?" She chuckled softly. "That will not be a surprise."

"Are you trying to remind me of your birthday?"

"Man, please."

He poked her side several times and she yelled. "Stop! Ty, stop!"

When he wouldn't, she slid off the sofa to her knees before him.

He chuckled softly. "You may want to...um...get yourself together. I have a reputation I would like to keep."

Just then the doorbell sounded.

"Ohhh." Madison jumped to her feet and started to smooth her clothes. No doubt, Mason and Kelani had arrived.

Tyler watched her, amused. "I'll hold them. You look..." A short snort escaped him at her say-it-if-you-dare look.

"Ugh!" she huffed, and he couldn't resist the grin that reached his face.

She cut her eyes at him, moved to grab her purse from the small sofa, and hurriedly made her way towards the bathroom.

"I love you!" he hollered at her back, chuckling softly.

CHAPTER 40

An hour later, Tyler and Madison tried valiantly to keep from constantly looking at each other. They shouldn't; after all, Mason and Kelani were sitting at the dinner table and they should be fully engaged in the chatter.

Madison's eyes swept the group as she spoke, "How about this—Kelani and I will stack the dishwasher and you guys can find the movie?"

"Sounds good, Em," Tyler said, smiling at her.

"Of course that would be good," Mason remarked teasingly. "I know she didn't lift a finger to help prepare this food. You're spoiling her to death."

"Hater," Madison shot at him, pushing back her chair and rising. "I did help."

"Yes, she did," Tyler jumped to her rescue.

Mason clapped. "That's my bad. We thank you both, for such a tasty meal."

Madison remained quiet.

"You're welcome," Tyler rushed in to respond.

Madison gathered some of the dishes. "Don't be saying that. We do not want him coming over every day. Kelani, you are welcome to do that."

With that, Madison moved towards the kitchen, plates in hand.

Chuckles broke out.

"I love you, baby sis!" Mason called out behind her.

Soon, Madison and Kelani had stacked the dishwasher and were wiping the cupboards.

At Kelani's "A-A-A-Ahem," Madison swung around and was greeted by girlish giggles.

"What did I miss?" Madison asked, puzzled.

"Oh, it's more like what did *I* miss?" Kelani clutched her heart, and playfully batted her eyes. "Yes, Ty.

Ty made this. Ty took me to see it. Ty, stop, you did not just say that." She clapped her hands. "I love it."

Laughter burst from Madison's lips. "You need to stop."

"No. *You* need to stop. Seriously!" Kelani shook her head. "I thought I was about to hear 'boo thang' next."

Madison cracked up. "Girl, stop. You need serious help."

"No, *you* stop. And thanks for the laughter, too. Felt so good."

"Lani, I understand, but as Ty said—"

"Ty. Ty. Ty." Kelani laughed aloud, then looked cross-eyed. "Good gracious, woman, get it together. Such boundless energy. Contain yourself. Geesh!"

"Shucks! You got me." Madison laughed self-consciously. "But as Ty said, God is watching over you. I believe He is watching over you and Mason," Madison ended in all seriousness.

A knowing smile curved Kelani's mouth. "I believe so, too. Some days are hard, but today is going great."

"I know we all said it, Lani, but we were all soooo very proud of your testimony in church today. You not only spoke, but ooh, that song! Girl, there was no dry eye in the sanctuary by the time you were through," Madison gushed.

Kelani had sang "Never Would've Made It" by gospel recording artiste, Marvin Sapp.

Kelani looked over her shoulder. "I had to. 'Never would have made it' sums up my mental state." She turned and leaned against the cupboard. "I spoke with Mason two weeks ago and asked if he was okay with me saying a few words about our loss. He said yes." She shook her head in amazement, her expression dreamy. "I love my precious husband. He has been supportive, kind, prayerful, and oh God—" she paused, choked up.

Madison rushed to her side and rested a hand around her shoulder. "It's okay, Lani."

Kelani managed to pull herself together. "Madison, he has been so caring. I am so glad he's my husband."

Madison waited as a tiny smile curved Kelani's lips.

"I know he's grieving, too," Kelani continued, "but he's open about it and he has helped me to face the fact that I miscarried." She released a deep sigh. "Everything is an effort. It's still hard, but I trust God."

"Amen," Madison said. "Tyler and I are praying for you both."

"We appreciate that. And we have been praying for you and Tyler, too." She bumped Madison with her hips. "You both look happy."

Madison smiled widely. "We are. But we're still working things through."

"We need some girl-time," Kelani furrowed her brows. "And, why do I have to hear from Mason that Tyler intends to take up the position of youth minister?"

"Uh-oh. Yep, let's get together one evening this week."

"Sure. I'll buzz you later so we can decide. Let me make sure my husband has no plans for me."

"Alright, wife. You do that."

"Girl, stop. You'll be in the same boat soon." She lifted a hand as Madison began to protest. "Oh, I knew there was something else," Kelani said. "I'm having lunch with author Pollick tomorrow before she heads home." She grinned self-consciously. "Her first name is Ava. I'm accustomed to thinking of her as Author A. M. Pollick. Do you want to have lunch with us?"

Madison smiled at her. "Sure. It was great meeting her. I can't believe she came to our church to see you and show her support. Good surprise, Lani." She hugged Kelani and released her.

"Love her!" Kelani gushed. "Like I told you, after I read her book—thanks to you—I reached out to her. She was wonderful. We spoke a few times and at the end of each of those conversations, she prayed for me. She has been a blessing."

"Indeed. It was great to meet her. She is one of my favorite authors."

Kelani slowly shook her head. "I still can't believe she came."

"She's indeed in ministry for the Lord."

"Yes. She said that she felt the Lord leading her to visit me," Kelani said, crossing her arms under her breasts. "You may recall she lives in Jamaica. She told me that she has relatives in Orlando, so she's staying with them."

"Just beautiful."

"She actually came in on Thursday, and we met on Friday, so we were able to chat and pray."

An incredulous expression filled Madison's face. "She came and you didn't tell me?"

"I didn't want to disturb your flow with Tyler. Plus, I had it covered."

"I forgive you for saying that."

Kelani chuckled. "Ava has a wonderful spirit."

"I can tell. She would not be able to write like that if she didn't. I'm going to see about setting up a book signing event for her. We can probably mention that when we see her tomorrow."

Kelani clapped her hands. "That would be great. I believe many women who experience miscarriage would benefit from all that she would share. I'm seeing her doing a couple seminars, too. We could talk with Pastor Fotola and see if the church wants to be involved."

"Yes. Great ideas."

"Uh-oh. Our men must be wondering where we are."

"Oh, yes." Madison smiled at her. "Let me finish wiping the counter."

"I need to finish wiping this side, too."

They completed the task and then dropped the disposable washcloths into the trash.

As they were about to move through the door, Kelani clutched Madison's hand.

"What is it?" Madison's head swung, the pressure on her wrist making her eyes pop.

Kelani swallowed hard. "We're thinking about adopting Malachi."

Madison's eyes filled with tears as she clutched Kelani's shoulder. "Oh, Lani, that would be awesome."

They hugged each other tightly, released each other, and then hugged again.

"You know how much I love Malachi. It was love at first sight for him and Mason," Kelani said, chuckling softly. "Mason and I have been praying about it for a while. The blessings of God may not have come packaged as we expected it, but we will not allow our baggage to stop us from receiving it."

"Amen. Amen," Madison beamed.

"It's not that we won't try again," Kelani told her, "but right now, we feel this is what the Lord would have us do."

Tears pooled and Madison wiped her eyes.

"Those had better be tears of joy," Kelani threatened playfully.

"Yes. Yes," Madison said quickly, tears trickling this time. "You just blessed me. Thank you."

"Praise God." Kelani smiled at her with hands akimbo. "You better dry those happy tears before you make Tyler think I was giving you a beat-down."

"Okay. In a minute, I'll have it together," Madison said, dabbing her eyes with her fingertips, and then wiping her cheeks.

"You better, Aunt Madison. Prepare for babysitting duties."

Madison giggled, throwing her hands in the air. "I'm up."

Kelani chuckled softly, looping her arm around Madison's waist as they moved towards the living room.

CHAPTER 41

Madison clutched Tyler's arm as they walked into a private room at Abella.

"All set as you requested, sir," the server said.

"Thanks, Kimberly," Tyler said with Madison attached to his side.

"Please let us know when you are ready," Kimberly added, bearing a practiced smile.

"I will," Tyler responded. "Thank you."

With that, Kimberly took her leave, closing the door.

"This is the best birthday celebration I've ever had," Madison said, smiling.

She should have celebrated her birthday in December, but with Kelani's miscarriage, the death of Tyler's father, and the disclosure about his biological parents still hanging over him, it was hard for anyone to be in a celebratory mood. Since then, she had entered a relationship with Tyler and he had insisted that she should celebrate her birthday at an appropriate time.

She rested her hands on Tyler's chest and turned smiling eyes up to his. "Thank you for making my birthday special in March," she said, giggling softly.

He slid a hand around her waist, a soft smile tugging at the corners of his mouth. "I'm glad you feel that way. You look enchanting."

Her eyelids fluttered as his gaze caressed her face.

She felt beautiful.

Glowing.

She saw the admiration in his eyes as he took a mental snapshot of her elegant sky-blue evening gown.

Style: Timeless classic.

Silhouette: A-Line.

Fabric: Chiffon.

Neckline: One shoulder with silver sequin embellishments.

Length: Floor-length.

Waistline: Empire with silver sequin embellishments.

To add extra sparks, she wore silver evening slippers and round diamond stud earrings with a matching bracelet. Her glorious curly hair was on fleek—tumbling around her cheeks before cascading down her back—just the way he liked it.

He had told her to dress up, and that she did.

"Let's sit," Tyler said, gently touching her arm.

"Sure."

He escorted her to the white leather loveseat in the spacious, open lounge area. She scanned the expansive room, noting the ornate detail of the architecture and furniture. Like several of the other private rooms at Abella, everything was white with a touch of gold.

She smiled when her gaze landed on the coffee table before them. It was home to a beautiful, tall floral arrangement of yellow roses and a gold tray with two wine glasses and champagne in a gold-trimmed wine chiller.

"Give me a moment," Tyler said walking across the room towards a table that was set for two.

"Ty, what is a girl to do after this weekend?" Madison asked, watching his back. "Friday was all day pampering—morning to evening. Then, dinner with my parents and close family members. You made sure I had heaven on earth." Excited all over again, she stood and twirled. "And again today, you're at it—dinner in this gorgeous place. What are you going to do tomorrow—to out-do yourself?"

Her head angled slightly upward as he moved towards her. He was oozing confidence. She noticed he had shaved off his sideburns but was sporting his usual thin moustache and beard.

A smile burst from her lips, and just like that, her heart recognized that this tall, suave, bowlegged, he-man, in his edgy, perfectly-fitted, black tuxedo—he was all hers.

He leaned in and kissed her cheek. "You deserve this and much more."

Her heart lurched to a fervent tempo, her entire being responding to him.

"These are for you." He pulled from behind his back a bunch of red roses, and handed them to her.

As she took them, a touching expression covered her face, and she tried to respond with a joyful, "Thank you," but the words seemed to have gotten wedged in her throat.

"You are welcome," he said.

She found her voice. "They are gorgeous." she remarked, bringing the flowers up to her nostrils.

He smiled at her. "Just like the angelic lady holding them."

Sweet Lord! Her blood was pumping now.

"Em," he said softly. "I love you."

"I love you, too," she choked out.

Her stomach tightened as their eyes met, and mutual admiration blossomed into uncontrollable smiles. In the next breath, he was on one knee before her.

Something flamed to life inside her. "Oh. My. God," Madison panted. "Wha-what...?" Her voice trailed off and her hands flew to her chest as she gazed at him.

The air was thick with expectancy.

"Em, living my life without you is not an option. I have loved you forever." Tyler took a ring box from his inner pocket and opened it. The Ritani eighteen-carat white gold, three-stone diamond ring gleamed in the black box.

He smiled up at her, vulnerability shining in the depths of his warm gaze. "You made me believe in miracles. For with you, I have found where my heart belongs. I love you. Will you marry me?" he asked, his voice deep with emotion.

Madison fell on her knees before him. "Yes. Yes!" she cried out, hearing the manic beating of her heart. A little laugh burst from her lips as she watched him slip the ring onto her finger.

For a moment, they gazed at each other without speaking, then instinctively, hugged each other, tightly...with enthusiasm and strength. Years of despair melted, replaced with the euphoric feelings of a new beginning.

"I love you," she whispered.

"I love you more." He held her tighter, kissing the top of her head.

A moment later, he rose and helped her up. A hundred thoughts spun in her head, with joy bouncing off every one of them. She smiled up at him and he placed his hands on her waist and lifted her off the ground. For the first time, she did not squeal, but grinned down at him. He set her back on the ground and kissed her.

It took what seemed to be a thousand measured breaths for their breathing to regain normalcy.

"I have a surprise for you," Tyler said, moving towards the table.

She slapped her hand on her forehead. "Another surprise? I'm in."

He threw a smile over his shoulder. "I'm glad for that," he said reaching for the iPad on the table to communicate with customer service.

Soon, he walked back to her. "Ready?"

"All yours."

"I like the sound of that."

He extended his hand and she took it.

Shortly thereafter, they walked out of the room and down a passageway.

She was smiling all the way. She couldn't stop herself, even if she tried.

Tyler halted at a double door with the words *Grand Ballroom* scripted in gold French-styled font.

Madison's head whipped up at Tyler.

He flashed her a spellbinding smile.

Her heartbeats thundered in her ears, but before she could speak, the door swung open. She sucked in a breath while gazing at the sea of smiling faces in the room.

It felt like a dream.

She heard herself exclaiming, "Sweet Lord!" Her heart jumped around as her insides knotted. And without warning, she buried her head in Tyler's chest, shivering.

He held her close, kissing the top of her head, and soothing her with gentle back rubs.

When he could pry her away from his chest, Kelani, Rebecca, and Laurie-Ann were on hand, straightening her dress and mopping her face while whispering encouraging words. Kelani took the bunch of red roses from her hands. Just as well, for the flowers had taken a beating in all the excitement.

Surprised laughter bubbled from Madison's lips, and her bewildered gaze returned to Tyler. He tenderly held her hand and quietly comforted her with his eyes.

Soon, her hand encased protectively in his, they walked the red carpet amidst cheers and applause. She returned the smiles and shared breezy small talk with their guests, whose eyes were glowing with expectation.

Madison paused, expressing her joyfulness at seeing the fireworks in the centerpieces on the tables.

Tyler subtly moved her along.

The energy level of the room amplified with each step they took.

They smiled and waved at the guests—church members, friends, relatives, grandparents, and parents—until they came to a standstill at the top of the room, near the head table.

A knot formed in Madison's throat.

Suddenly, the hundreds of guests seemed to fade away, and the huge stands of yellow roses and candles disappeared. There weren't cameras snapping photos of them, and the room wasn't filled with everyone who loved them.

For a moment, it was only Madison and Tyler.

She had to fade them away as she took deep calming breaths. When she came out of her breathing exercise, she realized that Tyler was still holding her hand. Their eyes locked, and the silence in the room was deafening.

He flashed her a charming smile. "Good surprise?"

He winked one eye slowly, and a soft giggle escaped her. She let out a tightly trapped breath before nodding.

"Ready to rock and roll?" he asked.

"Yes!" It came out in a rush.

He moved her slightly to the right to a padded chair fit for a queen, and indicated that she should sit. She offered no resistance.

Tyler took the cordless microphone from the table behind them. "Ladies and gentlemen, thank you for sharing this evening with us!" Tyler smiled proudly, then dramatically pumped a fist in the air. "She said yes!"

Their guests broke into wild and thunderous applause and cheers.

"I love you, Em," Tyler said, still smiling, "And I want to spend the rest of my life with you."

"I love you, too." Madison blew him a kiss, and held up her hand to display her engagement ring.

Their guests began cheering again.

"Em, my love, this song is for you. You are what dreams are made of." After flashing her a captivating smile, he lifted a hand, and instrumental music started to play as the introduction to "A Love Like This" by gospel recording artistes Phil and Brenda Nicholas filled the air.

His eyes never leaving Madison's face, Tyler belted out the song from his soul.

Deep.

Layered.

Sensitive.

Emotionally-rich.

Passionate.

Mesmerizing.

Masterful and timeless.

It was a promise of all things new—love on the edge of tomorrow.

By the time he brought the song to a blissful end, the guests were sniffling and even he had to wipe his eyes.

A warm glow on her face, Madison flew into his open arms.

He laughed softly, and held her close, kissing the top of her head.

She didn't realize she was crying until Tyler stopped raining butterfly kisses on her head and used his fingers to wipe her cheek.

She looked up at him, his dark-brown eyes smoldering with promise. Her eyes pooled again, and she shifted and found herself gazing at the heartwarming expressions and nods of joy from their guests. She didn't bother to hide her tears when so many of them were dabbing their eyes.

She managed to smile widely, with understanding and love, before shifting her gaze back to the man who held her heart captive.

He was beaming ear to ear.

She returned his smile.

With entwined fingers, they—the future Mr. and Mrs. Bradshaw—faced their guests.

"Ladies and gentlemen," Tyler said, "I awoke this morning with my face stiff. Do you want to know why?"

Pockets of snickering and several choruses of "No!" and "Yes!" reached him.

Tyler flashed a brilliant smile. "I was smiling while I was sleeping. All because I was thinking about my wife-to-be and this special day."

That brought hearty laughs and many broad smiles.

"Looking back," Tyler said, a wide smile across his lips. "I realized that my smile was definitely not overdone for this occasion."

Amidst more laughter, Reverend Joseph Tanner and Pastor Robert Fotola walked forward.

Tyler and Madison kneeled on the cushions that were provided. The pastors rested their hands on Tyler's and Madison's heads, and Reverend Tanner began praying.

"Oh Lord, our Lord, how excellent is Your name in all the earth. We honor and praise You, for all that You have done. You reign supreme in our hearts and we, Your children, are happy to call You Father, Savior, and Lord.

"Father, on this special occasion, we present Tyler Aiden Bradshaw and Madison Emma Kanate before You. We pray a special blessing on them and on this occasion announcing their engagement. God, we thank You that You have called and equipped them for a life together with You in their midst.

"We pray Tyler will continue to be a man of integrity, and not waver under the pressures of this world.

327

Preserve his life from the enemy and destroy any net that was set for him. May he continue to trust and keep his eyes fixed on You, Lord, and not be afraid of what man can do to him. Oh Lord, lead him, guide him, protect him, so his light will shine before men so that they will glorify You.

"Proverbs eighteen and verse twenty-two states, 'He who finds a wife finds a good thing, and obtains favor from the Lord.' We thank You that Tyler has found Madison. Teach him, oh Lord, how to love and care for her.

"Father, we thank You for Madison. We pray for a fresh anointing on her life. Anoint her with the oil of joy and refresh her by Your Spirit. Enable her to walk in the fruit of the Spirit. Strengthen her, Lord, as You work in her that which is pleasing to You.

"Unite Tyler and Madison in a bond of love, friendship, and commitment. Perfect their love for each other, Lord. Let communication be easy between them as You teach them to take their eyes off the circumstance and look to You. Remove feelings of inadequacy and negative emotions, and instead, fill them with more love, wisdom, discernment, revelation, and knowledge.

"May their dwelling place be in the shadow of Your wings. Help them to seek You first daily, to set their priorities in order. May the river of their worship be a sweet offering as it flows to You. Help them to be anxious for nothing, but with thanksgiving let their request be made known unto You. May they always sense Your presence, Your love, and Your peace. We pray Your blessing on them this day, and forever more. For this is Your doing, Lord, and it is marvelous in our eyes. In the name of Jesus Christ, we pray, amen."

A chorus of quiet "Amen" and "So let it be" filled the room and then was replaced by silence.

Too moved to utter a response, Tyler and Madison hugged each other… for a long time.

EPILOGUE

A year later

She had never been happier. Madison felt like twirling in the welcoming summer weather. Rays of sunlight bounced off her as she stood in their sprawling backyard, admiring the amazing landscape—the array of green trees, well-manicured lawn, and beautiful garden. She loved the lush landscape with its stunning colors and varieties of plants.

Satisfied, she moved towards the freshly-painted white gazebo, then stopped to fetch a yellow rose from the patch nearby. She stood, tracing a finger along the stem of the rose, while carefully avoiding the thorns. Her mind ran on her husband and a smile burst on her face. No doubt he was watching her...as always, from the huge, glass kitchen windows.

They had gotten married three months after their memorable engagement party. After their lavish wedding, they had lived at Madison's home for about six months while their elegant, two-story, contemporary French-styled home was being built. Of course, Tyler designed it with her help, and they decorated it together. *Unforgettable moments!*

The slight whisper of the morning breeze whipped around her, and Madison lifted her head to admire the beautiful touch of sunlight peeking over the rooftop. Her heart tripped unexpectedly and as she tried to contain her excitement, she felt movement on the inside.

A woozy kind of emotion—joy, crazy joy—was radiating from her.

She gently rubbed her belly.

Everything just felt perfect.

Perfect day.

Perfect weather.

Even a perfect husband.

Entering the gazebo, she retrieved her Kindle. She was about to move out of the gazebo when spontaneous praise burst from her lips. "Lord, You are awesome! Father, thank You for life, and love, and family…"

Mindful of her husband, she made her way back.

The back patio door opened before she touched the handle, and she couldn't help the smile that popped on her face. In that moment, her breath caught, because she remembered, Proverbs 13:12, "Hope deferred makes the heart sick, but when the desire comes, it is a tree of life."

Tyler flashed her an alluring smile. "I thought I would have to spend my Saturday alone," he teased, locking the door behind her.

His voice made her pulse throb wildly at her throat. "No such thing, honey," she told him, batting her eyelids.

"Happy me." He snaked a hand around her waist, cradled her chin with the other and lifted it to kiss her forehead.

She loved the authoritative manner with which he reached for her, and she sank into him, letting herself relax and enjoy the joyful stirring in her womb. His delicious woodsy scent assailed her.

Tyler kissed the top of her head, the way she loved, then hugged her shoulders and moved her through the kitchen. He stopped suddenly and looked directly at her. "Have you taken your prenatal vitamin?"

She pulled a sour face. "I hate taking pills."

"I know, but it's just for a few weeks to help cover the nutritional gaps in your diet."

She dropped her head on his chest.

"Do it for the babies and me?" His voice dripped with honey. "I'll even drop in a kiss or two, after you've done so."

330

She lifted her head and smiled at him. "Sure, but I'll take the kisses in advance, please."

In a split second, he pulled her close and brushed his warm lips against her forehead, her cheeks, and then her lips.

Fire sizzled through her veins and she wrapped her arms around his neck, moaning in contentment and pressing herself against him.

He gently pulled his lips from hers. "There's more where that came from, but I need you to take your vitamin first."

She smiled at him. "That's encouraging. I will take you up on that after we organize the babies' room."

"Awesome. And look at that, your vitamin and a bottled water are on the island." He moved her towards them.

"Slick. Very slick. You had it all planned."

He rubbed her back, chuckling softly. "Guilty, but I came up with the idea of the kisses at the last minute."

"Great incentive." She took the pill and downed it with water.

"Good job," he said, capping the water and placing it on the island.

"Thanks. Good job to you, too."

They continued out of the kitchen, down the passageway, passing the formal dining room.

"Are you still bent on keeping up your mom and dad's tradition?" Tyler asked.

"You don't want to?"

"It's neither here nor there with me."

In silence, they strolled across the living room with its glittering crystal chandeliers, stunning opulent walls and carpet, and French silk draperies. It was nothing short of whimsical and romantic.

"Do you want to think about it; pray about it?" Madison asked.

"No. I'm good if you are good."

They paused at the foot of the stairs, and she faced him. "Honey," she said placing her hands on her chest, "we have time, if you have a change of heart."

He ran a hand down her arm. "Babes, I'm at peace for now." His voice was a gentle timbre caressing her ears.

They would not fight over not knowing the genders of the twins his wife was carrying.

"Thank you, honey." She pecked his lips.

He flashed her a toothy grin. "You'll be happy to know I've been thinking about names."

Madison clapped her hands joyfully. "Thank You, Jesus."

"Well, tell me how you feel."

"I am thrilled. That's all." She playfully patted his back as they ascended the stairs.

"My list is in no way as long as yours," he teased.

Her lips swiped to the side. "You know I can hear you, right?"

They paused on the landing and he pushed away strands of hair from her cheeks. "I had to go there. You have two columns with names and we have another four months to go."

"I'm ahead of the game."

He smiled tenderly at her. "Yes, you are. Thank you, wifey."

His smile made her smitten heart skip several beats as they walked across the landing, and down the passageway. She hooked her little finger around his, and smiled warmly at him.

He chuckled softly. "How is it okay for you to hook my little finger and you're not okay when I hook yours?"

"Errr…"

He waited for a response, casting her a glance.

Nothing was forthcoming.

As soon as they entered the entryway to their master bedroom, Tyler lifted her in his arms.

She squealed with delight, hugging his neck.

The twins lurched in the excitement.

"Oh my, you're all getting heavier," he panted.

"Ooh! I can hear you."

He grinned at her. "Not to worry…yet."

"That's comforting!" she teased, hugging him tighter as the twins began a happy dance.

The door was open, so Tyler used his shoulder to push it further in, then used his feet to close it. He deposited her on the massive king-size bed.

"Ooh, yeah," she purred. "Just what I need."

The bed dipped as he settled beside her, and the twins continued to stir. She rolled on her side to face him. "You know what, I'm beginning to think the twins know when you are near."

Tyler came up on his elbow, slipped his hands under her blouse and gently rubbed her belly.

"Hmmmm." Madison rolled on her back, enjoying the warmth of his hands as they made music on her belly. "That feels so good."

His eyes twinkled as he gazed longingly at her. "Organizing the babies' room is on hold, I see," he teased, lowering his head and pecking her lips.

Instead of responding, she eagerly tilted her lips for more of his feathery kisses, moaning softly in contentment, her hands roaming his back. She had come a long way from her bashful days earlier in their relationship. Tyler had masterfully helped her to strip away all her inhibitions.

He gathered her closer, his hands touring her body. "You are so—" He searched for the right words as he gazed at her, "—plump...juicy...and nice, very nice." His voice, low and husky, was filled with amazement.

Tenderness swirled within her. "You like me this size, huh?" she asked playfully, guiding his hand to her belly.

"Mm-hmm. A lot." Her full breasts thrust forward and he ran a hand over them before caressing her belly.

"Mmmmm," issued from her lips and he kissed her belly, uttering a spontaneous prayer of thanksgiving before looking at her.

A smile flitted across Madison's lips as he gazed at her in wonderment; seemingly absorbed in a mixture of memories. She knew what he was thinking, for he told her often enough. His dream had become a reality. And he was intent on protecting the dream and the miracles growing inside her...and their happily-ever-after.

Amazing.

Their love story, which had faded to black because of life's storms, had been reborn through the grace of the Almighty God—to a collage of beautiful pictures with the vibrant colors of the rainbow as backdrop.

Happy, she reached for her husband. Simultaneously, he reached for her.

"I love you, my wife and children." He kissed the inside of her palm.

Breathless with delight, she rejoiced in the pleasure on his face. "I love you, too, my husband. You are always in my heart."

He gazed at her intensely—full of love.

Her mouth went dry as she took in the dilation of his pupils. It excited her to see the thrilling hunger in his eyes.

"I love you more," he said, pecking her lips. "You are—" he pecked her lips again, "—always in *my* heart."

Incoherent whimpers left her lips, signaling the fire he was stirring within her.

On cue, he showered her with delicate kisses as he moved her towards the edge of bliss.

Her pulse tripped, then kicked up, and her body arched against his like a taut bowstring, reveling in his touch—reveling in the feeling of being loved. The desire that he was awakening in her caused shimmering sensations to surge and swell throughout her body, only to surge and swell, over and over, again.

Exuberant.

Delightful.

Unhinged.

Unrestrained.

Their love…it was all-consuming.

At times, overwhelming.

But they treasured it.

It was strong.

It was deep.

It was passionate.

Definitely heaven-sent and full of wonder.

So they were joyful. Each moment they sank deeper, each minute they felt more, each second it took them further.

God had caused their hearts to feel and sing again. And a fulfilled desire is sweet to the soul. For love had found a way to give them precisely what they needed…each other. And for that, and many other blessings, they would always be grateful.

READING GROUP GUIDE

01. Which of the characters in *Where My Heart Belongs* did you identify with most, and why?

02. Tyler and Madison's relationship in college ended badly. Why do you think she gave him another chance?

03. What do you like and dislike about Tyler's character?

04. Madison had not seen Tyler for years, yet the bitterness had not faded. Why?

05. Was it strange that Tyler had self-esteem issues?

06. How do you think Tyler handled the betrayal of his trust?

07. Have you ever been betrayed? How did you handle it?

08. What do you think about Mason and Madison's relationship?

09. Were you surprised about the bond that developed between Larry and Tyler?

10. What are the similarities and differences between the twins? Do you think they were spoiled?

11. Why do you think Larry, the twins' father, did not want Rob to take them home?

12. What are your thoughts on the role that Larry Kanate has played in his children's life? Do you think he was overprotective? Why or why not?

13. Which scene moved you most in *Where My Heart Belongs*?

14. How does the title fit the book as a whole?

15. How well are you guarding your heart?

SONGS MENTIONED IN THIS NOVEL

Gloria
By Michael W. Smith
YouTube Link:
https://www.youtube.com/watch?v=fxEOxQYl-wY

You Deserve It
By JJ Hairston and Youthful Praise
YouTube Link:
https://www.youtube.com/watch?v=zxL1m0uG8x4

Amazing
By Ricky Dillard & New G
YouTube Link:
https://www.youtube.com/watch?v=D24fo1gIaXw

Endless Love
By Diana Ross and Lionel Richie
YouTube Link:
https://www.youtube.com/watch?v=JM_R1R28kLM

What A Beautiful Name
By Hillsong Worship
YouTube Link:
https://www.youtube.com/watch?v=nQWFzMvCfLE

Turning Around for Me
By VaShawn Mitchell
YouTube Link:
https://www.youtube.com/watch?v=ZzbKwcC-Xmo

Never Would've Made It
By Marvin Sapp
YouTube Link:
https://www.youtube.com/watch?v=7JXFg5KEoXg

A Love Like This
By Phil and Brenda Nicholas
YouTube Link:
https://www.youtube.com/watch?v=Rgu3ADZc5P8

A NOTE FROM THE AUTHOR

I am thrilled to continue the *Encounters of the Heart* series, with Book 4 – *Where My Heart Belongs,* a heart-stirring story about love deferred and rediscovered under unforgettable circumstances.

The series is based on Proverbs 4:23, "Keep your heart with all diligence, for out of it spring the issues of life." Although the books are in a series, they are also stand-alone novels. Book 1 – <u>*Shades of the Heart*</u> is a novel about the courage to love in the midst of broken promises, and ultimately about the healing power of forgiveness. Book 2 – <u>*Mirrored Hearts: Sealed by Fire*</u> is a deeply stirring and satisfying novel that recounts the struggles of two broken hearts, mended by enduring love, and sealed by fire. Book 3 – <u>*A Place for My Heart*</u> is an emotionally gripping account of a most unexpected love, and a marvelous reflection of God's grace.

Thank you for taking the time to read *Where My Heart Belongs,* and for your continued support. I pray that the story of Tyler Bradshaw and Madison Kanate touched your heart in a meaningful way, and that you caught a glimpse of God's desire to free people from life-altering events that haunt them. May God continue to bless you on your journey. Stay victorious!

With love,
Ann Marie

ABOUT THE AUTHOR

Ann Marie Bryan is a dedicated, graceful, multi-talented leader with a passion for excellence. She is the CEO & Founder of Victorious By Design, an organization committed to providing top quality professional writing services, comprehensive personal and professional development programs, and exceptional performing arts services to meet the unique needs of individuals and organizations.

A Christian Fiction author, Ann Marie writes to educate, inspire, and empower others. She desires to tell great stories with fascinating characters to show the awesome power of God in the lives of people and places.

Ann Marie's greatest passion is to empower others to succeed by tapping into their God-given potential. She enjoys writing, reading, dancing, teaching, meeting people, and traveling.

CONNECT WITH THE AUTHOR

I would love to hear from you. Please let me how *Where My Heart Belongs* may have spoken to you. As always, I would like to hear your testimonies about God's faithfulness.

Let's stay connected!
Website: www.annmariebryan.com
Twitter: www.twitter.com/authorabryan
Pinterest: www.pinterest.com/authorabryan
Instagram: www.instagram.com/authorabryan
Newsletter: http://eepurl.com/bOw6sr
Facebook: www.facebook.com/authorannmariebryan
Email: abryan@victoriousbydesign.com

JOIN MY FACEBOOK READERS' GROUP
Ann Marie Bryan's Reader's Café

CLICK LINKS & WRITE A REVIEW
Where My Heart Belongs

Amazon
http://www.amazon.com/Ann-Marie-Bryan/e/B008VTK62O

Goodreads
https://www.goodreads.com/author/show/6448888.Ann_Marie_Bryan

AVAILABLE TITLES

BY ANN MARIE BRYAN

Unforgettable, My Love Has Come Along
A Circle of Love Novel

Two paths, destined to cross. Friendship, faith, and love are intertwined in ways neither could have imagined. Can love conquer all things? Find out in the heartwarming and humorous pages of Unforgettable, My Love Has Come Along.
Amazon: <u>Unforgettable, My Love Has Come Along</u>

Mirrored Hearts
A Short Story

He is determined to keep his secret close to his heart. She is living under the crushing weight of her own secret. Will their marriage survive when mirrored secrets are exposed? Find out in the page-turner, *Mirrored Hearts*, a fascinating story about faith and love in the face of crushing secrets.
Amazon: <u>Mirrored Hearts</u> (FREE)

ENCOUNTERS OF THE HEART SERIES

Book 1 - Shades of the Heart

A riveting story about the courage to love in the midst of broken promises, and ultimately about the healing power of forgiveness.
Amazon: <u>Shades of the Heart</u>

Book 2 - Mirrored Hearts: Sealed by Fire

When life takes unexpected twists and secrets are laid bare, remember to breathe. Two hearts. Mirrored secrets. The ultimate solution – a marriage sealed by fire.
Amazon: <u>Mirrored Hearts: Sealed by Fire</u> (Kindle Unlimited)

Book 3 – A Place for My Heart

An emotionally gripping account of a most unexpected love, and a marvelous reflection of God's grace. Crushed by heartache and desperate for an escape, he makes a life-changing choice.
Amazon: <u>A Place for My Heart</u> (Kindle Unlimited)

COMING NEXT
Book 5 - Encounters of the Heart Series

VICTORIOUS BY DESIGN

Lighting the path to your next level

You are one of a kind.

You are fearfully and wonderfully made.

Embrace your uniqueness, talents, and abilities.

You are designed for your purpose.

You are perfect for your purpose.

You are Victorious By Design.

Visit http://victoriousbydesign.com for more information

www.ingramcontent.com/pod-product-compliance
Lightning Source LLC
Chambersburg PA
CBHW050733230626
47052CB00002BA/13